Enjoy! ♡ Dara

# HELL'S FURIE

NOVEL 1 OF THE HELL'S REJECTS SERIES

By

## DARA KENNY

# CONTENTS

**Hell's Furie**



**Published by Dara Kenny**



**Published:** Dara Kenny 2021
darakennyauthor@gmail.com
**Cover Design:** Dara Kenny
**Cover Models:** David Harris, Diana Madness

# Acknowledgments

*Thank you to the readers for taking a chance on a brand-spanking-new author and series. Your support and reviews on this journey are treasured gifts that I do not take for granted! Much love and ass smacks to you all!*

*Caraleigh, aka Carebear. You are the real MVP here, bestie! I likely would not have even entertained the idea of writing this book, much less finished it, without your daily cheerleading and motivational speeches.*
*I love and adore you more than words can express.*

*Don. You have no idea how much your constant words of encouragement and support mean to me. I treasure the ray of sunshine that you are, my good buddy.*

*Hollie. I'm so grateful that you were my first writing partner and showed me how fun creative writing could be. Thank you for helping to activate that portion of my brain and all of your contributions since.*

*Much gratitude to my family, friends and beta readers for your feedback, love and encouragement during this process of writing and publishing my first novel.*
*It means the world to me!*

*And last, but certainly not least, my Hubby! You da man, babe! I adore that you always go along with whatever scheme I've conjured up. Whether I was bringing home rescue dog after rescue dog, deciding we're going on some new adventure, or jerking the wheel to go out in left field and write a book, you always have my back.*
*You own my heart, always and forever.*

*Delia and Justus.*

*I couldn't be more thrilled that you are the ones to pop my author cherry. I adore the passionate immortals that you are, and the fact that you are constantly taking up real estate in my brain.*

*You've changed my mindset and the way I view things forevermore.*

*Rock on with your badass selves!*

# Here's your warning.

*This book is violent, gritty, and likely has triggers for some.*
*Torture and drug use run rampant through these pages.*
*Not to mention explicit sex scenes and F bombs galore.*
*Buckle those safety belts, it's a bumpy ride!*

# PROLOGUE

*Thirty years ago*
*Imprisonment Day, Hell*

*Delia Payne had always lived up to her name, dealing out pain without batting an eye. This situation had been no different. It had taken seventeen demons of various assortments to successfully deliver this bloodthirsty Furie demon to her new version of Hell. She'd decimated the first wave of lackeys who attempted to do so, but they kept sending more until she was eventually overwhelmed and incapacitated enough to transport.*

*The demoness had never spent much time here in the lower level of the realm; her charges rarely included slaves. She was familiar with the stench of purgatory, but the slave quarters took it to a whole new level. The air was thick with the acrid malodor of blood and suffering. Wails of agony and devastation were louder here, she noted, as they dragged her thin, nearly limp body down the coal tunnel that was illuminated only by random torches hung haphazardly along its gritty walls.*

*The oversized males accompanying her flung open the door to her new home and tossed her in. The approximately ten by fifteen-foot space was encircled by flaming walls, spelled to keep prisoners in, and a hard, coal packed floor littered with the long forgotten bones of previous tenants.*

*A real work of art it was not...nor was it fashioned with comfort in mind.*

*Delia took a moment to lie there and get her bearings. Struggling to breathe through collapsed lungs, she made a mental inventory of her injuries. Cracked skull and missing liver made the top of the list.*

*Searing pain scorched through her entire, abused frame. Blood laced tears escaped her onyx eyes as she writhed in agony, resulting in further misery. She wondered if there was a single inch on her body that was unharmed.*

*With strength called forth from deep inside her being, Delia managed to suppress her groans and cries, refusing to allow any of her captors the satisfaction of overhearing her blinding agony.*

*Wheezing in desperate breaths, she gingerly rolled to the other side of the putrid dungeon. Most of her bones broken, it took every last vestige of her strength to do anything other than scream in misery as she did so. Her long, raven hair matted around her shoulders when she was finally still again. Dark crimson pooled around her as it leaked from all of the gashes and slashes that had been gouged deep into her once flawless, porcelain skin.*

*When Delia heard the spelled door slam, locking her in, she closed her eyes and listened as the guards retreated. Satisfied they were gone for now, she succumbed to the black hole gnawing at her consciousness. Just before she passed out, her last thought was that HE would come for her. HE would release her and get her out of this predicament.*

*Justus. He would save her. Together, they would lay waste to anyone who stood in their way as they left this literal Hellhole.*

*Never had she been more wrong.*

# CHAPTER 1

*Present day.*
*New Orleans, Louisiana*

Hell's Rejects - that underground club was Delia's baby and one of the most lucrative establishments in NOLA. It specialized in everything illegal. Drugs, prostitutes, and gambling… just to name a few. The demoness had so many cops and city officials on her payroll; it was laughable. Oh, how easily the pathetic humans could be bought. It both disgusted and amused the tattoo covered owner.

"Hey! This drink isn't strong enough!" squawked a scrawny, young male sitting at the bar. Delia had scented him when he sat down. Damn stinky dog was what he was and he couldn't have been far past maturing into his immortality. Twenty-eight...maybe thirty? She had never been a fan of the Weres. All of the ones she'd met had been sketchy and unpredictable; that was before they shifted into werewolves.

The owner glanced up at the clock above the liquor bottles before addressing the complaint. 7 pm. *It was entirely too early for this shit*. Delia rolled her dove-grey eyes before spinning to face the male. Thick, periwinkle locks bounced along her shoulders and down her back as she turned and the blonde mutt's gaze met her own. "It's a fucking shot, pup. You want stronger? Order something different." Without breaking the stare off with his mud puddle eyes, she leaned and grabbed a bottle of Bacardi 151 and held it up. "If you're not a pussy then I suggest this." She smirked and grabbed a shot glass from the rack. "So?"

"I ain't a pussy! Give me that shot!" He pointed to the bottle Delia was holding, sounding like a sniveling, spoiled brat.

The owner snorted under her breath. Turning away from him, she added a splash of Satan Sake; it was potent as hell, and brewed specifically for demons. As for everyone else? Well, good luck keeping it down.

"Only because you asked so nicely," Delia informed the mutt as she faced him once more with a patronizingly saccharin tone. Behind a deadpan stare, she watched him throw the shot back and had to bite down on her lip piercings to avoid laughing in his face as his eyes grew wide and his face turned fifty shades of red in shock. "Mmhm, that's what I thought," she remarked, mildly entertained, as she slid him a glass of water. "The shitters are right behind you," she pointed over his head. "Don't puke on my floor or bar, got it?" The last thing she wanted to do was deal with his disgusting bodily fluids at the beginning of her shift.

Laughing, Delia turned to the other bartender, a relief fill-in that she didn't know very well. Not much could get the demoness to laugh, but inflicting pain on others usually did the trick... especially when they deserved it. "Ten bucks says he tosses his cookies and comes right back for more," she wagered, as she brushed past the other female to exit behind the bar.

It was still a little slow for a Tuesday evening, but she knew that would change at any moment. There hadn't been a day in the fifteen years since she opened the club that Delia could remember the place being completely dead. After all, this was a haven for those looking to revel in a taboo adult playground. And there was no shortage of patrons looking for a good time by whatever means possible. Her drug vault alone was a hot commodity. If this place burned down, she could still live quite comfortably from the proceeds of those sales alone.

Delia made her way around the large, mostly empty dance floor, through the hallway of private rooms, then to the rear bar where the strippers put on their shows. A large, triangular stage occupied one end of the room, with four smaller pedestals spaced throughout the rest of the area. Currently, only the main stage was in use and it would stay that way until the crowd grew more substantial. As the owner walked through the area, she checked in with the manager to ensure all was up to par before the floodgates opened.

Confident all was as it should be, Delia cut out through the hidden door behind the main stage. She deftly dodged oncoming kitchen traffic and exited the private hallway to hustle upstairs to the casino.

The space was quite expansive, taking up nearly half of the glamorized second floor of the warehouse space. Half a dozen each of poker, craps and blackjack tables were moderately spaced throughout, as well as two long walls lined with slot machines and a single baccarat table that were mostly unused but remained clean and stocked, ready to be occupied.

Pleased with the setup, the demoness disappeared into scattered molecules, voyaging invisibly to the office. After taking human form again by a bank of security monitors that covered the wall opposite her desk, she scanned them quickly to verify all were in proper working order. This was followed by a quick test of the communication earpieces the staff wore, which all passed her inspection.

Satisfied, she sat at her desk, leaning back and tossing her leather booted feet up onto the cherry wood surface while she read over and approved gambling markers for some of her high rollers. They were her real meat and gravy, best to keep them happy so their C-notes flowed freely right into her bank account.

There was a brief knock, then the door opened. Delia didn't bother looking up, she knew there was only one individual who worked there with the balls to just walk in like that...one of her two best friends, Rez. He'd been with her long before she opened Hell's Rejects, and he was one of the few whom she could tolerate. He'd become her big, little brother over the years. Sure, they fought like mortal enemies at times, but, when the chips fell, they always had one another's backs.

The voluntarily bald bodybuilder stood six-foot-three, and was a smoke demon with heavily inked olive flesh. He shut the door behind him and leaned against it with arms crossed over his broad chest. As he was heading up security that night, he was dressed in all black, tactical garb with 'SECURITY' in glowing white letters across the back.

His amber eyes nailed her gaze when she eventually shot him an inquisitive glance. "There are three male demons looking for...guess who?" His raspy, baritone voice had the slight twang of a southern accent to it.

Delia shrugged, disinterested, and guessed, "Santa Claus? Easter Bunny? Hmm...whoever could it be?!" She rolled her eyes and sighed as she went back to the paperwork. "Are they Luci's?" she asked, already knowing the answer.

She'd been hunted by Lucifer's scrubs since she escaped Hell. The ruler of the underworld had branded her with his mark in order to keep tabs on her after pulling her from the Breeding District to work for Justus in the Punishment Realm. Though, not nearly as many of his minions had come to seek her out as she would have guessed. She often wondered if the talisman that enabled her to bolt from that horrific plane also masked her somewhat from good ole Luci.

She wore it every single day, as a necklace, just in case.

Rez sighed wearily and ran a meaty hand over his scalp. "Of course they are. You handling them, or am I?"

Her brow raised with irritation as she met his glare. "When the fuck have I ever turned down getting my hands dirty, huh?!"

The strengthening Furie rose from her desk as her blue-purple hair gradually transitioned to jet black. Most of the demoness' Furie genetics had been suppressed since her imprisonment in Hell. Luckily, she still possessed lethal claws and most of her strength. In addition to this, when sufficiently triggered, her eyes and hair both morphed to the blackest of blacks.

She remained hopeful that one day the rest of her Furie traits would surface--no luck so far.

Rez rolled his shoulders, smirking as he stepped over to the monitors and pointed to the three demons. Their asses were planted on a plush sofa in front of the stripper's main stage, eyes glued to the dancer. Clearly, they did not get out of Hell very often. "There's your suitors," the demon grinned as he looked down to Delia who was then standing beside him. "If you ask me, Lucifer's ranks are in the shitter," he chuckled.

He wasn't wrong, either. These fellas looked to be straight out of boot camp. You could tell by looking at them that they were still wet behind the ears. Delia had seen boy scouts who looked better prepared to take her on!

This would barely be fun. Leave it to Luci to take all of the sport out of it. But blood was blood, after all, and spilling it would still up her mood.

In Hell, she'd had a reputation for being particularly ruthless and indiscriminately vicious. Where were the rest of her kind?! She needed some actual competition!

"Umm, yeah, I guess the Breeding District isn't exactly panning out these days, huh?" She snort-chuckled; another rarity only those closest to Delia ever saw. Unless, of course, you were on the wrong side of her claws.

She punched Rez in the shoulder; her version of a hug with him. "And off I go. I'd say wish me luck, but really, I deserve to die if those shit stains can manage to out maneuver me." With a shrug, she disappeared.

Materializing behind the sofa where her new buddies were sat, she leaned between two of the males and whispered, "If you call me 'Daddy', I'll consider taking it easy on you."

All three shot up from their perch and turned to face the yawning club owner. She stretched slowly, as if she were about to do a yoga class, while the demons stalked around the furniture to encircle her, just out of arm's reach.

Delia pulled a band from her wrist and quickly tossed her ebony locks into a much too high ponytail. This was THE ponytail that signaled staff and security to stay out of her game.

Taking stock of these pitiful excuses for demons, Delia pivoted on her heel. The one currently in front of her, nearest the main stage, stood six-foot at best. A bit wiry for her taste, not that she particularly liked men, but still. Shaggy, luminous orange hair hung down to his shoulders. She pointed at him and proclaimed, "I'm gonna call you Carrot Top." The guy's eyes flashed from hazel to black.

Good, they had something in common.

"You won't be calling me anything when you're back in Hell where you belong!" he huffed, but didn't move a muscle toward her. *Amateurs*.

Delia shook her head and turned to the demon on her right. This kid couldn't weigh more than a buck fifty, at most. In fact, had he even fully matured yet? She couldn't say for sure, but it didn't appear so. He had large, eager, dark blue eyes, which contained a glimmer of excitement. The eager ones always made the stupidest mistakes. "And you," she grinned at him, "You're…Thumper." Well, what do you know?! Those blue eyes of his suddenly began burning red; apparently, he *had* come of age. And, though he hadn't moved yet, she instinctually knew that he would jump first when they got down to business.

She continued turning to the one standing almost behind her, just to her left. Out of the corner of her eye, Delia noticed Rez and a few others from their security team ushering patrons and staff out of the area. Luckily, it was only just coming up on 8 pm, so their large crowd wouldn't be showing for another hour or two. That left plenty of time for her to handle this sitch, and clean up the aftermath.

The Furie locked eyes with number three. Well damn, this was rare! She had herself a Bambi AND a Thumper in this bunch. This demon had huge, chestnut brown eyes and ears that were disproportionate in size. Short, cropped, dark brown hair, and full lips the size of Texas.

Seriously, if this was all that was left in the underworld, she'd never been more thrilled to make it out. However, this one actually had some bulk to him. Not much, but considerably more than the other two. "Ok, Bambi, what do you boys have in mind for capturing me? It better be good. You're not exactly the first to try," she taunted.

Thumper darted around, flanked her, and put her in a choke hold. *Called it!* Delia didn't so much as flinch as a sinister smile spread across her midnight painted lips.

Carrot Top, still standing in front of her, cackled as if this thing were already over.

*Seriously?* Time to school these jokers on Furie demons. Her kind didn't react like others. Their deadly calm demeanor was only a mirage as their strength intensified. This often lulled opponents into a false sense of security and caused them to underestimate the severity of what was to come.

The demoness' inky, depthless gaze tracked the boys as the color overtook the whites of her eyes. Dark claws extended from her fingers, supplying her with ten serrated, razor-sharp talons at the ready, but still she waited to attack. Delia wanted them to really soak in that false sense of confidence and arrogance they were currently wallowing in.

A complete moron known as Bambi, stepped over and leaned down to laugh in Delia's face and mock her, "Yeah, that was really hard. I'm glad you warned us how difficult it'd be to bag you!"

Thumper had a pretty good hold on her, but that was hardly enough to restrain her actions. Without so much as a breaking a sweat, she impaled each of Bambi's peepers with her claws and plucked the bloody orbs straight from his head.

Before the other two had a chance to react, Delia's other hand speared through Thumper and relieved him of his spine.

What remained of Thumper crumbled to the floor, lifeless, making his best effort to imitate a useless sack of assholes while a puddle of crimson pooled around him.

Bambi flailed around, holding his bloody face in his hands, screaming, falling over sofas and knocking into stages.

And then there was precious, little Carrot Top, a.k.a. CT. He seemed to have lost his voice and the contents of his bowels.

*Damn.* Delia was *not* cleaning up that piss puddle!

All five-foot-six, one hundred and thirty pounds of the demoness strolled over to the last remaining foe, stopping a few inches from him, daring him to so much as cough. Hands on hips, she glared up at him, "I'mma make this quick because I have shit to do." Watching her intently, CT stumbled back and bumped into a couch. "Don't run and embarrass yourself any further." Delia hiked a thumb to the small crowd at the entrance of the room. "They're already laughing as it is."

"Fuck you, whore!" CT barked as he lunged for her, impaling her right shoulder all the way down to the bone with a dagger.

Delia glanced at the protruding handle and smirked as her left hand flew up and crushed his wrist; the sound of shattering bone making her giddy. CT yelped and punched her in the jaw with his other hand.

Delia laughed.

The burning of her shoulder only added fuel to her fire of destruction, and before the spindly male could deliver his next strike, she ripped out his throat in one swift slash of her claws. A fantastic waterfall of red erupted and cascaded to the floor. For good measure, the demoness kneed him in the ribs as he went down like the incompetent garbage he was.

Delia turned to face the chuckling masses and gave a little bow. She removed the dagger from her shoulder, spun on her heel, then launched it at a still floundering Bambi. The blade whistled through the air and lodged itself square in his temple. *Crunch*.

All three were officially down and out. But they weren't dead. The only way to kill most immortals was by decapitation or fire. And tonight, completely out of character for her, she was feeling generous.

A large presence came up and stood beside her to survey the damage. Onyx orbs turned to her friend, Rez, and she grinned. "Kill those two," Delia instructed as she gestured nonchalantly to Bambi and Thumper. "That one," she nodded to Carrot Top who was now draped over a sofa, "pin a note to his shirt that says 'LUCI, DO BETTER!' and have him dumped at the landfill. He'll eventually make his way back to his master. Maybe the Lord of Darkness will send some actual competition next time."

"Are you insane?!" Rez asked, shocked by how brash her instructions were. "He'll send a fucking army next time! Then how will you elude capture??" He glared at her in disbelief and shook his head incredulously.

"No, he won't. He's too lazy to go to all that trouble. BUT, maybe, just maybe, he'll send me the one I want." Delia waggled her brows, smiling up at Rez. "Merry Christmas in June, baby!" She chuckled and punched his shoulder. "Just do it, this is what I pay you for, remember?"

With that, she traced to her apartment above the club to change out of her blood-soaked clothes and take a few personal samples from the drug vault before getting back to work.

# CHAPTER 2

It had been decades since Justus Azrael stepped foot in New Orleans. In fact, he couldn't even remember the reason for his last visit. Standing there now, though, he recalled why it was such a hot spot. The city was a cesspool of criminals and altogether reprehensible immortals of every variety. It made Vegas look like the kiddy pool of sin.

A perfect playground for his death demon side to feast endlessly…if his other half would only cooperate. Death demons gained strength with each kill, though his angel side only permitted him to dispatch those who had heavily sinned. This presented a major conflict of interest at times.

The six-foot-five, heavily muscled male, emerged from the dark alley he'd traced into. Dressed in a navy blue, Gucci button down shirt, perfectly fitted black jeans, and leather shitkickers, he walked the two short blocks to his destination.

From the outside, it looked like a run down, abandoned warehouse, but he knew better. The place was spelled to keep the average joe from finding it. His company had been keeping tabs on the place, as well as his mark, for months.

The interior of the facility was a stark contrast to what he was currently looking at. On the other side of the mirage was a booming club, blasting loud music and flashing lights, with a mile long list of illegal activities taking place within its walls – a miscreant's paradise.

Justus came to a stop in front of a dingy set of steel double doors. Faded, black lettering spelled out 'Hell's Rejects' just above on a metal sign.

Raking a hand through his short, sandy blonde hair, he took a moment to center himself before entering. He yanked the door open and was met by yet another set of doors that were much more aesthetically pleasing than the last. He could feel the heavy bass vibrations of the music clearly now, and the trenchant stench of sex and drugs hung thick in the air around him.

The spinning, twirling lights overhead were a seizure waiting to happen, he mused, as three large members of the security staff surrounded him. Apparently, new faces here got a major examination. This made sense, considering the kind of establishment they were running.

As some bald guard checked his ID, which was fake, and another patted him down, Justus surveyed his surroundings. His hand was stamped with a black 'HJ' emblem and he was told to enjoy his evening. It was doubtful he'd enjoy anything about this wasteland but he was in, and that was all that mattered.

It was just after midnight and the place was crammed wall to wall with people. He was accosted countless times by dancers and prostitutes as he wove through the sea of sin. "Not interested," he grunted, shrugging them off. His angel half cringed with every interaction and grope.

Justus followed directional signs that pointed him around a massive dance floor and to a wide hall that led to a double set of stairs. At the top, the space opened into a lavish casino. The crowd thinned marginally in this room.

He scanned about until he found the 'man', though he used that term very loosely to describe this particular individual whom he was in town to dispose of. That would not happen here, though. Tonight was recon.

The half-breed purchased a tray of chips from the pit boss and heads turned as he strode with confidence across the room. Justus reached the poker table where his mark was playing and stood a few feet away, casually observing until a seat immediately left of the disgusting slob was vacated.

The bastard was the ringleader of a child trafficking operation and nothing disgusted Justus more than those who preyed on children. Luckily, he was a master of masking his emotions. This lowlife would never know what was in store for him until it was too late.

The buy in for this game was not for the thrifty; minimum wager was ten thousand dollars. The mark hid the proceeds from his operation behind his gambling earnings, so the payouts had to be big.

Justus bought in on the next round and intentionally lost to the child peddler. While the deviant raked the winnings over, Justus clapped him on the back in congratulations. The creep didn't realize the almost imperceptible sting he felt was a minuscule tracker being injected just under his skin.

"Well done!" Justus feigned praise with only a hint of his Sydney accent bleeding through. "Unfortunately, I'm low on funds now," he lied, something his angel side rarely allowed. "Just wasn't my night."

Justus excused himself from the table. Halfway to the exit, the scent of a ghost from long ago tickled his nose, stopping him in his tracks. He slowly studied the crowd, glancing in all directions, looking for her, but she wasn't there.

He let out a hefty breath he'd been holding and took one last look around. There was no way it was her. He had to have been experiencing some sort of strange flashback or perhaps...he didn't know.

He shook off what had to have been a sick trick of his mind, briskly jogged down the stairs and exited through a side door to the alley. Justus paused there and fired off a quick text to his office: Tracker placed, will follow-up tomorrow. Headed to my hotel.

After pressing send, he pulled up the map to his new home. This would hopefully only be his home for a very short time. The plan was to stake out the trafficker and dispose of him and his cohorts, pronto. He simply needed a bead on all of the players. The sooner he got out of this disgusting city, the better.

There it was again. The hair on the back of his neck stood on end when the scent of HER hit him once more.

---

Returning from negotiating new terms with her drug supplier, Delia materialized in her office at Hell's Rejects. The coked-out dealer arrogantly thought he could jack up the prices, but with a little demoness mojo, and possibly some shed blood, she convinced him to reconsider.

The Furie shucked her brass knuckles and tossed them onto the worn in couch, then walked over to the bank of monitors projecting the goings on of the interior and exterior of the establishment.

She froze when she saw a phantom.

HIM. The one she'd been waiting to show...the only demon half-breed capable of returning her to Hell. She'd killed most every other minion sent to retrieve or kill her, which had become a very long list over the years. But why was Justus here, why NOW? There was no way Carrot Top had already healed and made it back to Lucifer with her inflammatory note.

Delia watched as he made his way from the poker room, down the stairs, through the bar and to the exit. Her heart raced, breathing hitched. Vibrant eyes seeped to black.

Finally, he'd pay for his betrayal of her. She'd get revenge for all of the agony and misery he put her through; the physical torture.

FINALLY, she could shred his heart as he had done so callously to hers.

She continued her observation as he walked through the exterior door. Her eyes darted to the camera that covered the alley when he emerged there and seemed to be doing something on his phone.

He looked just as she remembered. A hulking beast of a male. Muscle on top of muscle lined his entire, dead sexy mass. His icy blue eyes reflected the coldness in his heart and soul. He was definitely an evil one. She still endured night terrors to this day of the things he'd done to her, so she rarely slept. Thankfully there were always drugs to help her along with that!

HE ruined her. HE pulverized her body and spirit leaving her an empty shell of what she once was. HE was every good and bad thing she'd ever experienced. HE was the worst of the worst.

She patted her boots quickly, reassuring herself that her poison tipped daggers were still safely sheathed there. With a deep, steadying breath, she traced to the alley, a few yards behind him, and lurked in the shadows. It took no time at all for his woodsy scent, with notes of dark spices and citrus, to reach her. When it did, she wanted to run to him...NOT to kill him, though.

She neared hyperventilating status as feelings she thought were long dead, resurfaced and clashed with her need to kill him.

She was beginning to panic over her reaction. Her mind told her to rip his heart out and mount it on a shelf in her loft.

The remnants of her black, shredded heart vetoed that thought.

Both sides wanted hands on him, but for diametrically opposite reasons. In that moment, she realized what true hate was. She loathed herself for hesitating to confront him. She hated herself far more than she could ever hate him for this weakness in the moment.

As the demoness stood there, mentally bickering with herself, Justus' head turned and their eyes met.

Her glossy, coal orbs held his now glowing gold glare.

Who would flinch first?

---

*Day 374 of imprisonment*

*"He'll be here soon," she muttered to herself through split, swollen lips as she lay trembling on the coal floor. This was a mantra she'd repeated countless times since being thrown in the dismal dungeon.*

*On her side, Delia stared at the flaming door of her enclosure. Dull eyes, unblinking.*

*She'd just endured her latest round of torture. The excruciating pain of broken bones and dissected organs had once again left her in a pool of her own congealing blood.*

*Her body burned and ached; something she was getting used to. Her pain threshold rose a little with each trauma.*

*This session, she had managed to kill three of her assailants before the other eight got the better of her. She'd been torturing souls for too many centuries to let them simply walk in and ravage her uncontested.*

*Delia had been the only female to ever hold high station in Lucifer's Punishment Realm for a damn good reason. She brought new meaning to the terms 'vicious' and 'ruthless'.*

*Originally, she'd been in the Breeding District. They thought, given her high quality bloodline, she'd make a good 'breed mare', so to speak. They were wrong.*

*Being a Furie demon, the fight only made her stronger, more lethal. She killed most who attempted to breed with her and the ones who were successful…well, she exacted her revenge upon them later.*

*She birthed no young. Not because she wasn't impregnated but because she refused to carry them to term. Each time Delia realized she was with child, and there were dozens of instances, she'd self-abort; clawing through her own abdomen and ripping the offensive creature from her body. No fucking way was she going to be treated like cattle and produce spawn for them!*

*After each termination, the Furie would be captured, weakened from healing, and sent for further punishment. Punishment in that realm was laughable, however, so it was hardly a deterrent.*

*Wash. Rinse. Repeat.*

*Wash. Rinse. Repeat.*

*For almost a century it had been that way.*

*Eventually, the higher ups took the dilemma to Lucifer himself, and Delia was reassigned to the Punishment Realm, under the rule of Justus Azrael, where her skills and diabolical personality could be put to good use.*

*As an added bonus, they sterilized her once she had proven her worth. Lucifer was convinced all demon females were whores and he didn't want her muddying the bloodlines, sleeping around with the impure.*

*The demoness was happy, as happy as a Furie demon could be, anyway, with the modification and reassignment. Things were finally good, for once in her existence. And she had HIM…the only being she ever cared for, loved even, in her own demented way.*

*Weary eyes blinked only once, peering at the door. "He'll come. He'll get me out," she murmured. "He'll be here soon."*

*Exhaustion and weakness from blood loss ultimately forced her to relent to the black hole of unconsciousness where she would relive her torture all over again in her nightmares.*

*No rest for the wicked and all that shit.*

# CHAPTER 3

Justus stared over his shoulder; his heart sinking like a lead balloon. He swallowed hard and blinked.

Still there.

But.

It was impossible he was seeing HER. This couldn't be real; his mind had to be short circuiting.

The faintest hint of cherries and dark chocolate invaded his senses and he inhaled deep. It was definitely her.

Fucking Delia Payne was barely more than a few yards away, and she was not happy.

Rage burned heavy in her dark eyes and seething aggression radiated from her form. She was looking for a fight. One he was in no mood for. But, apparently, he was in the mood for something else...he realized his pants were getting snug in the pelvic region.

Justus inwardly cursed himself and ignored the aggravating pinch of his jeans. The half breed masked any surprise that might have lingered on his face and turned to fully face the demoness he had successfully avoided for two decades.

Neither moved nor spoke for what felt like a torturous eternity, both silently evaluating the other.

Eventually, she spoke, which wasn't a surprise to him; she'd always had problems keeping her smart mouth shut. "Well, well, well...look what crawled out of Hell," her sultry voice was dripping with contempt.

"According to the history books, you're the one who crawled out; I merely traced," he stated matter-of-factly, his tone nearing boredom.

Delia rolled her eyes and leaned back against the brick wall of the building, arms crossing over her leather clad cleavage as she studied him further. He was ashamed to admit that he didn't mind studying her as well. It had been ages since he'd seen her in the flesh.

He'd only had dreams that turned to nightmares since their time in Hell. This was much better.

His ex-partner looked mostly as he remembered but with many more tattoos and piercings. No complaints here, he mused just before he gave himself another inward shake to correct his train of thought.

Guilt and shame slammed full speed into his conscience, replacing the previous emotions. This was dangerous territory, especially considering he needed his mind clear in order to handle this chance meeting.

---

Delia shifted her weight, doing everything in her power to avoid letting her eyes roam along his beautiful, ridiculously stacked body.

Don't even get her started on all of his lick-able tattoos.

She pinched her thigh, HARD, in an attempt to snap out of the eye-fuck. It was no use though, because she abruptly got a heaping whiff of his drool-worthy scent again. To ward off the favorable reaction her body was producing, she let her claws sink into the palm of her hand and felt the warm flow of blood seeping between her knuckles.

Back on track! Somewhat. Dumbass that she was, she should be sinking her claws into him at this very moment, but instead…she kept her distance for fear of doing something remarkably insane.

Sure, she did unspeakable things on the regular, but there was a hard limit, and this was it. *So much NO*.

"You need to trace on back to wherever you came from then, not enough room for both of us here," she sneered, unsure if she meant a single word of that statement.

Delia watched as Justus' fingers flexed; fists opening and closing by his tree trunk thighs. The faintest grin tugged at her lips. She couldn't deny that she enjoyed how her presence was affecting him.

To his credit, his facial expression remained even as they held unwavering eye contact. "Watch how you speak, Furie. You don't dictate my comings and goings. I'll leave when I've finished my mission."

The demoness kicked off the wall and started toward him, only to stop. She hadn't a clue if she'd end up killing him or ripping his clothes off. That scared her. She settled back into a casual stance, arms intertwined across her chest. "I'll speak to you any gods-damned way I please, prick." An ebony brow arched in defiance. "Feel free to attempt to silence me. I'm itching for yet another reason to gut you."

*Truth.* She needed to refuel her loathing for him to suppress all these stupid feels clogging up her revenge plan.

Mirroring her stance, Justus smirked. "You can certainly try but just like all the other bastards I've put down this week, I won't hesitate to do the same with you," he snarled.

The demoness hid her confusion well. She had deduced that he had come to town solely for her; on Lucifer's behalf. That didn't seem to be the case, however. If he was being truthful, of course; though she knew his angel side rarely allowed him to lie.

She scoffed at his cockiness. "You may want to note that I'm not drugged and haven't been beaten to a pulp by any of your pathetic minions. The playing field is a bit more even on this plane." She smirked, tiring of this exchange. "Good luck, though, I look forward to your best efforts to 'put me down'."

"If I wanted to, I would've already," he sighed boredly. "As for the minions you speak of, you forget their orders were the same as mine," he growled, rubbing the scar on his chest where Lucifer's brand had once been. "Not that it fucking matters any longer. What's done is done."

Drawing in a deep breath, Delia exhaled slowly. The building tension between them was growing unbearable with her conflicted emotions. "You can't seriously stand there and believe that both of us can stay in this city without dire consequences. One way or another, someone is checking out and it ain't gonna be me." She glared at him, itching for him to react, to show any sort of true emotion.

---

Justus strode over to her with purpose, stopping inches away.

Essentially boxing her in, he planted his hands against the wall, on either side of her shoulders. "Then I look forward to the chance to bury…" He hesitated as his glowing golds bore into her onyx gaze while she stared up at him. "…whatever this is, once and for all."

Periwinkle locks joined in the darkening department and morphed jet black. He'd pinged a nerve and she was about to combust. It was obvious, so he should have been prepared for what came next.

*Hindsight and all that shit, ya know?*

Delia's glare turned murderous. At the same time, one set of her razor-sharp claws gouged deep into his chest while her other hand threw a hook and caught him in the jaw.

An involuntary roar broke free from Justus as his own hands bolted with blinding speed, clamping her wrists. He adjusted his jaw while yanking her hard to spin around, preventing any further injury to himself.

Slender wrists crackled beneath his grip, but Delia didn't show any sign of it in her behavior. She whipped her head back to headbutt him, he dodged it.

With her frontside pressed against the wall, it gave him a perfect view of her shapely ass. What had been a minor issue for him before, had now turned to granite in his pants; which made absolutely no sense! After everything in their history, how the hell was she turning him on right now?!

He spat a mouthful of blood on the wall beside her face and snarled next to her ear, crushing her wrists into powder, "You cease breathing if you attack me again. CUNT." He shoved at her lower back as he released her and traced across the alley, cursing under his breath.

His ripped, bloody shirt revealed jagged slices carved into his pec, right above his heart. He knew what her endgame would have been; luckily, she held back, he thought. Justus was all too aware of what the demoness was capable of, and his surprise at seeing her almost caused him to make a fatal mistake.

He pivoted back to Delia when her laughter turned maniacal, but she only waved at him with limp, dangling wrists, then disappeared.

Relief flooded him as he, too, ghosted. That was one confrontation he had not been mentally prepared to take on.

# CHAPTER 4

*1799 A.D.- Approximately two centuries before Delia's imprisonment*
*Punishment Realm, Hell*

*Justus materialized outside his private quarters after a mission. Shock widened his gaze when he found Lucifer awaiting his arrival. It was quite rare for the King to bother with paying him a visit.*

*He bowed slightly as he addressed his guest, "Grandsire." He straightened and continued speaking in what he hoped would be perceived as a sincere tone, "To what do I owe this honor?" The half breed attempted not to choke on the words.*

*Lucifer, defining the phrase 'tall, dark and handsome', stood immaculately dressed, flashing Justus a deceptive smile. This was a smile that screamed ill intent. A smile not to be trusted.*

*"Justus the Fierce, my Grandson. You've kept me waiting." The fallen archangel frowned, disappointed. "Alas, here you are." His voice was capable of grating anyone's nerves, it was disgustingly smooth and calculating. "I have brought a gift for you, just inside. The guards are currently with her, but I imagine their time is winding down." Lucifer's crimson glare twinkled with mischief. "One might say she is a feisty one. She also does not know why she has been transferred."*

*Thuds and swearing could be heard from inside. Justus inquisitively cocked his head at his grandsire. It sounded as if a wild animal were loose in his home. Lucifer grinned, "That would be your new enforcer."*

*The King's hand knocked the entrance door wide and motioned Justus in. When Justus entered, his icy blues came to rest on a spitfire; he'd felt the demoness' eyes on him before he adjusted to the lighting to find her.*

*A strange feeling washed over him. One he couldn't name, mostly because while in Hell he rarely felt anything at all. Something about the realm suppressed his emotions.*

*Justus had to mask his expression when he focused on the female standing next to a downed guard. She was stunning, covered in a fitted, bloody, leather uniform that accentuated every curve of her body.*

*Best if Lucifer was none the wiser of his attraction to her.*

*The half-breed scoffed as he looked over to his grandsire. "Is this a joke? A female enforcer on my team?! The others will not tolerate this." He was cut off before he could say more.*

*Lucifer smiled, clapping him on the back as he turned to leave. "Don't worry, boy, she can handle herself. You'll thank me later when you see her blade work." He stopped then, and seemed to consider something for a moment before he continued. "And her affinity for playing with her prey." Lucifer's amused laughter faded slowly in his wake after he traced, leaving Justus to handle this odd situation.*

*"Leave us," he ordered the guards who were still standing. His focus then went back to an unhappy demoness. He had a sneaking suspicion that Lucifer expected him to fail this assignment.*

*Justus studied the female more closely as she did the same to him.*

---

*As the able-bodied guards filed out, Delia wiped her sticky hands and dagger on her dark pants. They, along with the matching bodice, were in stark contrast to the hideous, easy access gown she'd been made to wear in the breeding district. This animal hide was much better suited to her scathing personality and utterly malicious demeanor.*

*The demoness had downed numerous guards when they came to retrieve her from her living quarters. She could only assume she would now be punished again for killing her last 'suitor'.*

GAG. *It didn't matter how many times, over however many centuries they tried, she'd never willingly be one of their incubators.*

*Arriving at this new location, they'd given her the updated change of clothing and when a couple of the idiots decided to get handsy and help with her wardrobe change…well, it didn't end nicely for them.*

*She kicked at the unconscious guard at her feet. Delia had sliced him deeply. He was nearly decapitated. Too bad. She really should have finished him off.*

*Rolling her shoulders, she brought her attention back up to the brave one who had sent the others away. She tapped her palmed dagger against her thigh as she sized him up.*

*He was big enough, that was for damn sure; at least a foot taller than herself. In her station, she'd never seen any males with such pronounced muscles. They were almost hypnotizing as they flexed.*

*All in all, he was likely the most alluring thing she'd ever laid eyes upon. And those eyes of his...deliciously frigid and mesmerizing. Nice, this should be a formidable opponent, she thought.*

*"So what the fuck am I here for? You a new bloodline attempting to impregnate me or something?" Delia quirked a brow with a devilish smirk. "Give it your best effort, PRICK."*

*Long fingers flicked at him, daring him to come at her.*

---

*Confusion rattled around in Justus' brain for the briefest of moments as her words sunk in. Impregnate her? His gaze roamed about her lithe frame once more, he could certainly understand why someone would want to, but he dismissed the thought and answered her sincerely. "No, that is not in my job description. I am to help you redirect your frustrations and aggression in a form that is productive."*

*He pulled out a flask containing a corrupt politician's soul and held it up for her to see.*

*As she eyed the container, he noticed her body posture and how she was seemingly uncomfortable in her current attire. Perhaps she was unaccustomed to it? It certainly suited her well. It clung to her like a second skin drawing the eye to all the right...*

*Justus mentally slapped those thoughts away. According to her questions, she'd apparently come from the Breeding District. He was angry on her behalf, but kept his face indifferent.*

*Surprising the female, Justus raised his dagger and immediately dropped it to the floor, before kicking it to her. She bent down to grab it, when she straightened again, he held up the flask. "Follow me and I'll show you what your new assignment entails," Justus told her as he walked past.*

*He was relieved when she fell in behind him instead of attempting to stab him.*

*Justus lead them down a stone tunnel off of his home. It was well lit by staggered torches and wide enough for three of him to have walked side by side. They entered a small chamber that was similarly carved and brightly lit.*

*He swept his arm out, welcoming the demoness to the space. "Where the fun happens."*

*The female eyed him suspiciously before inspecting the rack and shackles on the far wall. She spun around, daggers raised, ready to fight when she heard Justus close them into the room.*

*He stifled a grin and uncorked the receptacle in his hand. He dropped it to the ground and stepped away.*

*A flickering shadow took form before turning corporeal. The politician stood in the center of the room. Wild eyes searched for something that made sense.*

*"Welcome to Hell. Tell us, have you ever forced yourself upon another?" Justus looked to the demoness as he queried the soul. His angel DNA knew the truth before the human surely would attempt to deny.*

*He preferred the female express her rage, so why not at this wretched scum? The man's eyes went wide, but Justus continued. "No?" He raised a brow in question.*

*As the man shook his head vigorously, Justus clicked his tongue. "Sorry, mister, I'm afraid I already know the truth. I have this little gift that allows me to detect human lies, you see. And unfortunately, for you, SHE…" he hiked a thumb toward the demoness, "very much has an issue with predators such as yourself."*

*Justus motioned toward the human, giving the female the all clear to enjoy herself.*

---

*Skeptical grey eyes never left the males as Delia allowed the scene before her to sink in. Was this muscleman serious? Or was this a bad joke?*

*A blade in each hand, her gaze narrowed on the big one. "I'm being given free rein to dole out punishments on this vermin?" The beefcake gave her a curt nod of affirmation. "If this is in any way a deception," she paused as her eyes bore into his, "...you'll go down with me. Got it, asshole?"*

*Her brow creased momentarily when his brow rose and she thought she might have seen the slightest tug at his lips.* Apparently, she was entertaining to him?

*"Make no mistake, I AM an asshole but not when it comes to business. And my name is Justus, by the way." He smirked and continued to stand back. "Proceed." He whisked his hand toward the shaking soul, prompting her to get on with it.*

*A nefarious smile grew as the naughty soul began hyperventilating. Delia shrugged and thought there surely could be worse tricks, so why not participate?*

*The soul began sobbing and begging as she twirled a blade between her fingers. Ignoring his words, she sauntered toward the crybaby. A quick look over her shoulder and Justus was in the same spot, near the wall, thick arms crossed over his chest.* Good.

*On a pivot, Delia flung the blade at the politician, seating it to the hilt in his pelvic region. She likely severed his little Vienna sausage, judging by the screams and wails that erupted from him as he fell over in a whimpering heap.*

*A sinister smile graced Delia's features as she walked over to the rapist and gripped the handle of the dagger. With ease, she yanked the serrated blade up through his abdomen, filleting flesh and muscle like jello. Blood and viscera gushed from the gaping wound while she laughed hysterically.*

*The Furie frowned when she noticed the little piggy was nearing blackout status. "What a pussy," she mumbled, while reaching to collect a length of protruding intestines.*

*Bone crunched as Delia punched the lowlife in the temple while he lay there, making pathetic sounds. Her bloody fist leaving crimson spatter across his puffy features.*

*"How do you slow unconsciousness in these weak fuckers?" she genuinely inquired, wrapping the entrails around the soul's neck making him a lovely necklace.*

*Grinning, Justus strode over, removing a vial from his pocket. "Ah, well, smelling salts can be magical, watch." He knelt and waved the open vial under the politician's nose. Immediately the guy jolted awake, struggling against his own innards that were choking him into a nice shade of blue.*

*Looking over at the dark-haired beauty with sincere interest, Justus held out the vial to her. "Here, this one is yours."*

*When her fingers brushed his to retrieve it, their eyes met. Another foreign reaction occurred as they touched ever so briefly; he felt heat spread down into his groin and inwardly cursed as his cock began to swell.*

*Justus immediately shook it off. Chemistry or not, he had a job to do.*

*"However, it's pointless to bring them back when they are this far gone," he informed her. His claws elongated and sharpened. In a few swipes, he had dismantled the soul's upper region and removed the lifeless head from the body. "Might as well finish them off and wait for them to regenerate, then go again a little slower."*

*"The fuck?!" The demoness hissed as her arm ghosted out, her dagger jabbing deep into the side of Justus' lower back. A roar erupted and he swung around on her. Delia narrowly spun out of the way, removing her blade as she jumped back and screamed, "You said that one was MINE! Asshole!"*

*"I was doing you a favor, you stupid cunt!" He bellowed in response, his hand reaching to put pressure on his wound. Had anyone else done that to him, they'd be dead already, or at least laying on the floor with a broken neck, but with her, his reactions were skewed.*

*He was just as much intrigued as he was angry. Justus knew this female was going to be nothing but trouble, and he honestly looked forward to it. "The fucker will be back in minutes! Be patient!" He growled, fists clenched as he nodded to the dissipating form.*

*Once it completely disappeared, it suddenly reformed, fully intact. The politician woke, standing a few feet away from them to live the next of a long line of deaths.*

*"Just shut up!" Delia walked over to the bastard. When his beady eyes peered into hers with terror, she smiled and stabbed him right between the eyes. Lights out.*

*Flicking blood off her blade, she twirled back to Justus. "Why the fuck do*

*I need patience when they come right back?!" She shook her head, disgusted with his logic. "Stupid fucking males."*

*Justus sluggishly dragged a hand over his face. This woman was going to be difficult, at best, and hard to keep off Lucifer's radar, no doubt. Frankly, they'd both be lucky if they survived this new arrangement.*

# CHAPTER 5

Bandaged hands rose, blocking out the bright rays that had begun breaking through the dark curtains. Delia groaned at the rude intrusion while she attempted to wake.

Rolling over to bury her face in a pillow, she growled at the sharp pain that shot up her arm when she accidentally knocked a hand on the headboard. Her wrists were healing well, but they still had a ways to go. Immortal or not, she didn't heal immediately, unfortunately. She'd already missed a day of work thanks to the altercation with Justus and would probably need to miss at least one more until she was mostly healed.

The night before, when she'd left the alley, she'd traced to her office where Rez was doing inventory on the drug vault. Perfect timing; exactly what she'd needed--not really due to the pain of her injuries, but mostly for the mindfuck she'd experienced.

Rez rolled up a joint containing just about everything but the kitchen sink and held it as she smoked, listening to her recount of the evening's events. The demon was livid and swore to enact his own revenge on the half-breed. Delia squashed that notion and made it clear that Justus was HER problem, and that she would deal with it. Everyone else was to remain hands off when it came to retribution. Needless to say, Rez wasn't happy about that order.

---

The demoness sighed, exasperated, as she sat up in the middle of the bed. Her dove-greys squinted, peering around the open floorplan of her loft, unsure what she was looking for. Then, as if her other best friend had been alerted to her waking, Zaylee appeared standing in front of her.

The shapely succubus' coffee-colored eyes narrowed on Delia and she raised a hand in question, gesturing to Delia's mittens. "Seriously?! Why the hell did I have to hear of your escapades from Rez?!" Thick, fire engine red hair flung around Zaylee's arms as the Latina beauty posed the question in her usual animated fashion. She was one of the few who were permitted to speak to Delia in such a disdainful manner without getting hurt.

Exhaused eyes rolled, Delia fell back into the pillows. "Oh, you didn't get my smoke signal, then?" The demoness snarked back. "Perhaps you've noticed…I don't have any fucking hands to call or text with!" Bandaged stumps waved to nail home the point. "Also, I'm flipping you off right now."

"You're such a bitch," Zay scoffed, and sat on the bed beside Delia. "What do you need? Besides that tool's head on a platter." Zaylee knew many of the details of Delia and Justus' sordid past. To say she wasn't a fan of his would be quite an understatement.

Many moons ago, only a couple of years after Delia escaped Hell, the two females had been a couple. Unfortunately, they weren't meant to stay that way, but had remained as close as two could be without the sexual intimacy. Mostly.

Delia smirked, looking over to the bedside table. She jutted her chin to the goodies. "Six oxycontin and water." Zay moved to retrieve the items, grabbing the pills and dropping them into the demoness' open mouth, then held a water bottle out with a straw for her to wash them down. De swallowed then continued with her requests. "Now a joint."

"Why don't I just directly pour the contents of the drug vault on you while I'm at it?!" Zay quipped sarcastically. "Damn." She shook her head as she lit the monstrously sized joint and held it to Delia's lips for her to take a hit.

Slow on the exhale, the demoness kicked the sheets off of her legs and scooted off the bed. "Pants and tee," she nodded toward the lump of clothing on a chair. "Those'll do."

Zaylee did as she was asked, with only mild commentary while she assisted her girl with getting dressed. Delia's mood and headspace were shit, and the only reason Zay wasn't truly giving her hell was because she knew her bestie well enough to know when NOT to push.

"When's the last time you ate, chica?"

"I have no fucking clue. But who needs food when I have all these drugs?!" That garnered Delia a hardcore death glare. *Whatevs.* "Listen, I need you to help me go through the security feeds to see what that prick was doing in my club and then track his sorry ass down."

"I can do that. Do I get to watch you kill him?" It was a legit question.

"We'll see. Come on." Delia slid her feet into flip flops then traced to her office; Zay was right behind her.

The Furie kicked a chair over to the monitors and told Zay what to type in to find footage of that evening. The women sat and played back a recording of Justus entering the club then going to the casino and playing at one of the tables. When Zay zoomed in, they watched as he brilliantly placed a tracker on the man beside him.

"BINGO!" Delia chirped. "That fucker is going to pay for messing with one of my high rollers right under my nose."

The two besties spent the next couple hours tracking down the hotel that Justus was staying at. It just so happened he was checked into a hotel owned by one of Delia's extremely loyal patrons. *What a stroke of luck!*

The demoness put in the order to have Justus watched and his comings and goings reported back to her. Once she was healed, he'd be graced with her pretty little face, again.

*SURPRISE, BITCH!*

# CHAPTER 6

"Yes, three out of the four," Justus confirmed over the phone to his business manager, Hannah. "The last ringleader, Kendrick, is proving elusive, but I'll get him soon enough."

The tracker he placed on the gambler nearly a week ago had been effectively high-yielding. So far, two of the four main players in the trafficking operation had been quietly assassinated and, as soon as he located the fourth, he'd wipe those last two off the grid and get back home to Sydney.

Away from HER.

"Only checking in to make sure you're well. It's unusual for a mission to take you this long," Hannah prodded. "Are you certain there are no other complications?"

His manager knew him well, and, while there most definitely were complications in town, he had no desire to share that information with her. The dark fae had a tendency to treat him more as a lover than a business partner. This was a tendency he did not encourage, as the feeling was not mutual and never had been. As far as he was concerned, sleeping with someone once did not lock you into a life-long commitment to them. Hannah had clearly missed that brief.

He ran a meaty hand through his hair while attempting to evade her inquiry as pleasantly as possible. "It's a complex organization, nothing more. These scumbags cover their tracks exceptionally well, but they'll slip up soon enough. When they do, I'll be there." His laptop dinged as he got an alert that the tracker was on the move. *Saved by the bell.* "I've got to go, but I'll send another progress report when there is something to divulge."

Justus ended the call before Hannah had anything further to add and kicked back on the hotel suite's sofa to inspect the tracker's activity.

Hannah had long desired a deeper relationship, but that wasn't who he was. Yes, since returning to live in this realm, his emotions had resurfaced and it seemed guilt and shame stayed at the forefront. The chain of events in Hell had left him majorly screwed up in the head; an anguish he masked expertly. Justus had no yearning for any type of intimate relationship other than a quick fuck here and there when he needed to unleash some pent up frustrations. Strictly nothing long term. Ever. It simply wasn't in the cards for him and he was happy to forgo the headaches that accompanied such affairs.

Shutting out ghosts of the past, Justus switched to the tracking app on his phone and traced along with it, to continue pursuing his mark in person.

---

If he wasn't in town for her, and he wasn't in a hurry to get out of her town… then that left the Furie with a conundrum on her hands. Delia had already proven to herself that, when it came to retaliating against Justus, she had a split personality. Her head and heart couldn't exactly get on the same page. So what did that mean?

Long nails drummed against her desktop as she weighed the options. Though there weren't really any to weigh as she could only come up with one.

Harassment.

Simply make him too miserable to stay in NOLA any longer. Good thing she knew just how to push his buttons.

The manager of the hotel had been keeping her apprised of his movements while she healed, and it was time she popped in on Justus herself. An anti-welcoming committee, if you will.

Amused by her decision, she paged Rez through the security comms to inform him of her departure. Within minutes, she stood in the small kitchenette of Justus' plush, temporary residence. The half-breed was not present.

*Hmm, where to start?* She didn't want her presence to be obvious, preferring to keep things subtle. Make him question his sanity a bit? *Ah yes, excellent tactic*. He deserved to be as batshit crazy as he'd made her. The only problem with that plan? Subtlety had never really been a strongpoint for her.

Kitchen cabinets opened and closed as she moved bags of chips out of place. Bottles of water got repositioned. Unfortunately, his refrigerator barely held any contents, other than Satan Sake and eggs. No fun to be had there, other than to partake in the libations.

Popping the lid off a bottle, she moved on. Next, she found herself in the bedroom area. After digging through his drawers, she snagged one of his t-shirts and a hoodie. *He'd never miss them, right?! Nah!*

Placing her cold brew on the nightstand, Delia plopped down onto the comfy, oversized bed. Justus' mouthwatering scent lingered on the sheets as she laid back on the pillows, making certain that her scent would linger there as well.

And no, she would NEVER cop to stalling a bit too long; fantasizing about the torrid sexcapades the two had once enjoyed. No, she definitely did NOT do that.

On to the bathroom. The demoness took her time milling through his toiletries; she may or may not have switched the contents between his shampoo and toothpaste. *What a savory surprise for him!*

Shaving cream in hand, Delia left a parting note to her traitorous ex-partner on the mirror: Blood is red. Your eyes are blue. Stay in town and I'll off you. XOXO

Wiping her now fully healed hands on a hanging towel, a chill ran up her spine. She felt his presence materialize nearby. Grey eyes grew large as she mentally debated staying or leaving…

---

With gritted teeth and clenched fists, outrage seeped from Justus' pores while he stood center room of his suite. HER scent permeated his senses and he could easily discern numerous items out of place. What in the nuthouse looney bin had she been looking for in his room?! And how did she find him?! He was staying under an alias.

He froze. She was still there. His body reacted in a very distinct way when he detected her energy lingering; a response only she'd ever been able to illicit.

Slowly turning, Justus' icy blues narrowed as Delia emerged from his bathroom. She sauntered over to him, a ferocious growl rumbled deep in his chest. The bitch had clearly lost her mind; more so than he'd assumed over the years. "What the fuck are you doing here, Delia?! Are you insane?!" *Rhetorical question, that last one.*

Hopping up on the kitchen bar as if she owned the place, the demoness grinned proudly while she leaned back on her palms. The deep V of her tight Slipknot shirt putting her ample cleavage on display. "What? I thought old friends were supposed to visit each other when in the same vicinity." Her brow creased as she feigned a frown. Long, toned legs, covered in snakeskin leggings, flailed back and forth as a hyperactive child does when made to sit still. "Aren't you happy to see me?" The faint whine of sarcasm in her tone was the icing on the cake.

A deadpan stare full of cynicism met her act of innocence and goodwill. Justus recalled how much the dark beauty enjoyed her games. These were games he didn't have time for. "No. Get the fuck out, Delia. Take your less than convincing side-show and hit the road."

Justus' thick arms folded over his chest while their gazes played chicken. Her plump, bottom lip jutted out in a faux pout, drawing his eye. The things he'd seen those lips do...*BLOODY HELL!* Justus quickly punted those thoughts away...for the most part.

The cocky wench chuckled when she won the stare-off and slid from the bar to stand before him. "Mmhmm. I see the wheels turning. You remember what these lips can do, huh?" Her forked tongue flicked between those delectable lips, flooding his mind with countless intimate memories. His jeans turned dreadfully tight. "Yep, there it is. You definitely remember." Her brows bounced as the steel greys beneath twinkled with mischief. This female was going to be the death of him, one way or the other, he was certain of it.

"It doesn't matter, those days are long gone." Where the hell did that load of gravel in his voice come from?! "Get. Out. NOW!" His arms remained firmly folded for fear of throwing her on the bed and fucking her stupid. "I don't have time for your bullshit, psycho bitch. LEAVE."

Without a doubt, he knew she hated him, so why was she here? And why wouldn't she leave?!

Hands on her heart, Delia whimpered, "Words hurt, Jussy. Here I am trying to mend fences and you shit all over it!"

Oh wait, did she actually sell that?! He seemed to be considering her words.

"Only you forget how well I know you. I'm no fool and I'm not buying this skit for one second."

A large hand snaked out and fisted the length of her blue-purple locks. *Now we're talking!* Oh, the fond memories as he yanked her head back and leaned down, nose to nose with her.

"Take your games elsewhere. I'm not interested!" Justus snarled in her face.

*Liar.* She had clearly seen the lead pipe in his pants; who did he think *HE* was fooling?! In fact...her own hand flew out and snugly cupped his gargantuan bulge. *Mistake.* Damnit to Hell, she was such an idiot.

Shock decorated his handsome face as he sucked in a sharp breath at the surprise groping. Meanwhile, a tidal wave of heat and desire assaulted her body; her nipples pebbled and ached as her thong grew increasing damp.

She should get a moron trophy for THIS stunt.

Both stood frozen, unsure where to go from here. Talk about a game of chicken…this was the ultimate play.

Their eyes locked, waiting for the other to flinch. After what felt like an eternity, Justus growled, "You've got approximately five seconds before I," his lips pursed as her grip tightened on him. He briefly cleared his throat before slamming the side of her head against the wall and continued, "fuck you into an oblivion." His brow raised in challenge. "Did you come here to get fucked, De? Because all you have to do is ask next time. No need for games."

A disgusted hiss left the demoness' mouth as she sneered up at him; she could feel a trickle of blood bouncing down her scalp where it'd met the wall. "If you want these legs to open for you again, PRICK, then you're gonna have to break them." Her own brow raised in defiance, as she inwardly berated herself for wanting him as badly as she did. "And you may want to consider the consequences of it. Consider how easily I could remove your beloved appendage at any moment." Her tongue clicked. "Decisions, decisions."

"Not a difficult decision at all, actually," he shrugged, releasing her hair and peered down at her hand, still cupping him. "Your turn."

*Arrogant asshole.* He hadn't changed a bit.

Delia released his length and took a step back with a wicked grin. "Glad that's settled. See ya around, jackass." With a flash of middle fingers, she disappeared to go drown her insanity in the drug vault.

# CHAPTER 7

*Nearly nine years into Delia's Hell imprisonment*

*The demoness sat dead center of her putrid cell, legs folded under her. Her naked form was disgustingly dirty, caked in soot and dried blood. She had grit in places one should NEVER have grit.*

*Her fingers burrowed into the grainy floor beneath to bring up charcoal granules. Out of sheer boredom, she would count the specks to pass time in between torture sessions.*

*Used to the drill by now, she had trained her nearly non-existent mind to go elsewhere when things got too horrid. Her pain threshold through the roof, they had to keep coming up with increasingly creative ways to get a reaction out of her. They had almost turned her into a zombie.*

*No one had come in a few days, best she could calculate, anyway. After a time here, every day seemed to run together, so she couldn't be sure of that timeframe. The demoness actually looked forward to them coming in; it gave her something to do. They tried to keep her as drugged up as possible but she always took at least one of them down with her. That was her entertainment.*

*Dark, empty eyes moved over her legs and arms. She couldn't remember the last time she'd had a proper shower or a bite of food that wasn't laced with something to disorient her. She had a constant rumble in her stomach; hunger pains ever present.*

*When she heard footsteps approaching, her gaze traveled over to the door that held her captive. Years she waited for HIM to come for her. She knew he would, KNEW it. But time and time again, he didn't. She wondered if something had happened to him, or if he just didn't care what her fate was. After a while, she didn't long for him as often. Only on occasion did she allow herself to think of him.*

*The footsteps ceased outside her enclosure and she heard muffled male voices. Several minutes later, the door opened and HE strolled in without giving her as much as a second glance. "I've got it covered, leave us," Justus Azrael, overlord of Lucifer's Punishment Realm, instructed the other guards that had accompanied him. They fell back and shut the door, closing them in together.*

*Delia's battered heart flipflopped as she wobbled to her feet. She couldn't believe he had ultimately come to release her! "You finally made it!" she exclaimed happily as she limped to him.*

*His hand halted her forward progress when he caught her by the throat, cutting off her airflow. She stared up at him, confused. He generally only choked her when they were fucking or fighting.*

*"Shut up," his voice was stone cold, and his gaze icy and full of malice as he glared at her. A beat later, her frail body was bouncing off of the unforgiving cell wall.*

*She crumpled to the ground in a heap, her body throbbing and burning with fresh anguish, but she barely registered the pain.*

*Surprised by his action, she wearily looked up at him as he neared. "Wha..what are you doing?!" Her whacked out mind tryed to make sense of the situation. Perhaps it wasn't Justus at all, maybe it was a cruel trick her mind was playing after so long in isolation.*

*She scrambled to upright herself, but he was faster. Her claws swung, getting numerous swipes deep into his bare chest and arms, but he gripped her throat again. This time, he raised Delia up briefly before he slammed her body to the ground, little poofs of soot kicking up from the impact. "I said, shut the fuck up."*

*Eyes wide, she gasped for a moment, trying to regain the breath he'd knocked out of her. Justus stood above her, peering down as if she were nothing more than a bug on the floor. Kicking out at him, Delia tried to garner the space needed to get up. Her strength wasn't the best these days, but her fighting spirit hadn't gone anywhere. The demoness landed a blow to his knee and heard the crack.*

*"That was stupid," Justus remarked, as he bent and grabbed her legs, knocking her hands away when she reached to dislodge them.*

*One at a time, he wrenched her feet backwards and busted her ankles with the hyperextensions. Delia didn't make a sound, knowing better than to show the slightest hint of weakness. It did hurt though, she couldn't deny that. Despite her pain threshold being high, she still felt things.*

*Mostly what she felt at this moment, however, was her heart shattering into a billion pieces.*

*Justus dropped her legs and stepped back with a slight limp. "Get up," he instructed her, knowing damn well she couldn't.*

*An astounded look passed across her sunken features as she stared up at him, still unsure if it was actually him or not. "Justus? Please, don't. I swear… I didn't know who she was!" Tears began to well in her hollow eyes, so many years she'd waited for him to come to her, to get her out of there.*

*Obviously, if this was indeed Justus, those dreams were just cruel nightmares.*

*Delia scrambled backward on her ass as Justus began to shake his head, malice glinting in his eyes. She knew that look. They'd known each other intimately and had worked together for centuries. He was treating her as one of his prisoners. He wasn't there to free her at all.*

*If there had been anything in her stomach, the Furie would have vomited when that realization hit her.*

*Possibly, just possibly, he didn't understand the situation, she thought. "Jus!" she screamed as her back hit the flaming wall again. "I swear I was set up!" Many of her male counterparts despised the demoness. "I had no way to know that was one of Lucifer's whores!"*

*Delia threw her hands up in surrender when Justus began slowly stalking toward her. His face giving away nothing other than menacing intent. "PLEASE, baby! Don't do this!" She yipped when he took her begging arms and torqued them, dislocating both of her shoulders with a sickening* POP.

*Before she could get another word out, he had her long, matted hair wrapped around his hand, which he proceeded to use to jerk her to his eye level. Though her feet were dangling on useless ankles, her knees were aimed to crush his manhood, but he batted them away before throwing her to the other side of the enclosure. This time she slammed into the fiery, spelled door and was immediately electrocuted, shooting her back over to Justus.*

*The half-breed stepped out of the way and allowed her to faceplant to the ground. The nauseating sound of cracking bones filled the air once again; her nose and jaw taking the brunt of the impact.*

*Delia lay there, silently, blood pooling under her cheek, mentally tallying her injuries, scrambling for a plan of defense.*

*No arms. No feet, although her legs still worked, she could still throw a knee. As soon as that thought passed her mind, Justus stomped on the back of her thighs with his large boots, instantly crushing both femurs.*

*Keeping her face to the floor, Delia soundlessly winced. She kept chanting to herself, "This can't be Jus. He would never do this to me".*

*The demoness gasped when she felt the impact to her splintering ribcage as he kicked her over onto her back. Grit assaulted her vision. The Furie tried to look up at him, but he was only a watery blur.*

*Justus knelt over her and Delia mumbled softly through her demolished face, "Baby.."*

*With that one word, Justus drove his blade deep into her chest, piercing her sluggish heart. Blood began gurgling up her throat as her soul cried desperately for him to save her.*

*Blood loss had her vision wavering, but just before she blacked out, she could make out his smile as he reached into the wound. Breaking the last couple of intact ribs, he plucked her obliterated heart from her body to dangle in front of her.*

*Tears cleared a trail down her soot and blood encrusted face as the life left her devastated gaze.*

No stranger to nightmares, Delia awoke in a familiar cold sweat and sat bolt upright on her sofa, still high from her raid on the drug vault the evening before. Trembling hands roamed around the cushions, fumbling for her phone.

Finding it wedged under her ass, she held it out while her eyes struggled to focus enough to see the time: 4:14 pm. "Shiiiit," she groaned, should have been downstairs at the club over an hour ago. Jumping up…and almost falling over, she quickly showered and threw on clothes before tracing over to the office.

Scowl in place, Rez was sitting at her desk, thumbing through invoices. "Nice you could make it," he snarked, not bothering to lift his gaze from the paperwork. "And a thank you for covering your shift last night would be cool, too."

Ignoring him and his attitude, Delia walked over to the adjoining room, straight to the drug vault and popped it open.

"Why don't you inventory it while you're cleaning it out. That shit doesn't magically appear, ya know." Always one to state the obvious, Rez didn't stop there. "At the rate you're going, we need to double our next orders." Delia clearly heard him grumble under his breath, "Fucking addicts."

Rolling bloodshot eyes, she threw together a quick speedball then grabbed a handful of benzos for good measure. Fuck it, whatever got her through the night; she wasn't concerned what her friends and co-workers thought of her coping mechanisms.

"How about as long as you're getting that big, fat paycheck, you keep your fucking commentary to yourself, hmm?" The demoness was in no mood for bullshit. "In fact, another shitty comment out of you and I'll demonstrate how quickly I can remove your tongue," she growled, shooting him a venomous death glare as she washed down the pills and walked out the door.

---

Sleep had been non-existent since the altercation with Delia the day before, but Justus had put those extra hours to good use by relentlessly tracking his marks.

Returning to his room, his jaw clenched tight. Her lingering scent still permeated the area. He debated with himself over staying or checking out and moving to a different hotel. The reluctant half-breed was hopelessly conflicted.

While he told himself he never wanted to see the demoness again, he also couldn't bear the thought of never laying eyes on her once more. Her presence drudged up every abhorrent memory that he tried to keep buried and yet, somehow, also stirred in him a need and desire he'd never experienced elsewhere.

As if his stomach knew he needed a distraction, it rumbled. Justus walked over to the kitchenette and frowned. He couldn't recall the last time he'd eaten. Rummaging through the fridge and cabinets, little sustenance was to be found. He had never been much of a grocery shopper. There were more than enough restaurants nearby, though. He'd find something, somewhere, soon enough.

Opening the door to exit his suite, he was caught off guard as a male stood there with an arm raised, braced to knock.

He could smell the fear on the guy when he asked, irritated, "What do you want?"

The kid stammered and held out an envelope with the name "Jussy" on it. *Great.* He knew exactly who it was from. "On-only to deliver this to you, sir," the small male stammered as he kept his frightened eyes low, staring at the letter.

Snatching the envelope, Justus barked, "Anything else? What, you want a tip?"

Why was Delia sending what appeared to be a teenager to do her errands? The boy needed a tip to stay far, far away from that Furie and her business dealings.

"N-no, sir. That is all!" The male speed walked away toward the elevator.

A faint growl stirred as Justus stepped back and closed the door. Reluctantly, he opened the envelope and unfolded the papers. A cover letter read:

*Jus,*
*I would love to say it's been great seeing you again, but… well…*
*Instead, I've enclosed your bill for my therapy. Since you refuse to leave, I figure you are responsible for the things I have to do to tolerate your presence in MY town.*
*You may pay by cash or credit card. Immediately, of course.*
*Fuck you, you prick.*
*-Delia*
*P.S. Since you're buying, I got the really high-quality shit.*

Justus gawked at the next pages. It was a bill for a laundry list of illegal drugs totaling a balance due of $172,000. That bitch was thoroughly fucked in the head if she thought he was going to pay this asinine invoice.

And who needs so many drugs?! Immortal or not.

Crumpling up the papers, he tossed them in the trash, shaking his head in disbelief at the balls on that female. Although, nothing about her should truly surprise him anymore.

Storming out of his suite to find dinner, he slammed the door behind him. That bitch had no clue the things he'd already done for her; he owed her NOTHING.

# CHAPTER 8

*"Yes, you WILL do it, boy! Or that wretched whore of a daughter of mine that birthed you will be no longer! CHOOSE. Which whore would you prefer stay alive?!" Nose to nose, Lucifer snarled in his face, "Make your choice, or you will end both of their miserable lives."*

*The loathing for his grandsire buried deep, Justus tried to reason with him. "Sir, Delia was set up. She had no knowledge of whom she was imprisoning. She was following false orders, issued by someone who is out to harm YOU." That was likely not true, but Justus was unsure of the particulars; so technically it may not be a lie. The half-breed's tone was not quite as level as he'd hoped for; his anger seeped through.*

*The king of the underworld took offense when Justus' fist slammed down onto the grand desk they stood before. Long, talon-like fingers encircled Justus' wrist and squeezed, piercing his flesh, causing his bones to fall to pieces. "CHOOSE," Lucifer growled. "And know that if you do not treat your sidekick as any other prisoner, I will take over. And if I have to take time out of my day to punish a fucking servant... Well, you cannot even begin to imagine the ways in which I will make her suffer. Your mother will be next." Lucifer slammed his grandson's mangled hand on the desk, then stared into his unflinching eyes. "YOU will make her pay for endangering my unborn or I will. UNDERSTOOD?"*

*Icy eyes, filled with flecks of gold, bore into Lucifer's infuriated, crimson gaze. Justus knew he had to make the decision quickly. His only friend and lover…or the mother who chanced her father's wrath to keep him safe?*

*His mother, Amara, never told his father, Azrael, the Archangel of Death, nor anyone else of Justus' conception. She'd fled to earth to birth him and left him with a wealthy, prominent family who were unable to conceive children of their own. Justus had only seen his birth mother once; when Lucifer brought him to Hell. She was the leverage his grandsire used to keep him working in the realm. Justus stayed, or Amara died. She had risked everything for him. How could he betray her now?!*

*Justus had no clue how he was going to complete the task ahead of him, but he knew he couldn't let them both die. "I'll do it." He nearly choked on the words, but he held steady so as not to show favoritism to the King. "I'll punish Delia for endangering our Prince." He would do what he must until he could get both females out of Hell.*

Sweat dampened sheets clung to Justus' mostly naked body as he awoke with a jolt. Sitting up, he drew long, deep breaths to calm his racing heart while focusing on the wrist that had healed long ago.

It was no surprise the nightmares had resurfaced since coming into contact with the Furie. He was certain that staying far away from her had been his only saving grace. The guilt and shame were now back, tenfold.

Delia hated him, that much was clear, and she would never understand or forgive him for the things he'd had to do. Nor would she believe the lengths he had gone to for her escape to have been possible. So, if hating him made her feel better, so be it.

That woman was as stubborn and bullheaded as ever. They hadn't seen each other in nearly a week, but he knew she was still stalking his room. Nearly every night when he came in, her lingering scent tortured his senses. And his psyche. Random things would disappear, while other, foreign items would mysteriously appear.

Every day, he lost another piece of clothing or personal item while a silly coffee mug or smart ass shot glass would pop up on his table, counter, or in one of his cabinets.

Don't get him started on the toiletries. Delia had a real knack for switching those out. She wasn't attempting to be stealthy in the slightest. She'd leave notes on the mirror in black lipstick or his shaving cream.

Justus assumed these visits would keep occurring until he left the city. Moving rooms at this point would only be a waste of time. He knew she'd find him, wherever he wound up.

Breathing normally again, he got up and got ready for the day. He had to find this last player in the trafficking ring. It wasn't clear if the guy was actually good at hiding, or if Justus was completely distracted by his past.

Regardless, the half-breed knew he had to wrap this thing up sooner rather than later.

ALL of it. The case and the ex. He was getting extremely tired of all of Hannah's questions surrounding the situation here. And she had many, every time they spoke.

Fresh out of the shower, dressed in perfectly fitted, faded blue jeans and a black t-shirt, he checked his texts and emails before logging in to peek on his mark. He'd placed cameras and bugs at the degenerate's residence and the locations where numerous private meetings had taken place. Currently, the bastard was snoozing away in his plush, gated McMansion, which meant it was as good a time as any to hunt down some lunch and get in a workout.

---

Glassy grey eyes scanned the main bar area from the balcony above. It was an average crowd for a Thursday afternoon at the club; a few dozen regulars were either perched and watching the dancers, or saddled up to the bar, drinking away their worries.

Delia stepped back a few feet, crawled into her private booth and fired up a blunt as she observed, distracted. She was jonesing to pay Jus another visit. She had been popping in over there at least once a day.

She took a hard drag of the heroine laced weed and murmured to herself, "Rotten bastard always has been my greatest weakness."

Reaching up, she depressed her earbud, alerting her second in command. "Rez, I'm jetting for a bit." She didn't wait for his smart-ass reply, she ghosted immediately, materializing beside Jus' bed.

She meandered over to the cushy sofa that had somewhat become her 'spot'. She plopped down before a shadow outside the floor-to-ceiling, sliding glass doors caught her attention. Heavy, thick, maroon drapes obscured most of her vision, but through a gap she caught sight of Justus on the oversized balcony. Elbows resting on her knees, she leaned forward to gauge what he was doing. Apparently, he'd had a high bar and some other workout equipment installed.

Taking another hit before stamping out her blunt on a plate with remnants of fresh food, the demoness wandered over to the refrigerator and got herself a Satan Sake and popped the top. After a long chug, she traced onto the balcony, a couple feet in front of Jus as he did pull ups.

Delia was just blitzed enough to let her eyes roam unchecked as the growl rumbling in his chest grew louder. "What are you doing here?" he'd asked, she realized after a moment.

Snapping out of her eye-fuck, which was unfortunate, he was a damn fine specimen, she replied nonchalantly, "Ah, ya know, I sensed you missed me so I stopped by to grace you with my delightful face." She flashed him a Cheshire Cat smile. Her midnight painted lips twitched with amusement when he growled again. Jus dropped to the ground, swaggered over to a weight bench and sat down. "Say, did you get that mini bar restocked yet? It was pretty low last time I was here."

Icy, incredulous eyes pinned hers as Justus shook his head. "You're fucking certifiable. You break into my room every single day and steal shit.."

"I also bring gifts! Don't forget that part!" she interrupted him with a wicked grin.

His deadpan stare nearly had her chuckling. "What. Do. You. Want?! This act is getting old quick, De."

"What act?! I check in every now and then to remind you that you need to be leaving. Until you do, might as well have some fun, yeah?" Delia unleashed a million-megawatt smile. "But truthfully, it appears you need to call in backup. It kinda seems like you're pretty shit at your job. I'm just sayin'...from an outsider's view."

Frigid blues narrowed on her. "You don't need to be worrying yourself over my missions, I'll be done soon enough and then out of this deplorable town and far away from YOU. In the meantime, keep your grubby hands off my stuff, psycho wench."

"Words. We've had this discussion before, Jussy." A faux pout crept across her features. "Words hurt. Be nice."

"Why would I be nice now? You have done plenty to earn my bubbly personality. The fact that we are sitting here, chatting, if that's what this shit is called, and I've not killed you…that means I am, indeed, being NICE." Irritated fingers stabbed through his sweat soaked hair. "Oh, and lay off the drugs. They make your scent reek." His nosed scrunched briefly to show his disgust.

"Ohhhh, is that why you haven't paid the invoice yet? You think that will slow down my consumption?" *Pfft. As if!*

Justus stood abruptly and come to a stop inches from the demoness, glaring down at her. "I will never pay that ridiculous bill. Ruin yourself with your own money." Delia let her fingers do the walking along his slick, bare chest and let her eyes track the action. She grinned when she saw movement in those very revealing sweatpants of his. "Stop it. Stop it and get out, Delia. I'm not fucking with you!"

"Yeah, but…" Delia's fingers kept trailing along his overly defined pecs, then down to his eight-pack abs. "I'm fuckin' with you, see." Large hands grabbed her wrists, halting her movement any lower. "Spoil sport!" she huffed, winking up at him, entirely aware of how she affected him.

And herself. *Damnit!*

---

The half-breed was astounded by her behavior. What game was she playing at this time? Because he could play, too, if that was the way of things now. There was no way he could hide the growing length in his pants, and he sure as shit could sense her own level of arousal. She couldn't hide hers any better. *So let's put the screws to her.* Justus inwardly cringed at the analogy. Wrong time for thoughts such as the ones he was having.

The suppressed emotions in Hell were in full force nowadays. Everything about his ex was stirring him, in one way or another. He was feeling foreign things he couldn't name, because it'd been centuries since he'd felt anything at all. Even living in this realm for decades hadn't woken in him anything close to what the demoness had done to him since seeing her in that dark alley.

Torture. This was his torture. She was unwittingly getting more revenge than she realized.

Justus dropped her hands and smirked as his fingers combed through her long periwinkle locks. "Okay. I'm in." His brow raised in question as he asked, "Shall we take this inside or should I undress you here for all to see?"

The dark beauty struck him with great force across the face, not entirely surprising him as he burst into insidious laughter. "Ya know, you REALLY are a prick!" Delia shoved at his chest. "Finish your job and get the fuck out of my town!"

Justus couldn't help but feel both joy at 'winning' this round, and a distinct sense of sadness at the situation they were in as she ghosted away.

Grabbing a towel from the bench, he traced to the shower to cool down and get his head straight. He had to finish this mission and he had to get away from Delia before something far worse happened.

# CHAPTER 9

Three days straight of non-stop stake-outs and tracking finally revealed the missing player Justus had been waiting for. Kendrick, the last of the trafficking cohorts. He was back in town, meeting with the greasy ringleader in a small, seemingly abandoned warehouse down by the river.

Darkness had converged on the area and the interior of the space was lit by nothing more than a single, hanging lightbulb on a chain. On the floor above the two scoundrels, Justus crouched in a heavily shadowed corner of rafters, watching and listening.

"So, what the hell happened to Arik and Feltz? Neither have answered any of my texts or calls." Kendrick inquired, as he scowled deeply.

"Uh, yeah, about that..." Mr. Potato began, shaking his head. "Both of 'em turned up in the landfill a couple days ago. They'd been worked over pretty good. Those idiots probably took the wrong kid and got caught." He shrugged to show his indifference. "Doesn't matter, though, the shipment is still on track to move out," the greaseball checked his watch, "…in five hours. Right on time."

Long, auburn hair fell over his shoulders as Kendrick whistled low in relief. "Perfect. South Shore, with the usual crew?"

"Definitely. Yacht is fueled and full of supplies. We're good to go."

"How many down below? Did we meet the quota?"

Justus' blood was boiling listening to the sick assholes discuss their 'cargo' as if they were discussing fruit and veggies. His eyes glowed gold as his claws extended.

"You know it! Plus a few extra," Mr. Potato barked with a husky chuckle. "Never hurts to have spares, am I right?!"

Game over. Justus couldn't listen any longer.

With a growl so deep it reverberated through the thick rafters and echoed throughout the space, he traced. Suddenly he stood in between the two guys, each of their necks gripped in his lethal hands. As their eyes bugged out in horror, he squeezed, allowing his sharp claws to pierce their flesh. The two struggled as much as they could, but his grip was solid.

"Sorry to break up the party here, boys. I got a tip that the rats were getting out of hand. Are you ready to join your buddies at the landfill?" Justus looked back and forth between the two as they fought to speak; pathetically scratching and hitting at his steel trap arms. "No?" He allowed them to struggle a bit more. "Okay, I can put it off a few minutes more." Justus slung Kendrick into a discarded pontoon boat, knocking him out.

Turning back to the greasy louse still under his grip, he reached into a tactical pocket of his pants and produced some heavy-duty zip ties.

After securing the guido to a girder, he stalked over to Kendrick and dragged his lifeless body by the hair, to lay alongside his partner. Justus grabbed a lone, metal chair and wrangled the unconscious sicko onto it, before turning back to Mr. Potato. "I hear you like to watch. So, you should really enjoy what's coming next." Justus winked and grinned before digging smelling salts from his pocket.

Kendrick immediately startled awake and Mr. Potato groveled, "Look man, I don't know who hired you, but we'll double…no, no, we'll triple your fee! Give you anything you want!"

"That's very kind of you, bud," Justus sneered, "but the only thing I want is to see you both dead. Don't you worry, though. I'll see to it that your money goes to the victims of that shipment that's never going to move tonight."

Justus' fist slammed into Kendrick's jaw, knocking him out again. This time his mouth was left hanging open. A trail of blood oozed from his nose and joined the one from his mouth, before collecting in his lap as his head lolled to the side.

"They'll kill you for this!" The guido had changed his tune, he spat meaningless threats now. "We are an international operation! You'll be hunted and tortured in ways you can't imagine!" Mr. Potato thrashed against his restraints while he attempted to maintain any sort of dominant demeanor. "Then, just when you think it's almost over, they'll throw you to the hogs so they can finish you off!"

Unconcerned, Justus glanced at him as he ran a sharp claw around the edges of Kendrick's face. This effectively woke him again, while, at the same time, removed all of his heavily tanned flesh. Screams and bellows rang out from both men as one felt the horror and the other witnessed it. Justus smirked as he peeled, then dangled the deflated mask on his finger between the hysterical scumbags.

"Maybe it's just me, but I think this is a real improvement. Wouldn't you say, buddy?" Neither of the men answered. They only cried and plead for mercy. "Anyway." The face flopped to the ground and Justus propelled it with the toe of his boot, flicking it up onto Mr. Potato's lap, causing more theatrics. "The more you carry on, the more joy it gives me. So, please, do continue!"

Crouching beside Kendrick, Justus produced a long dagger from his hip holster. Sternum to pelvic bone, he effortlessly sliced, as if gutting a fish, all the while reveling in the depraved carnage. Kendrick was out like a light, while his nauseous compadre began crying harder, gagging, and eventually hyperventilating.

*Amazing how the tides turned when you were on the receiving end of the torture, eh?*

After decorating Mr. Potato with intestinal contents, including some kidney earrings from the toy box, Kendrick left the mortal world for his next home in Hell. Justus swelled with power from the kill.

Now it was the ringleader's turn. Right as Justus was about to give the meatball a tour of his own body cavity unveiling, a single set of police lights lit up the exterior. Bummed by the intrusion, Justus covered the guido's mouth with a hand while cutting through his khaki pants with the other. He dismantled the twig and berries awaiting there. Moving his hand from the barely conscious scum's mouth, he replaced it with those useless parts and crammed them down his throat.

Radio activity and voices were quickly moving closer to the warehouse. Justus patted Meatball's head, "You got lucky, ole boy. I had so much more in store for you. Enjoy the Underworld, asshole." With one last glance at his handy work, he traced to the location of the yacht and called in an anonymous tip to the cops.

Justus stayed to watch the chaos that ensued. All thirty-eight victims were recovered and all perps arrested. Not a bad way to end a nice night, he mused, before ghosting.

# CHAPTER 10

"Why am I still here?" Justus grumbled into his hands as he sat back on the sofa in his hotel room. He should have gone home last night when the mission was completed. Yet, here he still sat. Every time he'd attempted to pack, he'd stop and have a seat as his thoughts ricocheted in a million different directions. He hadn't slept, eaten, or done anything productive in the last twelve hours. The half-breed was stuck in limbo.

Alerts began blaring from his phone and laptop.

Hannah. On FaceTime.

Great, exactly what he didn't need in this moment. He knew, however, that if he didn't answer, she'd only call repeatedly until he finally did. Biting the bullet, he opened his laptop in front of him and accepted the disturbance, "Hey, what do you need?" He tried to keep his tone even.

"Oh my gosh! Justus, are…are you okay?" Hannah overreacted, her light green eyes widening on the screen before him.

Slightly puzzled, he answered, "Uh, yes, I'm fine. Why the worry?"

Her long, curly blonde hair sprang about as she shook her head. "You haven't checked in for days! And, um, well, you look like you've been through the ringer, honey!"

Before he could reply, his buxom manager was standing before him in all of her royal splendor. Her bloodline was among the best of the best; he still muddled over why she worked for him. Other than the obvious. She'd never made it a secret that she wanted to be his, and, quite frankly, that exhausted him. He didn't have it in him currently to play this little charade with her. "Hannah, there is no need for you to be here. Please, just leave." His voice was firm, but not harsh; he probably should've gone with the rude tone he preferred.

Justus stood and walked over to the kitchenette, Hannah on his heels, to get a Satan Sake from the fridge. Ignoring her close proximity, he popped the top and chugged the cold drink. The dark fae wound her arms around his waist and stared up at him; her chin settled on his chest. "Talk to me, J. Please tell me what's going on?"

"For the last time, nothing is going on that concerns you. Please, leave." What was it with having to tell females to get out of his room lately? This was turning into a really bad rom-com. "I've got some loose ends to tie up, then I'll be back in Sydney."

Justus' head turned sharply toward the sofa when Delia appeared there and he cursed under his breath, "Shit. Here we go..."

*Understatement of the year, that one.*

---

It was the middle of the afternoon and the club was slow, what better time to dip out and see what Jus was up to? It'd been a hot minute since she trusted herself to be around him. That last go on the balcony had ended dismally, but she assured herself that her ducks, er, squirrels more like it, were back in a row...jumbled, but still.

Before Delia ever fully materialized in that hotel suite, she'd detected the scent of another being in the room. A female. A dark fae. She'd know a scent like that anywhere, considering she'd been poisoned with the race's blood for the majority of her incarceration in Hell.

The good part? She'd built up quite the tolerance to the putrid lifeforce over those years. GAME ON.

"Who in the world is *THAT*, J?? Is she a vagrant?" Hannah asked impishly, stepping closer into Justus as she locked eyes with Delia. The demoness wasn't buying her naïve, wholesome act, though.

Delia glanced down at the Guns N' Roses tee, red leather pants, and black boots she was sporting. She glared back at the blonde; the bitch knew damn well Delia wasn't homeless, nor a stranger to Jus. Justus stood in silence, ready and waiting to see what the demoness was going to do. "Oh, Jussy, you're into Dolly Parton rip-offs now? Tsk Tsk. What a disappointment to see you settling for such unoriginality," Delia shook her head in disgust.

Hannah sputtered; *her acting skills needing much work if we're being honest here.* A muscle in Justus' jaw ticked a moment before he made any remarks. "Hannah, leave NOW," he barked, as he unwound her arms from him. "Delia, don't start shit. She's done nothing to you." Hannah turned with a smirk, and pressed her back against Justus; taunting. "Hannah, NOW!"

*Too slow.*

Delia traced and grabbed the dark fae by the throat, slamming her against the same wall Justus had previously knocked her own head on. *Just look at how things turn-about, would ya?!*

Hannah screeched, throwing fists, but Delia was oblivious to any blows she landed. Her attention was fully on Justus. "I mean, seriously, Jus...pathetic."

"Cut it out, De! Her blood. Stop fucking around!" Eyes glowing that ethereal gold. "Her blood is royal and quite potent! Do you have a death wish?!" Justus grabbed her arms, yanking the demoness off of Hannah and allowing the bitch to ghost out of the place; infuriating Delia further. "Stop being stupid, De!"

The laughter began light, then increased in volume and pitch. Justus dropped his hold on the Furie and took a step back, fully aware that those were the sounds of insanity cranking up and he had no clue where it would go next.

Delia spun around to stare up at him; her hair and eyes having long ago morphed to black. "Stop being stupid?" She giggled, then her face turned to stone. "I'll fucking kill her if I see her again." Depthless eyes floated down his body to the ever ready, rapidly swelling appendage in his jeans. "And if she ever touches you again, I'll feed her own hands and eyes to her first."

Justus' gaze widened before his brow furrowed. "You're off your rocker, psycho. You have no claim on me, nor have you ever wanted one. Why would you care who I spend time with?!"

That was a question Delia didn't have an answer to. All she knew was that Justus was HERS and always had been, as far as her demented logic was concerned. Did she still hate him? Absolutely. Did she also go mental at the thought of anyone being with him other than herself? Yeppers!

Unquestionably, she'd utterly lost her mind. The Furie had one thousand percent boarded the crazy train and apparently would be staying aboard for quite some time.

Delia traced and torpedoed into Jus' thick form, slamming him against the full-length mirror mounted on the wall behind him. Shards erupted and sprayed all over them, though he quickly recovered from the surprise hit.

Justus snatched a huge section of her long hair, wrenching it around his fist. His other hand went to her throat and returned the favor of ramming her against the opposite wall. He held her there, his heavenly body wedged up against her lithe frame.

Dangerous territory.

Both panted for breath as their enraged glares remained unwaveringly locked, his shaft turning to granite as it nudged at her stomach.

Surprise flashed across her face, Delia felt the familiar swelling of her gums, then her fangs sharpened and elongated. Breathing ceased for the demoness. It took a good few seconds before she rallied, remembering to do the ole inhale/exhale again.

A return of one of her long lost Furie traits! Those puny canines were no more, hello precious FANGS! A sinister smile grew along her features as the sharp points dipped past her lips.

Justus took notice.

---

The half-breed's hands tightened their grip as he growled, "If you think I'm going to let you rip my throat out with those new playthings," he nodded to the displayed fangs, "think again, bitch. Not going to happen!"

Justus slammed her against the wall again when she began to snap them at him. He had no idea what he had gotten into here. He'd never seen Delia act this way.

Sure, they'd been together for centuries in Hell, before the clusterfuck happened, but they'd never been anything serious.

Had they?

Admittedly, he had basically no emotions whatsoever while in the Underworld, it was some strange side-effect that realm had on him. But had SHE thought they were a couple this whole time?

He supposed anything was possible, but she'd never been the possessive or mushy type. They'd certainly never discussed being anything more than work and bed buddies.

Now his mind was all over the place again. Had she felt more for him than he realized during that time? He'd definitely had plenty of conflicting thoughts and feelings emerge since getting his emotions somewhat back. How oblivious could he have been about them both? How do you gauge the true nature of a relationship when you'd had your emotional grid removed from the equation?

Bloody hell, he was so fucked in this situation. Obscenely clueless. The only thing he knew for a fact was that she had always meant something to him. She had to, for him to have given up what he had...she had to have meant something.

What in the Lorena Bobbitt was going on?!

Justus snapped back to the present when he registered that the demoness had begun to roll her hips into him. Her claws had snaked around his back and were digging into his ass, anchoring him firmly against her.

A feral moan-growl, one he had never heard out of himself, filled the air. He fought against common sense and began to move his own hips in opposition to hers. The friction on his overly engorged shaft was some sort of heavenly hell.

This wench was the only one who had ever been able to get him this turned on and amped up.

That was why she was TROUBLE.

He released her hair as the fragrance of decadent dark chocolate and cherries assaulted his senses, nearly overpowering him with need. His hand trailed down her side and in between her legs to cup her sex. The heat and dampness felt through her pants almost had his knees buckling.

Delia hissed in a sharp breath, then moaned while he teased her, working them both up into a frenzy.

Justus decided that if this was her ploy to kill him...well, he couldn't think of a better way to go.

---

The next thing Delia knew, she was flying through the air, landing backside first on the bed. Justus loomed in front of her, at the foot of the bed; his glowing eyes laser focused on her. She didn't fight it. Couldn't have fought it if she wanted to.

And she did not want to. Even if it was the single most asinine act she'd ever participated in. *And that was sayin' a LOT.*

With a quick sweep of the arms, she'd pulled off her t-shirt and tossed it aside. Jus' eyes flared and he ripped off his own shirt.

*Fine by her!* She would never tire of ogling the plethora of dips and swells his physique displayed, and all of it covered in that lick-able ink that painted such a beautiful portrait along the canvas of his body.

The demoness' fingers brushed over the black lace covered mounds of her breasts and continued down, across her toned midriff, to find the button of her leather pants. Justus tracked every move with anticipation.

His own hand moved to uncage the beast trapped beneath his zipper. As his jeans dropped and he stepped out of them, Delia purred at the fact he was going commando. It was indeed her lucky day.

Staring at her favorite appendage, standing proud and erect, she seemed to have lost her train of thought. Not once had she ever anticipated seeing him like this again.

He was magnificent.

Justus grabbed the waistband of her pants and, in one fell swoop, removed them, leaving her in a matching black lace thong. Gold hues devoured every inch of her feverish body. The groan he emitted when he palmed his shaft and began to slowly stroke, nearly made her whimper with desperation. She couldn't peel her eyes away from the action as she leaned up on her elbows.

Delia was torn, though. She didn't understand how they'd gotten here. How could she forget all of the things he'd done to her? How could she ever trust him again?

Her body was so overheated, she couldn't think straight! The demoness leapt from the bed and strode to the kitchen, shaking her head, fighting tears that wanted to spill. She tried to ignore his escalating growl as she kept her back to him.

---

Justus could only guess at what insanity was going through that little temptress' head as she stood there with her perfectly rounded, firm ass taunting him. His cock was about to explode for fucks sake! If it was possible, she was even more alluring and gorgeous than he'd remembered. And damn if he didn't recall a great amount.

But yes, he'd definitely let this go too far. He should have sent her home long ago. "Clearly this was a bad idea," he muttered, as softly as possible with all that grit in this throat. "Hannah was only he-…" He never got to finish that sentence, Delia launched herself at him.

The momentum of her attack landed them on the bed again. This time with him on his back and Delia straddling his hips. The heat of her thonged sex was mind scrambling when she settled on him; his length throbbed blissfully under the weight.

"Don't you ever say her name again," she hissed, her fangs along with her forked tongue giving her a slight lisp. The wildness in her eyes momentarily struck fear in him, but then her hips began to undulate and he lost all capacity for entertaining sensible thoughts.

Delicate hands with those lethal claws latched onto his pecs, piercing his skin. Fangs dug into her lip while those depthless eyes watched the blood trickle down his chest.

Justus felt zero pain. In fact, quite the opposite. Much to his approval, he watched her mystifying body take him over as she rose, ripped her thong free and impaled herself on his aching cock.

Their long, drawn out moans echoed around the room as she worked herself up and down…up…and…down the thick member until her tight depths allowed him to fully submerge.

When she was finally seated completely, Justus' hands gripped her waist and held her there a moment to calm himself, before he lost his load in record time. No one but this amazing creature could illicit such a response from him.

Watching her grind down on him, he knew for certain, she'd be his ultimate undoing.

---

Everything about this was disastrously wrong.

Yet, epically right.

The conflicting thoughts warred as she teetered that line of euphoria and hatred. Justus felt mind-blowingly amazing.

Too good. Too perfect.

Delia's hips began to move again and, with each stroke, her brain short-circuited a bit more.

Sweat dotted Justus' brow as he strained for control. It was quite a turn on as he groaned and grunted, keeping a vice grip on her hips.

No longer concerned with anything other than dominance and pleasure, Jus turned feral.

He raised and forcefully pounded her down on his pulsing shaft. A vicious growl reverberating in his deep chest as he manhandled her, triggered Delia's own instincts.

Dark eyes widened as her fangs began to swell larger. Venom seeping from them.

Mating venom.

A scenario she'd never encountered before. It made no sense! She'd been with Justus countless times in Hell.

WHY NOW?! No. NO. NO. NO! This could not be happening.

Furie demons only have one, true, fated mate. When that being is found, the venomous bite claims them for all immortals to recognize. The venom leaves a scar, a visible TAKEN sign, if you will.

The Furie tried to break their stride but Justus was hopelessly lost in it. He continued to perfectly ravish her, her body beginning to tense as a release was building.

Jus assaulted her sweet spot relentlessly, as no one else ever had.

Waves of a rapturous orgasm soon overtook her and juices flowed over him like the crashing of a tidal wave. Instinct overload spurred her to lower her head to the roped bands of muscle between Jus' neck and shoulder. With absolutely no thought to consequences, Delia impaled her throbbing fangs deep into his flesh, letting the venom flow, catapulting Justus straight into his own shuddering waves of release.

Together, they rode them out, oblivious to anything else.

As the aftershocks and tremors subsided, Delia released her fangs before sitting up. Both of them panting for breath.

It appeared that clarity finally fell upon Justus as his eyes shot wide and he reached to feel where her fangs had been. A deep growl rumbled before he roared, "What the fuck have you done?!"

No warning, no theatrics. Delia's deadly claws abruptly harpooned through Justus' chest. The shock on his beautiful face likely appearing much the same as hers had been in Hell, back when he betrayed her.

Ribs fractured as the demoness yanked his heart free. A gorgeous crimson waterfall gushed from the chest cavity.

Holding the still beating organ out, for both to see, tears streamed down Delia's cheeks as she rasped, "Apparently, I loved you."

# CHAPTER 11

Nearly a week had gone by and Delia was reminded of some mating details the hard way.

By experience.

All races of immortals had varying methods and rituals for claiming their fated mates. Furie demons, as well as numerous other types of demon, marked them with venom, as she had done to Justus. The hideous side-effects of that little gem? Well, if a Furie was not claimed in return, they basically went into withdrawal after a certain period of time elapsed with no contact from their mate. And these withdrawals made those caused by narcotics feel like a grand vacation in comparison. The demoness would know; she'd tried to quit the myriad substances in the vault many times over the years.

Since leaving Jus in his hotel room that disastrous night, unconscious, minus a heart, she'd been back to check on him several times a day. As much for her benefit as his, really.

So far, he had yet to wake, but his flesh had healed, meaning soon, soon Delia would have to face the music and endure his wrath. She'd also instructed hotel management that under no circumstances were anyone, including the maid service, to enter his suite until she gave the 'okay'.

Now she waited for the inevitable moment of reckoning that was to come when he awoke.

A knock brought her back to earth. The heavy office door opened and Rez came creeping in, shutting it behind him and leaning against it. He knew something was up, but Delia hadn't the stomach to tell anyone details.

No time better than the present, she figured and got dialogue started, "You need something or what?" *Ok, so that wasn't really jumping into the dreaded topic, now was it?*

Rez eyed his boss and friend suspiciously. "Yeah, I need to know…what the hell is going on with you? You're barely working, and acting very strangely. Did you get into some bad H or blow or something?" *The concern on his face was legit.*

With pale, clammy hands, Delia knuckle rubbed her exhausted eyes and then picked up her phone. While texting Zaylee to come over asap, she answered Rez, "Well, it's a clusterfuck of epic proportions, even for me. And I don't want to go over this twice, so I'm getting Zay here. I can fill you both in at the same time."

His large hand scrubbed over his bald head and Rez groaned, "Fuck. Now I'm not sure I want to know."

"Trust me, you don't. I don't even want to know." The Furie's periwinkle hair plummeted around her as she lowered her head to rest on the desktop, wondering if a few good bangs would make this all go away. "What the shitcicle is *this* asshatery?!" She sat back up holding a thick chunk of white hair.

Purple-blue? Cool. Jet back? Awesome. But WHITE?! *Hellllll naw!* "Great, another side effect," she whimpered to herself.

"De, you're kinda freakin' me out," Rez mumbled as he walked closer, his accent bleeding through.

Dove-greys rose to him. Rez's worried amber gaze looking back at her was almost too much for her to continue. The demoness whisper-confessed, "I'm long past that stage, bud. I'm royally fucked."

Slowing the momentum of words for a much needed moment, Zaylee materialized, standing in front of her desk. Delia met her bestie's frantic glare as Zay erupted, "What's wrong?! What happened?!" Some Spanish words were thrown in there also, while Zay's arms whipped around, fully animated as she remarked on the sorry sight before her. "A la chingada! You look like you're two steps from the long sleep! WHAT. IS. HAPPENING?!"

Dear gods, she loved her girl, but Zay was a LOT. Right now, Delia just needed to get this over with.

"Enough!" Delia stood, slamming her fist down on the sturdy desk, splintering it.

Zay clammed up quick and Rez swore under his breath as they both moved away. Rez put it in reverse to lean against the door and the fiery succubus took a seat on the arm of the sofa. Both stared and waited for Delia to elaborate.

After a beat and a composing breath, the demoness continued in a shaky voice, "I'm going to say this fast, and to the point because it's all I can manage." Her eyes neglected to meet theirs, knowing this would go over like a lead balloon. "About a week ago, I was at Justus' hotel and we fought…and then we…uh, kinda fucked." The demoness ignored the following stream of outraged expletives from her friends and continued to quickly speak over them, "AND I also marked him and ripped out his heart."

De cringed when the room went nuclear, but spoke louder until she was screaming. "NOW I AM GOING THROUGH HORRID WITHDRAWALS AND CAN'T DEAL WITH THIS SHIT! BEAT ME UP LATER!!" With that, she disappeared to the only place she would feel both better and worse--Justus' room.

---

Ice blue eyes cracked open as light streamed in through the opening in the curtains, scorching his retinas. Justus reached for his phone, only to find that apparently it was not on the bedside table as it should have been.

Pain in his chest lit up. Memories flooded him. Maybe it'd been a dream…turned nightmare.

He palpated his chest, then his shoulder. No, it was reality. The cunt had fucked him, marked him, then jacked his gods-damned heart!

Deep breaths.

Deep breaths.

The half-breed gingerly sat up and slung his legs over the edge of the bed. Standing and gaining decent balance, he spotted his phone on the bar.

Baby steps. This shit really hurt, but he felt immeasurably grateful for his angel side at that moment, it allowed him to heal much faster than most immortals. Without it, he'd likely be laying here for a month or more.

Actually, how long *HAD* he been out?

Slowly making his way over to the kitchen, he checked the time and date on the phone.

A week. He'd been left unprotected and vulnerable for an unforgivable WEEK! Anything could have happened to him in that time!

Bloody hell, he was going to kill that wench for what she'd done!

His head began to swim and Justus grabbed onto the bar stool, nearly landing on his face.

After a few minutes of simply breathing, he was able to stand upright. Methodically, he trudged to the shower and stepped in, cranking up the hot water. As long as the warmth held up, he had no plans of exiting anytime soon.

---

Delia materialized beside Justus' bed; only he wasn't there. The Furie slumped in relief when she heard the shower running. She looked around the room. It didn't appear he'd been awake long, as everything, minus his phone, was still as she'd left it. The sheets she'd changed yesterday were still clean; no signs of fresh blood.

Realizing he must be starving, she traced quickly to the club's kitchen. Minutes later, she returned with drinks and sandwiches.

Justus was still in the bathroom but the shower had been turned off.

Dread flooded her. Luckily, he was still too weak to rip her to pieces, but he had a sharp tongue and would no doubt lash her with at least a few choice words.

Grey eyes darted to the closed door, where a growl was emanating with growing ferocity.

She took a seat on the sofa; no way was she running to poke *that* bear! He could come to her. She heard his words before he breached the doorway of the bathroom. "Delia Payne, if you are in my hotel room then your balls are bigger than your brain," came the growl.

In her defense, though, he knew her balls had ALWAYS been bigger than her brain, so this really shouldn't come as a surprise to him.

Honestly, she only wanted to touch him so her nasty chills and nausea would subside a little. The entire time he'd been out, she'd lay cuddled up against him when she checked on him. He was the heating blanket to her block of ice. He was her fix now; her addiction. Only he could sooth her. And he was NOT going to like that fact.

Heavy footfalls turned her head back to the bathroom. Delia ceased breathing when she saw him; he was more glorious than ever in nothing but a towel. And pissed.

Oxygen moving again, she stood slowly. "Jus…"

He raised his hand silently, warning her to quiet. And she did.

Fingers wrenching one another, the Furie waited for what felt like an eternity for him to make his way back to the bed.

Justus sat at the bottom corner for a breather. He didn't make a peep nor look at her.

"I only..."

"Not another word from you, Delia. You marked me and ripped my heart out."

"You ripped mine out first, remember?" she mumbled under her breath, but he heard her just fine.

"Well, you got your revenge, didn't you? And, in true Delia fashion, you did so in the most wicked of ways."

"I swear, that wasn't premeditated."

Icy blues cut over to her and he grunted, "That makes it even worse." But then his eyes softened, just the slightest bit. "You look worse than I do, wench." His gaze lowered to her anxiously fidgeting fingers, then gave her a once over, not missing the faint, but constant, trembling of her body. "Drug vault not treating you kindly, huh."

Delia sat down…on her hands. "You could say that." She looked away from him, to the draped window. "Turns out being an unrequited mate has some hellacious ramifications."

Jus scoffed. "So, yet more misery you've brought upon yourself that you will somehow blame me for. Fantastic."

"No." She kept her eyes hidden. "No, I'm fully aware I only have myself to pin this one on." Delia stood, wrapping her arms around herself as the trembling worsened. "And now that I know you're okay, I won't bother you again."

"You fucking marked me! How exactly do you think we're to work this out?!" His disgusted, vile tone felt like daggers thrusting into her soul. "I'm fucking stuck with you now! It's clear you're already suffering! Now you're seriously just going to pretend it didn't happen?!" A sinister laugh, devoid of any joy, erupted from him. "And what exactly am I to do, walking around, sporting this oh-so-obvious mark?!"

Tears welled in her eyes, dangerously close to spilling. "Just tell anyone who asks that your mate died." She ghosted.

There was no need to wait on his response. She knew this was an unthinkable situation. She could berate and punish herself like a pro; she didn't need help from anyone else in those departments. Justus could live out his life just fine without her; she'd let him go.

# CHAPTER 12

"If I kill him, will that make this all go away?" Rez genuinely asked. The hot-mess-a-palooza demoness was sprawled out on the floor beside the open drug vault with an outrageously sized joint, full of all the things that would fit, hanging from the corner of her mouth. Delia proceeded to randomly pop pills as she rummaged through the goody bin. There was a literal pile of blow on the hardwood beside her that she'd made a considerable dent in. "De, you can't keep going like this. Immortal or not, you're going to kill yourself."

Glassy, hollow, horribly bloodshot eyes raised to Rez. A voice no one recognized replied, "I was as good as dead when I marked him. I'm just speeding along the process." A faint shrug of her shoulder caused her to slump over a bit, landing her free hand in the white powder. She shrugged again and went face first into the snow.

"Lucifer's arsehole!" Rez blurted as he charged over to her. "This is insane. Come on!" He scooped her up as she was still inhaling the powder and licking it off her hand. "Cut that shit out!" He knocked her hand away. "Shower time!" The smoke demon traced the Furie to her flat and set her in the clawfoot tub, then cranked up the water.

"OWWW!" She kicked at the knob, turning it back off. "It HUUUUURTS. ERRRYTHIN' hurts! Don' you unnerstan'?!" Delia pleaded with him through slurred words. "Lemme diiiiiie. Sooner, not later," she whined in such a pathetic way that it nearly choked up the burly demon. He'd never seen his best girl this bad off.

Crouched down, he kissed the top of her disheveled head. "De. It's only been a few days since you last saw that jerk." Tears flowed down the demoness' cheeks. "We will figure this out. You don't need to die."

Delia's pitiful gaze lifted to his. "A few days and it's already this bad, Rez. I can't sleep or eat. I'm freezing. My body and heart literally ache. Like constant acid ice picks to the chest. I'm hurting worse than any torture I endured in Hell. And NOTHING helps." She sighed heavily. "Except him.

How's that for a cruel joke? He gets to torture me all over again, and I did this to myself." The Furie slumped to the side, arms wrapped around herself, trembling as if she were laying in ice. She had no more energy to talk this out.

Rez attempted to move her again, but she hissed in pain. Instead, he went to the bedroom and gathered blankets. Returning to her, he bundled her up as much as was allowed and declared, "We will figure this out, De. I'll consult with the witches and that sorceress you like. Please, just don't die on me." He kissed her head once again and disappeared.

---

Justus absently roamed the streets of the French Quarter. Thus far, he'd been unable to make himself leave this ghastly city. Warring thoughts incessantly plagued his mind. Feelings he couldn't identify taunted him. He had no clue how to process the chaos. Strangely, the more he healed, the worse his chest hurt. It didn't make a lick of sense.

Browsing store fronts, a pang hit his chest so harshly, it nearly toppled him. Justus had to stop and compose himself briefly. Add to that, he felt a pull that he was no longer able to ignore. In that moment, he concluded it must somehow relate to the mating.

Was it a trick she had figured out to hurt him further? A trap of some sort? Or was it something more? The pain came in increasingly harsh waves, he knew he didn't have a choice but to investigate.

Ducking into an empty alley, Justus stepped into a shadow and traced. He allowed the pull to guide him. The half-breed materialized in a bathroom, mildly confused as to where he was.

Then her faint scent registered; it was sullied by enormous amounts of narcotics. His brow creased when a lump of blankets in the tub moved slightly and the pull became overwhelming.

Justus darted to the bath, confused; all he could see outside of the mound was a mess of matted, platinum blonde hair. Delia? He picked her up and kept her cradled in his arms as he uncovered her face. He gasped at her sickly features. Eyes, barely open, were sunken and vacant, heavy with dark circles. Skin so pale, she could almost pass as transparent. The Furie's frail body convulsed and he felt the coldness of her leeching through the layers of thick fabric covering her.

What in all the hells had she done to herself?!

Without further thought, he traced them both to his suite and carefully laid her out on the bed. Sitting down beside her, Justus uncovered her head completely. He swept a few stray tendrils of white hair back as he spoke softly, "Delia."

Nothing. No reaction.

"Delia, come on wench. Yell at me."

Nada. Her breathing was shallow, pulse faint.

Justus stood and paced for a few minutes. No one had ever accused him of being a caretaker, or even a remotely comforting being, but he had to figure out something. He wouldn't allow her to simply give up and end up back in Hell for her soul to be tormented for eternity. He had to at least keep her alive long enough to remove Lucifer's brand. Then she'd truly be free; she could decide from there whether to continue putting one foot in front of the other or not.

He unbound her from the blankets and removed her dirty clothes.

The Furie was a literal bag of bones. The scene before him was a shock to his system and he had to force himself to stop staring at the quickly declining female.

He removed his own shirt. A loud *WHOOSH* echoed around the room as his ethereal wings erupted from slits between his shoulder blades. Justus climbed in bed, pulling the demoness into his lap, keeping her cradled. Giant feathers swept around, blanketing her. A tiny sound came from Delia, though he couldn't make out what it meant. As he leaned back onto the pillows, he noticed her trembling was easing.

Good sign, he figured.

---

Heavy eyelids fluttered as Delia attempted to rejoin the land of the coherent. Dark spices and citrus rattled her senses, waking her brain. She'd know that scent anywhere. Her cheek against Jus' chiseled chest, curious greys finally opened and peeked around.

They were covered with some type of heavy, ebony silk? *Wait. WHAT?!*

The Furie's' gaze widened as she wheezed in a rattly breath. Were those…FEATHERS?!

Slender fingers tentatively reached out and stroked the awe-inspiring beauty and a mild rumble kicked up in Justus' chest. "Da fuck.." she whispered in a raw voice that barely registered. She'd never seen or touched anything as hypnotizing as these wings. She'd never even considered the fact that the half-breed possessed wings. In Hell, he'd never revealed them. That made sense, though, she supposed. What use were they there?

Justus shivered and Delia jerked her hand back, whispering, "Oh, oops."

"Don't apologize. Continue," he sounded half asleep, but Delia reached out again and fondled the lustrous quills. Jus moaned softly. Okay, apparently, he enjoyed that. That was good news, because she wasn't sure she'd be able to make herself stop. "Are you warm, now?" he asked.

It took Delia a second to comprehend his question.

She realized that, yes, she was indeed toasty and comfortable. More so than she'd ever been in her entire wretched life. "Yeah, very much so, it seems," she answered absentmindedly, as she continued caressing his feathers. "Um… Where are we? And… Why am I naked?" *Both, fair questions*!

"The hotel. Don't worry, you were only brought here out of necessity to warm you. You were beginning to resemble a corpse."

Why did that answer cause her heart to ache anew? "Mission accomplished. I suppose I need to go home now." Justus' arms and wings tightened around her, but he didn't say a word. Given this felt like being in a luxurious, soothing cocoon, she wasn't going to fight the issue. She'd never felt more at peace. "Or, I'll just stay a bit longer. By the way, how long have I been here?"

She felt Justus' arm move and a few seconds later, he replied, "I'm not certain when I picked you up, but it's probably closing in on a full day."

Shocked greys popped wide. "You've been lying here with me, keeping me warm and safe for almost 24 hours?" His arm came back around her and she felt him shrug but he didn't answer. "You should have left me to die," Delia mumbled. She truly couldn't bear to go through that whole experience again.

A deep growl reverberated. "Do not ever say that again. I will save you. Every time."

"Unless Luci tells you to torture me, huh."

Sable wings unfurled, Delia was nearly blinded by the light in the room. Justus sat up, holding her at arm's length to face him as his glowing golds bore into her. "Do not speak of things you do not fully understand. Far more transpired than you realize. I did what I had to do and, as a result, you are no longer in Hell. That is all that matters."

Delia shook out of his grasp and stood, retrieving her clothes from the nearby chair.

Just before she ghosted, she weakly replied, "No, that is not all that matters. But thanks for prolonging my death, don't bother doing it again."

# CHAPTER 13

Pulsating, spinning lights bathed the mostly empty dance floor below in a sea of colors as Delia sat, lost in thought, in one of the second floor VIP booths. She was cramming nachos into her piehole while she contemplated life. Did she truly want to die? Not particularly. Did she see this whole mate thing working out with Justus? Nope, not at all. So, what was the alternative?

She was faced with the literal dilemma of- can't live with him; can't kill him; can't kill herself.

The demoness had been away from Justus barely more than a day, but was already having chills from the separation. And it was royally pissing her off.

"Damn, puta, you've really done it this time, yeah?" Delia turned to her bestie who'd just materialized, sitting beside her. "At least you look better. Would hate to see you go down looking like a goth troll doll," Zaylee snorted, shoving De's shoulder playfully. "Seriously, though... What happened?! Rez nearly had a stroke when you disappeared. He tracked your phone to the hotel, but couldn't figure out how you'd managed to trace in your condition."

The Furie glared at the inquisitive Latina and shoved her back. "I didn't. Somehow Jus got me."

A torrent of irate Spanish gibberish spewed from Zay as her arms went supersonic with their animation. Delia didn't comprehend most of it, but there were a few things she understood: "that rotten bastard", "I'll cut his dick off", "deliver him back to Hell" etcetera, etcetera. One might say the Succubus wasn't Justus' biggest fan.

"You done now?" The demoness asked, when the redhead began winding down. Nope, apparently not, because she continued even louder. Hurling her feet across the bench seat, De sat back, and proceeded to finish her nachos.

When Zay shoved her again, Delia's clammy hand shot out, gripping her girl's throat. "Keep pushing, bitch, and I'll throw you off this fucking balcony." It was a legit threat. Zaylee simmered down when the demoness released her and went back to eating. "Trust me, I know what I've done, and I'm paying dearly for it. I don't need you or Rez piling on your opinions."

Zaylee grumbled a few more curses under her breath before switching back over to English. "You do understand that we are only saying these things because we care, and you scared us really badly, ya know? So, talk to me!"

The concern etched in Zay's expression nearly had Delia bolting for the door. She didn't handle concern, sympathy, nor support well. The demoness had spent too many centuries hardening herself from all of the pain and misery she'd lived through to accept such luxuries as the love and care of others; even those closest to her. She'd always dealt with everything on her own and had the "I'm fine; I got this; I don't need any help" routine down to a science.

But this sitch? This was different. This was something she absolutely couldn't beat or ignore. "What am I supposed to say? I told you what happened, and now I'm wading through the consequences. Story over."

"Puta madre!"

"Pretty much."

Delia felt Zay combing her fingers through her shower damp tresses, but kept peering down at the dance floor. "At least you got your pretty color back." De knew her bestie was trying to bring some light to their convo, but, at this point, it hardly mattered. "Fine. What can I do to help?" Zaylee scooted up against Delia's side and put her arm around her; De allowed it. For a minute, anyway.

"Just promise that if anything should happen to me, you and Rez will take care of things around here. This club is my baby and I've worked too hard to let it go down the shitter."

Zaylee grabbed De's chin, wrenching her around to lock eyes. "Cut that shit out! Nothing is going to happen to you!"

Delia shrugged out of the grasp and shook her head. "There is no guarantee of that now. I've officially nuked my world and anything is possible." She slid out of the plush, leather booth and turned back to her girl. "I've got to go check on everything downstairs before I get 'sick' again.

I'll catch you later, babe." A brief nod, and De traced to the main barroom to ensure everything was on track for a successful night.

---

It had only been a few days since he'd last seen Delia, but Justus' heart was pulling him. Worse than before. Everything in his being screamed to go to her, but he needed a better plan before he did so. Their last powwow had not ended as he'd hoped. After holding her, protecting her, and adoring the feel of her wrapped up in his wings for nearly 24 hours, she'd just bolted. He'd supposedly said something wrong, but he'd yet to fully comprehend what exactly that was.

*Social and emotional cripple, much?* Indeed. And he was afraid that applied to the both of them...which should make for an interesting and potentially dismal life together, at best. He couldn't allow her to suffer in such a heinous manner, though, even if she did bring it upon herself. He would once again come to her aid. It was hardly a choice now. Justus knew he'd never let any harm come to Delia, at least, none he could prevent.

Local realtors had been contacted and, with a hefty finder's fee on the line, he'd been receiving a steady stream of real estate listings that were half-assed matches to his list of preferences: large historic estate, substantial acreage, secluded. There was one that ticked all the boxes though, one that caught his eye in a major way.

A 1935, fully restored, 39,300 square foot stone castle with modern amenities. On the outskirts of New Orleans, it sat on twenty-five acres, which included bayou waterfront views. It featured 14 bedrooms and 16 bathrooms of which most, he assumed, would never be inhabited or put to proper use.

It was the ambience and space he was looking for. If he and Delia continued to fight then they'd have plenty of areas to avoid each other when needed, yet remain close enough that she wouldn't end up debilitated, as she had when he last found her.

Two days ago, after a two hour tour of the property, Justus instructed the agent to draw up the sales contracts for a cash buy. He had the deed in his hand that evening. Justus had to pay a righteous amount to get it closed that quickly, but fortunately the half-breed had been stockpiling riches for centuries and had, until that day, little use for them.

If he couldn't keep Delia happy in any other way, then he'd at least spoil her beyond belief. It wasn't as if his sparkling personality had done the trick lately. Time to throw money at their conundrum and see what occurred!

---

So far, so good, Delia thought, as she slung bottles behind the bar. One of the bartenders didn't show, and the evening crowd had picked up fast. Drink orders were coming in dozens at a time. The demoness' sour mood and ever worsening health woes were shelved as she concentrated on the task at hand.

Nearly dropping a tray of Irish Car Bombs, Delia passed it on to a server as her glittering eyes scanned the crowd.

She felt him. His presence was like a breath of fresh air, even though she'd yet to spot him. "I'm out. Do the best you can and don't take any shit from 'em," the boss-lady called out to the other alcohol chefs as she exited from behind the expansive bar.

Weaving through the dense crowd, she did her best to avoid the not so unintentional brushes and blatant gropes of male patrons. Yet another ramification of this mate asshatery was that any skin on skin contact from members of the opposite sex resulted in a searing burn that lingered for several minutes. Not that she was a wimp by any means, but she had more than enough on her plate already without piling that steaming shit on top of it.

The club owner followed the tug of her spirit, and as she meandered through the hallway of private rooms, Justus stepped in behind her. She startled, but recovered quickly. The chill of her body lessened greatly when his rough hand went to the small of her back and guided her to an empty suite, shutting the door behind them.

They stood staring in wordless conjecture as the bass of the music resonated through the space.

Jus reached out and caressed Delia's faded, blue-purple hair that currently included large sections of white, which framed her face. It tumbled around her shoulders as the demoness began to shake her head solemnly.

"You shouldn't have come," her words barely registered above the music. "I don't need the disruption here; I'm trying to work."

She could only assume he was there to see if she was still kickin' it above ground. Her mental stability was incredibly erratic, and being near him stirred up too many conflicting thoughts. She couldn't bear the whiplash inducing, yo-yo effect of her feels.

"May I take you somewhere?" Justus asked, with an uncharacteristically nervous voice.

"Please don't make this shit any harder than it already is. Just leave me alone and let this mess play out. I don't need your pity. That is the *LAST* thing I ever want out of you."

The Furie sighed and let her head fall forward. She truly didn't have the energy to do this with him. But the closeness to him; his scent invading her senses...felt so good. Far too comforting for her liking. The frigidity of her blood was beginning to dissipate, giving way to a soothing warmth.

It was all too much.

"Delia." Justus lifted her chin with a finger, catching her sorrowful gaze. Gold flecks bounced to life in his eyes as she stared up at him. "I need to show you something. Actually, more than that. Come with me. Please."

*It seemed they were both throwing out the niceties tonight, huh?* 'Please' was a word that had quite likely never been exchanged between them before all of this madness transpired.

In that moment, Justus was stunningly beautiful as he projected tender vulnerability. How could she possibly say 'no' to this man; the only man she'd ever cared for? "Fine. Let's get whatever this is over with."

# CHAPTER 14

Delia stood in the middle of a grand foyer, with winding staircases on either side leading the way up to places she couldn't imagine. Gorgeous black and silver swirled marble floors and matching polished banisters immediately caught her eye.

Straight ahead appeared to be a sitting room, the likes of which she'd never seen in person. Long, wide hallways lined by high, dramatic arches, branched off to their left and right and seemed to extend for days.

"What do you think?" Justus asked from behind her.

She hadn't a clue what she thought. She had absolutely no idea why he would bring her to such an extravagant location. "Uhhhh…" The demoness peered up…and down…and all around. "I mean, it's jaw-dropping but…" She turned to face Jus, bewildered. "Why would you bring me to a place like this?"

"I bought it," Jus stated flatly. An answer she wasn't expecting.

"You what, now??" Stupefied, she went back to perusing her surroundings. Soft golds and varying shades of maroon were the dominant palette adorning the entrance hall, sitting room, and attached aisles. The arches were rendered in lighter shades of gray, with zig-zag and rolled molding embellishments accenting the joinery.

The demoness raised her eyes to the ceiling. A magnificently painted scene depicted dragons in the throes of battle with an ominous, cloudy backdrop. Vibrant hellfire strategically highlighted the arena. "Wow." The word little more than a breathless whisper.

"De." Oh, Justus was speaking, wasn't he? Her attention wandered back to him. "You marked me. Did you honestly believe I'd be able to just cut out and leave you to suffer?"

Delia folded over, hands on her knees, as a raucous bark of nefarious laughter escaped her. She was thoroughly amused by his question!

After regaining some composure and straightening again, her vexed gaze met his. "Well, it sure as fuck wasn't an issue for you in Hell, you righteous prick! You not only allowed my suffering but led the charge in my torture!"

*That touched a nerve.*

Delia smirked up at him as she watched Jus' face contort before he snapped. His punishing hand snaked out and caught her by the throat, shoving the demoness against the massive, mahogany entrance door, holding her there. His face to hers, icy eyes burned with indignant rage. "Lucifer made it quite clear that if I didn't punish you for your transgressions, then he would. He would also kill my mother who was down in those dungeons with you. I did everything I could to save you both...but he still killed my mother!" With his free hand, Justus plucked the demoness' talisman necklace, hidden beneath her Nirvana t-shirt. He dangled it on his finger. "Where the fuck do you think this came from?! The gods-damned get-out-of-jail-free fairy?!"

The world stopped spinning, but the Furie's brain took on the task. If she weren't pinned, Delia would've slumped to the floor in shock. She hadn't a clue that his mother had also been a prisoner. Nor, obviously, that he'd been her key to escape. It was as if everything she'd known had now ceased to exist.

Black was white. Dogs were cats. And Justus was her savior.

---

*After years of secretly conferring with the most powerful witches, voodoo priestesses, sorcerers, and angels he could track down, Justus had been able to remove Lucifer's brand from his chest. Without the brand, his grandsire could no longer keep tabs on his actions or whereabouts; allowing him to ghost into the wretched realm, semi-undetected. After the successful brand erasure, he purchased spelled amulets to liberate Delia and his mother, Amara, from their dungeons.*

*The half-breed materialized into Delia's chamber first. She was pitifully filthy, so much so that it wasn't readily apparent that the demoness wore no clothes. She was laying in an unnaturally contorted heap, unconscious on the barren ground. Justus knelt down beside her, brushed the matted hair from her barely identifiable face and straightened her tangled limbs a bit.*

*It was clear she'd recently suffered a round of particularly virulent torture. She wouldn't recover enough to wake for hours, at least. He'd have to leave her to escape on her own. As much as he wanted to whisk her away, he could only transport souls in to Hell. With her brand intact, they'd never make it out if he tried to trace with her. The talisman would allow her escape under her own volition only.*

*Reluctantly, he placed the amulet in her bloody, broken hand. Carefully, he wrapped her fingers tightly around and wedged it under her side. He prayed she wouldn't drop or lose it before she woke.*

*He needed to leave and find his mother before he was detected and detained. Lingering for even a minute longer and waiting for Delia to wake was out of the question. A few beats later, he forced himself to rise and trace.*

*Peering through dungeon door after door, he searched for Amara. Nothing. Perhaps Lucifer had her moved, he mused.*

*Fearing he would not find her, Justus had the inclination to search the private quarters he'd resided in. Cautiously materializing in the deserted space, it took no time at all to receive the message his grandsire had left for him.*

*There, on his workbench, near the fire pit, sat his beloved mother's head.*

*Justus had come too late.*

---

"You…you left it in my hand…" The demoness was working it all out, though she was having difficulty wrapping her head around these new revelations and their implications. Justus' grip on her eased when he saw the look of understanding registering in her eyes, but he was still holding her upright. Legs had turned to jello, and the Furie felt grateful for the prolonged support. "He…he murdered your mother because you le-left... I-I wish I'd known she was there…"

Delia could grasp why she didn't know, however. She and Jus had never had the 'share all the horrors you've been through or are currently going through' kind of relationship. They'd been as close as two emotionally crippled beings could be, but sharing personal baggage was just not their M.O.

Words couldn't describe the grappling round her mind was in.

In a matter of minutes, how was one supposed to abandon everything they'd known as fact and accept the complete opposite as true??

The demoness blinked, and was thrown another curve when they were suddenly in another part of the… mansion? Castle? She wasn't sure what to call this place yet, but it was spectacular. Justus had traced them into a music studio that was filled with every instrument you could imagine. A piano, a full drum set, guitars of every type, a cello, violin, and a saxophone. Those were just the ones she could see from her seated position on what was possibly the most comfortable lounge chair she'd ever had her backside occupy. This space was her version of paradise with its soft earth tones mixed with whites and vibrant reds.

How had Justus known she'd need this space, she wondered.

Her breathtaking mate had managed to, in a matter of minutes, change her entire life and irreversibly transform her whole worldview. Dumbfounded, and stunned speechless, Delia could only observe Justus as he sat at the piano and played a hauntingly beautiful piece. The heavy notes hung in the air, clutching her heart in a way that only music could.

Without her consent, profound tears tumbled down her flushed features as she absorbed the soul moving performance.

She hadn't a clue that Justus played any instruments, much less so expertly. If she hadn't loved him before, well, she was a definite goner now! Music had always been her direct link to escape and soothing in this world, outside of drugs, that is. And here Jus was…both.

Untapped reserves of mental fortitude and strength from some unknown source assisted Delia as she rose and walked over to the piano. Sitting on the bench beside her mate, she threaded her arms around his enormous bicep while he continued to play.

Words fell from her lips as her tears turned to waterfalls, "'Thank you' will never be enough, baby. And I am unfathomably sorry that you lost your mother."

'Baby'. It felt like a lifetime since she'd called him by that endearment.

Justus continued caressing the ivories, but leaned and kissed her temple with a tenderness she'd never felt from him. "Thank you, Dove."

Delia nearly fell off the bench when he returned with his own long-lost pet name. She didn't realize, until that moment, quite how badly she'd needed to hear her mate call her that.

# CHAPTER 15

They spent the better part of the night roaming from instrument to instrument, indulging in a jam fest that did more for them than talking ever could. Meaningful words were difficult to come by, but pouring your heart and soul into musical notes was one medium through which they could meet in the middle.

At one point, Justus played a rowdy ballad, shredding an electric guitar. It left the demoness sitting in awe behind the skins, drumsticks dangling between her fingers, with her jaw hanging wide.

Prior to that, Delia had left the half-breed in a similar state after she'd wailed on a cello.

This would be their common ground room, she imagined. A place they'd come to when nothing else was working. The Furie couldn't imagine a better communication method for two emotionally defective hotheads.

Moving once again, Delia picked up a Gibson acoustic and let herself fall into the plush lounger, then began playing at a soft melody, her fingers tentatively flicking at the strings. The demoness raised her head when Jus walked over and sat beside her outstretched legs. His hand went to the bare ankle peeking out of her jeans, and squeezed gently, causing her to smirk at him. "You approve of this half assed tune?" she asked as she kept with it.

She lowered her eyes again when he only stared at her in response.

After a few moments, Jus' words aired, "You understand I bought this place for us, true? You and me…"

There went the music. She accidentally strummed a bit too hard and broke most of the strings in one go.

Delia cleared her throat and swallowed, bringing her cautious gaze back to meet his. His expression appeared to be a hopeful one. "Uhhh… No, I didn't get that memo." For a second, she nibbled nervously at her lip piercing, debating how to traverse this situation. The saying 'too good to be true' seemed appropriate, as she weighed the gravity of this conversation.

"So, like... What exactly are your plans for us? You expect me to move in here at some point, I'm guessing?"

"Tonight." He squeezed her ankle again. "My plans are for you to move in tonight." A rarity for him, Jus smiled sincerely. A brow raised inquisitively, as if to imply that this were a 'DUH!' moment. "We already know we can't be away from one another long periods of time without dire consequences."

He had a point, but DAMN. It didn't sound as though claiming her was a part of his agenda. It was akin to dangling a huge, gorgeous, juicy steak just out of reach of a starving person. "Uhhh..." Delia's brain was toast and her voice caught in her throat. She hadn't a clue how to respond to this grand gesture, nor how she truly felt about it. "How about we think on it for a hot minute? I need to get back to the club, anyway."

Confusion fell over Justus' face. "Well. Okay. Yes, I suppose there is no immediate rush. I do not want you getting sick again, though. At least promise you'll come here, right away, before that happens. Deal? Then the rest will come as it may, I reckon."

She could live with that. For now. "Deal. I swear I'll be back when the pains call for it." Delia put down the guitar and stood. Before she could leave, she had to do one last thing.

She leaned down, taking Jus' face in her hands and lightly nipped his lip with her fang. "Thank you. I don't know what this is we've got going on right now, but I believe we're on the right track." She kissed him softly, then disappeared.

---

The following evening, Delia was back behind the bar, slinging liquor again.

It'd been nearly 4am by the time she'd left Justus that morning. After checking on the club, she'd crashed hard. Surprisingly, she slept pretty well, considering everything that was up in the air. She felt somewhat rested as a result, and only had minimal aches and frostiness. Work kept her mind occupied. Somewhat.

"You snap your fingers at me *one* more time, Fizzy, and you'll lose them. Got it?" The demoness snarked to one of her regulars; an older warlock that had been frequenting her club since she opened it many moons ago. He was lowkey one of her favorite patrons.

"Now, now. I was simply attempting to get your attention on this busy night, Miss Delia. No need to resort to violence, Sassy. How about a smile instead?" The silver fox teased. He knew smiling was not on the menu for the demoness, unless it involved roughing someone up. Rolling eyes and a smirk was all he was going to get. "Fine. How about a whiskey sour, instead?"

"Noted, Fizz. I assume you expect me to jump over these other orders that are waiting and place you at the front of the line?" She knew the answer to that.

"But of course, my favorite, most beautiful, meanest buddy." Flattery. Usually didn't work but it did in his case.

The demoness winked at him and started on his drink. As she poured, two sharp beeps emitted from her comms earpiece. The deep voice of one of her newer security team members transmitted, "Delia. There's an antsy female out here at the rear loading dock. She's insisting she speak with a 'Justice'. I don't know who that is, but she told me to ask you."

*Da fuck?!* WHY would anyone be looking for Justus at her club??

Hold the damn phone. "Does she look like a Baywatch Pamela Anderson ordered from Wish?" If it was Hannah, Delia knew her night was about to turn fan-fucking-tastic.

"I don't know what 'Wish' is, ma'am...but yeah, she kinda looks like that chick."

"On my way." This was turning into a ghetto fabulous week! First, Jus with his grand gestures and now Hannah, popping up so Delia could rip that over-bleached hair from her head and feed it to her.

The club owner finished Fizzy's drink and slid it over to him. "You know the drill, warlock. Tip big." She gave him another wink before happily exiting from behind the bar.

It was too packed to trace, as many humans were present, but she hightailed it through the crowd.

*Ponytail up!* Delia snatched the band from her wrist and tossed her ebony locks high as she charged across the industrial kitchen and burst through the exit doors to the dock, ready to do some major damage.

Unfortunately, she didn't get the chance. The exact moment she got an eyeful of Justus' whore, there was a snap, crackle, pop.

Lights out.

The phone rang and rang. Justus kept hanging up and calling again. Texts were left unanswered, as well. "Gods-damnit, De! Fucking answer!" The half-breed roared at his phone.

Something was off. It felt as though his heart had stopped and horrible pangs were constant. The demoness had to be hurt, or in trouble. It was the only explanation he could come up with.

"Um, hello?" Came a soft-spoken voice on the other end of the line. He could hear music blaring in the background.

"Who the fuck is this? Where is Delia?!"

"Oh, um, I'm not sure, sir. She left her phone under the bar. I just noticed it kept going off and answered."

He immediately traced to Delia's flat. No one there. No signs of a struggle, either.

Next, he materialized down at Hell's Rejects, and grabbed the first person he saw in the hall of private rooms that appeared to work there. A server, he assumed. "Where's Delia?!" Patience long gone.

The young male stuttered, obviously flustered by the huge, pissed off guy in his face. "I-I...she...she was at the main bar last I saw her!" The server seemed proud of himself that he could be helpful.

"She's not there. Point me to her second in command." As the kid pointed to some bald meathead lingering in the hall of suites, Justus bolted toward the guy. He was dressed in black fatigues, with glowing white lettering across the back that spelled out 'SECURITY' in block capitals. Why the hell would Delia have a quadzilla bouncer as her next in line? He was stumped.

Justus tapped him on the shoulder forcefully.

The other male turned, highly annoyed by that tactic. "What the fuck do you want?!"

"Delia. Where is she?!" Short and to the point. There was no time to dick around with these people. The ache in his chest had worsened and he was beginning to feel the pull that accompanied it whenever she was sick. The direction of the pull was what perplexed him, though.

"Who's askin'?"

Justus wrenched his button-down shirt to the side, revealing a mating scar. "Her damn mate. Now, where the fuck is she?" The bouncer turned with a snarl and walked away. Justus stalked after him, none too happy, sporting his own sour face. "WHERE IS SHE?! Something is wrong. I can feel it!" Justus asserted, as he grabbed the meathead's shoulder. That didn't go over well, but Justus didn't care. He had to find her.

The security guy stopped in his tracks and growled, "Listen, asshole, the only reason your blood isn't painting the walls right now is because Delia made me promise to leave you alone. But, keep pushing and it'll be a forgotten vow." He jerked out of Justus' grasp and continued walking, the half-breed stalking right on his heels.

Upstairs, the manager opened what appeared to be an office door and stepped inside. He pushed the door wide, allowing Justus to follow, and the half-breed did. As the door closed behind them, the guy peered at a bank of security monitors. "I'll find her and then she can kick your ass out of here, herself," the male grumbled.

"I am trying to tell you something is wrong. I can feel it and she doesn't have her phone." Panic was setting in now. Justus' gut screamed that she was in danger. He noticed, as the meathead scanned the screens, the scowl on his face deepening. "She's not here, is she?!" Justus let his own eyes inspect every single image in front of him; anxiety peaking.

The guy typed commands on a keyboard and then spoke into a microphone on the desk, "Has anyone seen the boss-lady within the last fifteen minutes?"

After a few seconds, several replies of 'no' came back from numerous voices.

"Fuck." Baldy turned to Justus. "When did you get the 'feeling'? How long ago?!"

"Maybe half an hour." Justus pulled out his phone and scoured the calls and texts to Delia, looking at the timestamps. When he raised his head, he noticed the feeds were being rewound. Icy hues combed the screens and the half-breed saw her. "Stop!" he barked, pointing to the monitor in the bottom corner. "I saw her for a brief second right there!"

"The loading dock? What the hell is she doing out there?!" Meathead replayed the footage at normal speed.

Both men growled in unison. The feed showed Hannah appearing, and then Delia bursting through the exit door. No sooner had she made it through when a large male materialized behind her, snapping her neck. Before she fully hit the ground, the good-as-dead male caught her and all three disappeared.

Justus thought he was going to vomit; the pull made sense now. He loathed having to breathe the next nugget of intel to the bouncer. "I know where she is. I'm being pulled to her. They delivered her…back to Lucifer."

The half-breed heard the crack before he briefly saw stars. That bald douchbag had punched him in the jaw!

A rabid growl echoed throughout the small room as Justus returned the favor and sent the bouncer flying with a stout uppercut. When baldy jumped up and came at Jus again, his angel DNA rose to the occasion and he snarled, "We can either beat the shit out of each other, or I can go find Delia, cunt. What's it going to be?"

The ape backed off, narrowing his eyes as he grated, "Save her or you're dead, too, asshole."

# CHAPTER 16

The stench roused her, but her eyes wouldn't cooperate and open. They didn't need to. Delia knew exactly where she was: Hell. The waves of heat and howls of agony that surrounded her were all too familiar. A weak hand reached out to investigate as she lay on her side. The grit she dug into beneath her was no surprise.

She immediately reverted back to her former self and buried the terror bubbling up in her mind. Panic attacks would do her no good right now.

Minutes, hours, or perhaps days passed before she was finally able to crack open her eyelids and sit up. Her entire body ached; especially her neck. And how one could feel cold in Hell was beyond her comprehension but it was still her reality.

The demoness peered down at her ripped leathers and torn Nine Inch Nails tank top. "Son of a bitch," she grumbled, pissed off about her ruined ensemble.

The Furie's panicked fingers raced to her chest. Her necklace, it was gone. A wave of trepidation washed over her as she fell back onto the coal-packed floor. Without her talisman, she would be unable to escape.

How the flippity-fuck was she supposed to get out of *this* conundrum?!

Voices out in the corridor interrupted the thoughts and fresh waves of dread tangled in her mind. There was a particular voice among them that stood out. She recognized it easily.

"Yes, I was alerted of her revival." Then another voice spoke, but she couldn't make out the words before the first voice continued. "Do I appear incompetent to you, boy?! I, alone, shall welcome her back. Step away!" His regal, dark tone was unmistakable.

Delia managed to get to her feet and steady herself before her host and first visitor breached the doorway of the dungeon. She wondered if this was it, her last day as a living, breathing soul. She figured it was pretty much her luck, anyway. She was just getting somewhere in her personal life and then BOOM! Back to the drawing board.

The spelled barrier between the demoness and those in the corridor evaporated, and Lucifer strolled through in all of his arrogant, narcissistic glory. He stood feet before her; his demure hands tipped with shiny, pearl talons loosely clasped in front of him.

A sadistic smile played on his lips as he greeted her, "Ah, what have we here? Did you lose your way, little girl?" He chuckled. He'd always been his own biggest fan. "Did you enjoy your time away? I know you must have missed me and my hospitality, greatly," he boasted, in his perfectly tailored white suit that magically repelled the dirt and soot surrounding them.

Arms crossed over her chest, Delia regarded him with a deadpan stare. She'd be damned if she was going to bow to him. Her Hell motto of 'show no fear' was firmly in place. Regardless of what she did, the results were going to be the same.

She knew better, yet she still couldn't stop herself, "I'm sorry, who are you again?"

Claws gouged deep into her face as Lucifer bitch slapped her. Delia took it like the Furie she was, and didn't flinched or cry out. The sensation of warm streams trickled down her face and began dripping from her chin.

She knew it was all downhill from here. Why not enjoy the little things while she could, yeah? "Dude. You slap like a schoolgirl."

Luci threw his head back with an ominous laugh before punching her in the temple, knocking her to the ground, where he proceeded to kick her in the ribs with his Gucci loafers. Delia wouldn't lie, those splintering bones? They were going to hurt for a while.

"What was that, whore?" He laughed as he kicked her in the throat, snapping her head back, causing her to cough and choke. "Oh dear, has the little bitch forgotten how to speak? What a shame." Lucifer reached down, grabbing a fist full of half white, half faded periwinkle hair and used it to force Delia to her feet.

The demoness stared back at him with watering, onyx eyes and smiled, baring blood-tinged fangs. As one might imagine, the King of the Underworld became enraged, and threw her across the enclosure.

Bouncing off of the flaming opposite wall, she rolled and landed on her hands and knees, then proceeded to muster the strength to stand again. No stranger to unfathomable pain, Delia blocked it out and faced him. The Furie panted for breath through broken ribs and a collapsed trachea. Flesh blistering from contact with the fire. Wobbling slightly, she recrossed her arms and glared at him tauntingly.

Smoldering red eyes bore into her as Luci stalked around the weakened demoness. "I understand that you marked my wretched grandson and claimed him as your mate. It must be terribly embarrassing and humiliating that he did not return the sentiment. Perhaps I did pass some of my good sense along to him, after all."

*Ah, on to mind games now.* Delia rolled her eyes. Whether his statements held water or not was irrelevant. She refused to allow this overgrown child the pleasure of witnessing her reactions. Although, she would much prefer he shut the fuck up and return to hitting her.

Luci stepped up behind her, putting her in a choke hold, cutting off her oxygen completely. It took every last vestige of vigor inside the battered Furie to resist gagging and struggling as his nose buried in her mane. Lucifer inhaled deeply while stepping between her legs, kicking them further apart. "For a swamp hick, you smell surprisingly nice," he whispered eerily in her ear. "I still wouldn't contaminate myself by fucking you, though." He shoved her away. "That is more suited for the guards. They will enjoy you immensely," he laughed as she tripped over her feet and landed on her knees. "Get used to that position, whore. I wager they'll remove all of those pearly whites and keep that mouth very busy."

The demoness willed herself to block out the aches and burning as she struggled to gain any minuscule amount of oxygen. Pushing herself to stand again, she faced off with the archfiend and wheezed, "The almighty Luci is afflicted with E.D., huh? Noted." Delia doubled over in gasping, choked laughter.

Retaliating as she knew he would, Lucifer palmed the back of her head and proceed to slam her face into the coal floor until any signs of life were extinguished.

---

An actual plan of action would have made more sense but the half-breed couldn't remain topside knowing what was happening to his mate down below. *Yes, MATE.* There was no denying the longing in his soul or what he felt in his heart for her any longer.

Justus half materialized in the tunnel to the dungeons, attempting to stay undetected as long as possible. Being a close descendant of Lucifer, the half-breed could come and go in any area of the realm without the spells blockading him; aside from the royal grounds.

The spelled doors were transparent from this side and he was able to make quick work of finding her cell. A heavy boulder sunk in his gut when he saw her. She appeared to be lifelessly contorted in a mangled pile on the floor, pulverized, and surrounded by a pool of congealed blood.

Justus traced inside and knelt beside Delia, cautiously rolling the demoness onto her back. A pained gasp left him when he brushed her knotted, crimson soaked tresses from her normally beautiful face. She was unrecognizable. Her features were nothing but a mess of demolished, scattered puzzle pieces. "Oh, Dove," he whispered. "I'll find a way to get you out."

Schemes riddled his mind as the half-breed sought to formulate any plausible strategy. It would be pointless to move her to a hiding spot as long as she was without her talisman. She would be found with little effort because of her brand. He had to either find her necklace or, against all odds, procure the magic to remove the brand entirely. Given it had taken him years to accomplish that for himself, he may want to focus on the first option.

Justus assured the demoness he would indeed be back, "Dove, I will not leave this plane without you. I am going to find your talisman. I love you," he whispered in her ear, hoping she heard him. With any luck, it would lend her strength, knowing he was in the realm. Not one spot from her waist up was clear of spilled ichor, but he kissed her tenderly in the least damaged place he could find, just below her ear.

The half-breed bit into his wrist and sprinkled his blood over her poor face that much resembled ground meat, and then into her gaping mouth. His angel DNA would facilitate a speedier recovery. "Keep healing until I return, love." His heart was completely ripped to shreds upon exiting that dungeon empty handed, but he had to get her jewel.

The only location Justus could conceive of Lucifer hiding the talisman was in the royal castle's vault. This endeavor would most certainly be a Hail Mary. The half-breed would succeed or die trying.

He appeared just outside the ground's boundary; from here on, he would not be able to trace.

The few hundred yards between him and the castle were a barren landscape of, what appeared to the eye, solid ground made of a brown-red clay. He knew better than to trust that visual, though. He heavily inspected each step before taking it. Palming a dagger, Justus gingerly tip-toed along the eroded region, treading carefully so as not to fall victim to treacherous booby traps in the desert of bones.

On one misstep, the half-breed triggered the launching of a poison coated arrow. He couldn't pinpoint where it had come from on his right, as it whizzed past his head, brushing the sweat dampened hair on the back of his neck. He slowed his progression with hyperawareness.

A few feet later, he nearly fell victim to a camouflaged patch of quicksand.

Sweat beaded his brow, beginning to trickle down his face, blurring his vision at times. Just as he went to wipe it away with his forearm, a flaming spike erupted from the ground on his left.

Jumping forward to dodge it, devlins converged on him. The little bastards looked like raccoons who had survived a nuclear holocaust, with skin melted off and huge red eyes toggling around frantically. Razor teeth snapped, and greedy, tiny hands fought to seize him as his shitkickers stomped at them, crushing their putrid bodies into the dirt.

Yards later, a handful of slithering snakes hissing in Demoni, circled his perimeter, threatening to strike unless he retreated. No turning back now, though. He had finally reached the manicured --he used that term loosely-- portion of the property. Justus patted his pockets, then remembered he had throwing stars in hidden sheaths on his boots.

Retrieving the four small weapons, he observed as the serpents moved closer. Once within striking distance, Jus launched the stars. Three heads were deeply impaled and the rest of the snakes slid away, going back to their hidden holes to lurk.

From here, the traps were fewer and he was able to use the shadows of the burning bushes and toxic fruit trees to traverse the final yards to the castle. The structure towered high above him, with gargoyles patrolling the sloping peaks.

Justus kept his back against the west wall of midnight granite as he inched along, ducking windows and listening for voices while he traveled toward the north entrance. At the corner, he peeked around and located two guards pacing the extensive stoop. *Easy enough.*

Observing their patterns, Justus belly-crawled in the shadows along the castle's front perimeter each time the guards' faced away. He'd never been more thrilled to have coincidentally dressed well for an occasion; black jeans, black button down, black shit-kickers. He was perfectly camouflaged.

As the half-breed got steadily closer, he realized what he'd be dealing with: disgusting slug demons. They weren't terribly fast, but the slime they could secrete and project was both putrid and toxic. Once Justus was within spitting distance, he plunged his dagger deep into the first guard's temple, rendering him unconscious before the slug could react.

The monstrosity, which much resembled an overly obese, bald buddha who had been burned beyond recognition, collapsed to the ground. His twin slithered toward Justus, excreting and spitting revolting, venomous loogies. Justus ducked and dodged the missiles as he ran up on the demon. Unfortunately, the half-breed took a puss ball to the shoulder before he could drive his blade into the demon's throat. He wrenched the dagger deep and twisted it to sever the fowl creature's spinal cord.

Slumping against the wall as the demon plummeted to the ground, Justus ripped his shirt off and wiped as much of the slimy poison from his skin as possible. He was already feeling the effects of what had seeped through the fabric. Luckily, he'd recover from it shortly, but his throat felt as though it were already closing and he was slightly dizzy. The half-breed allowed himself a few short moments to acclimate to this new state until he heard the gargoyles scrambling down the walls.

Hyperaware of the scents and sounds surrounding him, Justus bolted to his feet. He cracked the entrance door enough to listen a few beats, then entered, closing the door behind him swiftly. All seemed quiet. Justus didn't detect any servants or guards, nor any of Lucifer's playthings in the immediate vicinity, and moved forward on feet that he begged to remain steady.

The corridor was long and dim; the walls and great, round columns, decorated in ornate gold carvings, inset with rubies. Justus cautiously passed by the drawing room, followed by the library, storeroom, and two pantries before he finally reached a stairwell that led below.

If memory served him correctly, the vault was located two flights down and to the left a couple dozen paces. The problem from here? Guards and hellhounds. Justus had no clue how many would be on duty, but he could sense a multitude of both.

Bring on the fireworks, he thought, as he crept down the stairs.

# CHAPTER 17

"Not even a salutation from my bastard grandson before he trapses through my living quarters on a scavenger hunt, hmm?"

Justus froze where he stood, on the first landing of stairs. Speculating what was to come next, he inwardly sighed. His grandsire had materialized on the floor above, leaning over the banister of the staircase, peering down at him. Justus did not bother meeting his gaze as he responded with a tight lip, "Your Grace."

"And considerably underdressed, as well," Lucifer added. "It appears, since your departure of my realm, you've misplaced all of your manners and etiquette, boy." Justus continued to impersonate a shirtless statue while his elder droned on. "That's one nasty mate mark you've got there, son. Perhaps that is the purpose of your social call on this glorious day? Might I remove it for you?"

An involuntary, low growl rumbled deep in the half-breed's chest. Justus would fight to the death before he allowed that precious declaration to be destroyed.

"Ah. I see," Lucifer chuckled as he descended the stairs. "Shacking up with the undesirables appeals to you still." The ruler came to stand before Justus, hands on hips. "I suppose it makes sense. Your mother had the same affliction."

A gold gaze met the crimson stare on him. "Do not speak of my mother; YOUR daughter," Justus snarled. "It would be a shame if death were to come to your beloved, illegitimate heir."

Lucifer joined with his own growl. "Dear boy, you think to threaten my blood and your kin a wise ploy, considering your current predicament? Perhaps your whore down in the dungeons will pay for that reckless miscalculation."

Turning, only to immediately spin back, Lucifer gut punched Justus. All of the air was expelled from the half-breed's lungs, but he righted himself quickly, staying his ground, and glared at his grandsire. With a slow shake of his head, Lucifer turned once again. This time, he snapped his fingers above his head as he yelled, "GUARDS!"

A bevy of demons and hellhounds converged from both above and below; obviously waiting to be called on. Lucifer stomped up the stairs, instructing his troop, "Escort my wayward grandson here to the cells below. Feel free to use force, if warranted."

Lucifer disappeared as the small army descended upon Justus. They pushed and shoved the half-breed mercilessly down the steps to the rather narrow, stone passageway. The hellhounds, with their flaming, matted fur, nipped at Justus' legs to goad him onward. When they reached his prison chamber, Justus was shoved roughly into the space, even though he had been cooperating.

He knew when to pick his battles.

The slate door slammed behind him and he took a seat on a thick, stone block that had been carved to resemble a short pew. Nothing else was in the room. He supposed, in comparison to the location Delia was being held, this was relatively luxurious.

Justus raked his hand through his hair as he spun scenario after scenario of escape plans and possibilities.

After hours of plotting, a plausible theory eventually took shape.

During his time spent running the Punishment Realm, he employed hundreds of hellhounds. They were extremely loyal beasts, and, in human form, quite the party crew. If he could track down one of his former workers, then he may have a shot at freeing Delia and himself. The hounds moved freely throughout the entire Hell plane since Lucifer regarded them as the perfect pets because they were faithful to a fault.

---

Tangled tresses hung around Delia's discolored, bloated face as she sat up. Her head and body thumped with anguish, like a bass drum pounding. Not a recommended sensation, if she were being truthful. She peered around, though could barely see anything as her eyelids were swollen almost entirely shut.

Yep, still in Hell. Not a nightmare.

Although, she could have sworn that Justus had been with her at some point. Actually, his scent still faintly clung to her, she noticed. She breathed a slight sigh of relief. If anyone could get her out of this conundrum, it would be her mate.

In between the cymbals clashing in her brain, she tried to map out how long she'd possibly been here. Time passed in this realm much differently than it did on Earth. A day in Hell roughly equated to an hour on the other plane. Given how badly she'd been beaten and her current level of healing, she'd guesstimated the amount of Hell time would be a few days, perhaps a week. Lovely, she thought as she rolled her eyes, cringing with the action when additional pain zapped her brain.

Her entire form, from the waist up, was one giant OUCH.

Fingers to her chest, she checked again to ensure there was still no necklace. Nope, nada.

What now?

She hadn't a clue.

Time passed.

And passed.

And passed.

Dear gods, she'd forgotten how utterly boring being locked up could be. Luckily, her injuries and wounds were healing exceptionally well. Only minor pains around her ribs and face remained. The swelling everywhere was much improved. Her eyes were fully open; her mouth in good working order. The Furie's nose had miraculously formed anew, and her throat actually felt remarkably clear.

She got to her feet, listening closely as footfalls and voices neared. She'd been awake quite some time. She was certain it was minions coming to remedy that, but they walked right by.

Minutes later, one came back. Only one?! Delia couldn't help but chuckle. What moron had they punked into coming to her cell alone? Aside from Luci himself, it had always taken a minimum of ten to fifteen stooges to put her down. The demoness was impossibly fast, and her lethal claws even faster.

A tall male moseyed through the spelled door. Delia gave him a good once over. He was on the slim side compared to Jus and Rez, but still nicely muscled and toned.

"Hey there, Miss Delia! You doing okay?" he asked in his smooth as butter voice, all happy and shit.

Delia stared at the lunatic. *What in the Mad Hatter's top hat was this guy about?!* With his not-quite-short, curly blonde hair swaying this way and that, he bounced on his toes. *And why was he only wearing a pair of gym shorts?!* The demoness had soooo many questions. But she'd start with this one, "What the fuck is your angle, knobhead?"

The guy laughed, then feigned a pout. "Come on, Miss Delia, no need for name callin'! Mr. Justus sent me to retrieve ya." The fool beamed with pride. "I'm afraid I'll have to get rid of that pesky brand before I can move ya, though, and well…that's gunna hurt, ma'am." His handsome face grew sullen.

*Was this guy for real?* "Come again?" Then the lightbulb went off. He was a hellhound. Delia recalled working with them from time to time when they'd bring in a soul. But how in all the hells was he going to remove her brand?! "I'm going to need more information, kid. Let's start with where Justus is and who you are."

"Oh, yeah, sure," he chuckled huskily. "Mr. Justus is down the way," he hiked a thumb over his shoulder, "locked up at the castle, ya see. And I heard through the grapevine that he was looking for anyone in my specific pack to come visit him. Can you believe it?!" There he went bouncing, again. "The Dark Master's grandson wanted to hang out with us!" *Talk about muchness. Wow.* "Anyway, I stopped by and talked to him a couple times. Ya know, we talked 'bout some of the good ole days when I worked for him."

"Wait, wait, wait," holding her hand up, Delia interrupted him. "How long has Justus been here?" That answer would give her an idea of her own timeline.

"Umm, I'm not sure."

"Well how long ago did you first visit him??"

"Hmm. I reckon 'bout four or five days," the half-naked pup shrugged. Delia nodded, figuring that sounded about right. He continued talking, "And boy was he happy to see ME!" The hound lit up like a damn Christmas tree on that statement. Delia had forgotten what a celebrity Jus was down here. "So, he asked if I could help him get you out, but he had to find a way to get rid of your brand, first." Did he breathe when he spoke? It seemed never ending words and they really needed to get on with this show. "And I got soo excited, I said 'I can help with that!!'" Delia understood why people loved dogs. As much as this guy annoyed her, she couldn't help but find herself taking a liking to him.

"Listen, what is your name?" The demoness needed a name to go with all of this…energy.

"Sorry, ma'am, I'm Blayde!" he smiled down at her and extended his arm.

"Uh," dove-greys went to his expectant hand, "I'd love to shake with you, but I figure it'd probably hurt about as badly as that brand coming off. Mate issues; story for another day. But look, thanks for helping. Now, tell me how this is going to work so that we can get home."

Concerned baby blue eyes regarded Delia with genuine sincerity. "Ok, so. I'm gunna shift into my beast. Now, when that happens, ya know I'm gunna have fire on me and other stuff but don't worry! I'll make sure nothin' hurts ya, okay?" Delia nodded in agreement, wishing he'd get on with it. She knew what a damn hellhound transformation entailed. "When you're ready, show me the brand and I have to lick it a few times." *HOLD UP! Was this for real? He was serious?!* "See, my drool can either be binding *OR* acidic. The Dark Master used it in the brand's spell itself. Therefore, hellhounds can remove brands." *Was he ever going to stop fucking talking?!* "I think it's a fluke. I don't think Mr. Lucifer meant for that to happen."

"Got it, got it!" She had to interrupt him or she feared she'd be moving in permanently. "Justus knows the full details of how this works and he's okay with it??" *It's a rather intimate area!* Delia wasn't even sure how *she* felt about it. *BUT SHE SURE AS HELL WASN'T* OKAY *WITH IT.*

"Yes, ma'am," Blayde nodded adamantly. "We went over it several times, step by step." He tapped his temple, grinning. "I got this! Plan is memorized." Gods love him, he was actually kind of adorable. And Delia *HATED* 99.7% of all males. She wondered if it was possible to adopt hellhounds… "Once your brand melts --sorry again-- then jump on my back and we're outta here! Mr. Justus told me to take you to a place called Hell's Rejects in NOLA and leave you with the big, bald bouncer."

Delia full on snort laughed. "Oh shit. Jus and Rez met… Can't wait to hear about that," she snickered. "Okay. Let's do this. Get your shift on, pup."

He smiled wide, with deep dimples blaring, "Will do, just back up a little, okay? I don't wanna accidentally hit ya! And remember, I won't let my fire hurt ya!"

Smirking with amusement, Delia did as requested and took a couple steps back. Blayde beasted out, shifting into what appeared to be a cross between a monstrously massive Rottweiler, and a grossly overgrown black bear. Charcoal hair, with short flames dancing from its tips, took the place of skin. As the muzzle and face transformed, teeth and canines layered and sharpened like those of a great white shark and about the same size, too. The once baby blue eyes now glowed a neon red-orange.

Blayde shook off what was left of the tiny remnants of fabric from his shorts, and sat down. Due to his enormous size, he was just below eye level with the demoness. Big, flickering eyes settled on Delia's. He waited for her to initiate the next task.

The Furie stood there, mentally preparing herself for what was to come. Jus was the only male she'd ever voluntarily allowed to touch her in that vicinity. And currently, she'd rather take a blade to the gut, but she was a beast herself. She'd manage.

Unbuttoning her leathers, she cringed as she lifted her tank hem and pushed the left side of her pants below her hip bone, exposing the intricate brand in the V there. It was approximately four inches in diameter, showcasing Lucifer's sigil: a silhouette of a dragon and a viper entangled, with his name inlayed over it, written in ancient Demoni symbols.

The hound's gaze never left hers. Blayde refused to lower his eyes until she gave the go ahead. "Yep, just do it," Delia grated, before she took a long breath and held it. She stared up at the coal packed ceiling when he stepped closer to her.

The demoness felt his boiling, velvet tongue lap over the curse. "Son of an assbadger," she hissed, and uncharacteristically flinched. Her skin felt as if it were being fried off. The wince had more to do with the location than the pain, though.

Another lick, and another. The burning sensation kicked up a few notches with each swipe. After the fourth go, she felt Blayde take steps back and gathered the fortitude to look down. What once was there was no more. Unchecked tears dribbled down her cheeks while she stared at the red, angry, rapidly blistering spot. The pain was forgotten as decades worth of relief flooded her. “Thank you,” she murmured quietly.

Shaking out of her moment, Delia refastened the leathers, scrunching her nose and inhaling sharply as the contact with the wound caused it to flare up worse. She stealthily wiped the dampness from her face as she cleared her throat. “Breathe a word of that to anyone and I’ll neuter your ass. Got it?” She narrowed savage grey eyes to the hound. He softly whimpered and nodded his big, block head. “Perfect. Let’s get out of here.”

He stepped over to her side, crouched, and Delia happily hopped aboard. The flames that ran along the fur on the hound’s back lost their heat when contact was made. The demoness gathered a fistful of his pelt tightly and they ghosted.

# CHAPTER 18

Heavy footfalls echoed as Justus paced his fifteen by twenty-foot prison.

What was the delay? Had they been caught? Perhaps the brand had proved more difficult to remove than anticipated? Sizeable hands clenched into fists as he grumbled to himself.

The half-breed turned toward the door when it was jerked open, allowing a couple dozen demon guards to enter. They filed in, lining the wall, facing off with the captive, blades drawn. "We've orders to move you," announced the last one to enter.

Justus stood in the center of the cell, feet planted hip width apart and fists raised. As he assumed his fighting stance, the taunting flick of his fingers beckoned them to approach. "Jump when you're feelin' froggy, underlings," he sneered, his Aussie accent thick.

The instant those demons thought to charge, a large pack of hellhounds materialized. They circled Justus, with their backs to him. Reinforcements. The half-breed nearly choked up at this heartwarming show of loyalty and solidarity. He knew these mutts had respected him, but he had no idea to this extent.

A ring of blazing fur attacked as one; it was rather beautiful to witness. Cascades of fire moved in sync while the echoes of growls and breaking bones mixed with screams, culminating in a cacophony of carnage. Stunned and impressed by the beasts' battle practices, Justus pivoted, waiting for a guard to break their line. None had.

Blayde appeared beside him. The pup nudged into him with a hip, urging him to board the Hellhound Express.

Justus grabbed onto the pelt and slung a leg over his back. They traced to the outer edge of the castle's grounds, where Justus would then be able to trace himself. "Listen hound," the half-breed patted Blayde's shoulder after disembarking, "when the battle is over, bring your pack to me. I'll ensure your safety and assist any who need jobs or shelter."

What those mutts had done in that cell had ensured their demise if they did not also flee Hell. Lucifer would do unthinkable things to them before they bled out. In return for acting so selflessly, Justus and Delia were indebted to the pack and swore to provide anything and everything they could possibly need.

Blayde chuffed and bowed in acknowledgment and gratitude, then ghosted to rejoin the melee.

Justus traced quickly to his old living quarters. He needed to retrieve something for his mate.

With that task completed, he traced to find Delia. He'd never wanted to hold anyone in his arms as badly as he needed her in that moment.

---

The demoness had been back on Earth maybe an hour at most, just long enough to meet with Rez in the office and show him that she was still alive. Delia gave him a detailed report of her time away and the events that had led up to it. Afterwards, she went down the hall to her apartment for a much needed shower. She was well past ready to wash off the disgusting Hell funk.

As Delia stepped under the delightfully hot water, she felt Justus make landfall. She turned, and there he was in all of his ethereal glory; kicking and shredding out of his gritty, blood spattered clothes. Glittering greys quickly shifted to black, as did her platinum blonde hair.

She admired his rippling muscles as fabric flew and fell to the tile floor. "I had a thank you speech prepared, but it seems I've forgotten it..." Her fang pierced her plump, bottom lip while a purr began building in her throat when her beefcake bent over to rid himself of a stubborn boot. His firm ass begging to be bitten.

The arctic chill in the Furie's blood quickly began to warm and boil over when Justus righted. Golden eyes bore into Delia's as he stepped into the shower with her, filling the entire space with his drool-worthy scent.

Justus took her face gently into his hands and laid a kiss on the demoness that she'd likely never forget. His tongue slipped through parted lips to dominate hers as she submitted fully, turning to putty in his hands. To do with as he wished.

Justus met her gaze again, a million emotions swirling in his enchanting orbs, then he sunk to his knees. Greedy fingers dug into her hips as he studied the ruined brand with a low, rumbling growl.

Searing eyes lifted to Delia's as she stared down at him with nothing but love and adoration. "Does it hurt, Dove?" She nodded gingerly, biting her lip ring. "I've got you now, love." Justus' gaze lowered back to the angry wound and he sliced through his tongue with a sharpened fang.

The demoness let her head fall forward, watching intently as he began kissing and licking the offensive mutilation. Healing blood swept over, eliminating the pain and bringing the flesh back to its former porcelain hue. Shivers ran down Delia's spine while moisture pooled between her thighs.

A hefty moan poured from the Furie when his talented mouth meandered along her quivering stomach and continued south.

Justus slipped his tongue between her folds and worked his magic. Electric tingles overtook Delia's body, causing her legs to tremble as her fingers speared through Jus' thick hair, fisting what they could in an attempt to stay upright.

At first, the languid licks of his tongue were slow, measured, concentrating on the swollen bundle of nerves pleading for his attention. Whimpered pleas for more from his female quickened his pace. His tongue delved in drawing up sweet honey, Jus groaned like a starved man having his first meal.

The vibrations radiating through him had the Furie withering and wavering on her feet. Tongue lashes quick-fired against her throbbing clit, and two thick fingers slipped into her wet depths, assaulting her release button from both sides.

When the demoness' knees buckled, Justus rose, wrapping his arms around her hips, picking Delia up. He hugged her to him as if he'd never been more relieved or grateful to hold someone. Long legs wrapped around him, her sex coating his shaft in delectable juices as her hips rocked.

The Furie nibbled along his stubbled jaw, panting, "You did..the impossible..and saved me again, baby." She suckled his luscious bottom lip before she kissed him with a frantic desperation. The taste of her essence on his tongue, driving her to madness to have more of him. Teeth and fangs clattered as greedy mouths begged and battled for a deeper connection.

The fragrant scent of cherries and dark chocolate filled the room, mingling with his citrus top notes, and their moans and groans of ecstasy formed a multi-sensory symphony for their passionate soundtrack.

Justus backed her against the steamy, ceramic wall and met her gaze as they broke the kiss to pant in much needed air. "Dove, you're wholly free now," he groaned. His lead pipe of an appendage grinding against the Furie's sensitive bud, elicited needy cries from her. Delia's head fell back, if this was a dream, may she never wake from it. Nothing had ever felt so exquisitely sublime as Justus growled, kissing and biting along her neck and shoulder.

His hands lowered to her plentiful backside, fingers gripping hungrily, he lifted her slightly as he lined himself up for a divinely intimate intrusion. "Only, you're not free of *me*," his teeth raked along her earlobe, "...you're MINE, Dove," he snarled just before he simultaneously breached her tight entrance and speared her shoulder with his overgrown, mammoth fangs.

Screams rang out as mating venom coursed into the Furie's system. Jus' over-engorged length caressed and obliterated her sweet spot in a monumental show of dominance and claiming declaration.

This was everything Delia had ever wanted but feared would never come to fruition. The only man she'd ever loved had now claimed her as his mate. Warm chills and fluttering butterflies flooded her system. Euphoria washed over her soul as Justus imparted to her a serenity that annihilated the steel walls that had sheltered her damaged heart for centuries.

Wave after wave of rapturous orgasms tore through Delia for what seemed like days.

After yet another onslaught of intoxicating pleasure catapulted through the Furie, Justus rocketed past his ability to hold himself back. Bucking wildly, he captured her mouth once more in a fiercely passionate kiss as he filled her with rope after rope of his seed.

Kisses turned to breathless pants. Movements slowed as the demoness turned into little more than a writhing, mewling mass of satiation. When her form eventually went completely lax against him, Justus traced them to their castle's master bed.

The couple materialized on the plush black and silver bedding, laying on their sides. Disengaging their bodies tenderly, Justus turned the demoness in his arms and pulled her tightly against him, making her the little spoon. Her slender arms wrapped over his at her waist as she snuggled further into him with a satisfied purr.

Jus buried his face into her damp locks, greedily inhaling the decadent scent of her. A heart he'd once regarded as faulty, now swelled with love, pride, and gratitude. His fated mate was where she belonged. It had never occurred to him that this day was a possibility, and yet, here they were.

"You're mine, Dove. We'll never part again," he spoke softly against her neck with a voice full of gravel. Justus pressed a kiss there and nipped a trail down to her mate-marked shoulder. "I'm sorry it took me so long to see what was in front of me all along." He nearly choked up before he finished the sentence.

He'd been a fool for far too long.

Delia shivered against him as his words sank in. Herculean arms tightened around her when she stared back at him over her shoulder. The sight of her shimmering eyes filled with tears, nearly gutted him. "I've waited so long," she whispered, as a loan tear trickled down her flushed cheek.

Sitting up, he pulled the Furie into his lap and draped a blanket over them. The half-breed cradled her protectively. Soft, sweet kisses met her damp features as an unsteady hand reached up, cupping his jaw.

"I'm here now, love, and I'll never let you go again," Jus reassured, before mercilessly kissing her.

In that moment, everything around them was turned upside down. Nothing made sense apart from their union.

Hours later, the couple roused. Delia raised her head from his chest when his thick fingers sifted through her tousled hair. Resting her chin on his pec, she stared up at him, smitten.

"I have a surprise for you, Dove," Justus hoarsely announced, grinning.

"I forgot it at your apartment, though. Can I leave you for a beat to retrieve it?" He winked at her, his grin growing into an enchanting smile.

Delia lifted up on her elbow and cocked an eyebrow. "When the hell did you have time to get me a surprise?"

"It was something I was able to grab, while in the Underworld."

Now the demoness was curious. "I can't imagine what in the realm I'd want, but sure. Surprise me, baby." Delia bit his pec then rolled off of him. "Any longer than ten seconds and I'm coming to look for you, mister." She feigned a pout when he quickly kissed her and disappeared.

Seconds later, Justus materialized and sat on the bed beside her. He kept an arm behind his back. "Ready?" He asked, knowing she certainly was.

Curious eyes searched the half-breed. What had he been up to? "Of course." She flashed that rare smile that melted him.

Justus revealed two books and handed them to her. The Furie knew by the covers exactly what they were before they touched her hand. Appreciative tears instantly poured as Delia brushed her disbelieving fingers over the faded and cracked, brown leather cover with gold trim and a center emblem. She raised her gaze to Justus and clutched the Lewis Carroll 1865 original Alice's Adventures in Wonderland and its sequel, Through the Looking Glass, to her chest. Speaking through tears, Delia proclaimed, "I have my muchness again." That statement carried endless meaning for the demoness.

Centuries ago, she'd found the books in Justus' small library and learned to read with them. Delia had read them countless times since, but it had been over three decades since she'd last held them. These literary works connected with her on a level nothing else had; until mating with Jus. She'd lived in a constant rabbit hole before she went to the Punishment Realm. During the rapes, she'd fade away to another world, one in which interesting creatures interacted with her. Then, after her imprisonment, Delia would often escape her gruesome tortures by retreating into the safe corner of her mind to chat with the Mad Hatter or have a smoke with the Caterpillar.

Aside from her mate, the books were her most treasured valuables. "I-I can't...can't even... " Delia's words trailed off when she could no longer form more. The emotions overtaking her, left her speechless. Nothing she could ever say or do would accurately convey the love and gratitude she was filled with.

Justus pulled the demoness in for a comforting hug. "I know, Dove. I know." He kissed the top of her head, holding her tight, and allowed her this moment to cry out everything she'd been holding onto for far too long.

# CHAPTER 19

The following weeks were a blur. If anyone ever thought the demoness had hit the drug vault hard, well, that paled in comparison to how much she'd worn out Justus. There was no exaggeration when she said he was her unwavering addiction. He was her church, her religion, her guiding light, and the Furie was making up for lost time in the best way she could fathom.

They'd christened each and every room in that ridiculously large castle, some numerous times. The music studio, for instance, was a choice pick. That comfy lounge chair gave way to many creative positions that had to be tried out. It quickly became their favorite piece of furniture in the whole place. No contest. Delia had plans to buy more for other rooms.

In between their sexcapades, the couple finished moving their things in and did some minor redecorating, while also managing their businesses from afar. They'd attempted to track down Hannah, but Justus had trained her well, so she remained successfully hidden.

She had to surface at some point, though, and Delia would be there when she did. Payback was an ass-badger, and the demoness had lovely plans in store for the deserving dark fae. And the longer she waited, the more time to dream up varying retribution tactics.

For now, it was time to get back to the club and give Rez some much needed time off. It was early in the afternoon and she had a surprise to set up, as well, for her mate. It was something she swore she would never, ever do again, but this time she'd actually enjoy it.

"You'll come to the club when you're done, baby?" Delia asked, as she materialized in Justus' expansive walk-in closet where he was getting dressed. Leaning a hip against the dressing table, she gave him a thorough once over.

Then another.

Gods, he was gorgeous as he stood before her buttoning a crisp, white shirt, that he'd paired with a perfectly tailored pair of black slacks and polished, black loafers. The demoness chuckled inwardly; she thought of how much of an odd couple they appeared to be. She glanced down at her black, tightly fitted Halestorm tank and shredded, red skinny jeans. Black and red leather knee high stiletto boots topping off the look.

But, opposites did attract. He was the light to her dark. The proper to her funky. The calm to her madness. While his temper could rival hers, his control over it was impressive; whereas she tended to let hers run amok.

Justus' icy blues briefly flared glowing gold as he watched her watching him, then strode to her, scooping her up into his arms, and kissing her before answering. "Nothing could keep me from it, Dove." He grinned in that way that made her knees weak, then nipped her lip. "Shouldn't be more than a couple of hours."

She nipped him back with a grin of her own. "Perfect. That'll give me some time to get things done before you show up, distracting me with all your sexy."

He set her back on her feet, kissing the top of her head, "I don't know about all that. You're the wickedly tempting siren I must attempt to block out to accomplish anything. It's an impossible task, but I'm going to give it a try." He winked down at her and kissed her once more. "I'll be back with you before you know it. I love you, Dove."

Delia swooned. Those words did indescribable things to her heart and soul. She could listen to that declaration on a loop, day in and day out, and never tire of it. "L word you, too, Jussy," she replied, hugging him tight. "Now we have to leave or we're going to end up all naked and sweaty...you know it's true." She chuckled softly and he joined in the amusement.

"Yes, I do know. See you later, babe." After a last kiss, he disappeared. With a dreamy sigh, the Furie followed suit.

---

"The boss-lady is back. Go home!" Delia announced when she materialized in the office to find Rez sitting at her desk.

His amber eyes and a dark, crooked brow rose from the computer he'd been working at to peer at the demoness. "You DO remember where this place is? I was beginning to wonder." The smoke demon smirked as he stood and stretched.

*Insert eye roll here.* "Keep talkin' and you can sit your ass right back down and stay." Hands on hips, Delia gave him a challenging glare as she walked closer.

"Well, I can see that being mated hasn't changed your sunny disposition any." Now he rolled his eyes. "What a pity." That earned him a punch to the shoulder.

"Shut up, jackass. You'd quit if I started being all nice and shit."

Arms crossed over his chest, Rez cocked his head at her, contemplating. "You may have a point," he agreed. "Luckily, we don't have to find out." The slightest grin played on his lips as he tidied up the desk.

Delia plopped into the desk chair and kicked her heels up; hands clasped loosely over her stomach. "Seriously, though. I'm going to make some changes around here and ease up your workload. I realize, up to this point, we've both lived and breathed this club, but that's coming to an end. We both deserve a life outside these walls."

Stumbling back in feigned shock, Rez gasped, hands clutching his heart. "You're a doppelgänger, aren't you?! De's still in Hell, isn't she!" He dropped the act and recrossed his arms. "That sounds great and all, but I'll believe it when I see it." Rez stared at her disbelievingly, as if he'd heard it all before. And he had, but Delia was going to follow through this time.

The boss-lady gave him a middle finger salute. "Scout's honor," she sneered. "You think Harper is ready to move up to management?"

Harper was the head DJ, but she practically ran the strip club portion of the building. She was a spunky, little harpy with a different hair color every night. She hadn't quite come into her own yet, but she was a hard worker and never met a stranger. The Valkyrie and siren dancers and patrons even liked her. Considering that those three species typically warred at any given opportunity, that was saying a lot.

The look of surprise left Rez's face quickly and he nodded. "She'd do well. She already knows the ins and outs of it all. Only need to teach her the accounting and inventory side."

"Cool. That's what I thought, too. I'll get her up here and feel her out.

Now, go home. Or anywhere but here. BYE!" Delia spun in her chair, flipping him off as he disappeared.

Opening the top drawer of her desk, she retrieved an ear comm, turned it on and put it in place. Pressing to activate, she spoke after the double chirp, "Harp. My office." In less than a minute, she heard the harpy bounding up the stairs. A knock at the door sounded before it opened.

"You rang, your royal highness?" De heard, as neon green hair and bright lemon-colored eyes appeared in the doorway. And yes, her inquiry was a play on words; a nod to the fact that Delia was often hella high.

"Yeah, come on in." Delia moved from her chair to the sofa, folding her legs pretzel style as she sat. Harper crept in, shutting the door behind her, then sat at the other end of the couch. "Two things." The demoness could read the anxiety on the chick. Usually, you didn't get called to the office unless you were about to get your ass handed to you. "...actually, three. First, chill out. This is a pleasant meeting." Delia chuckled, and Harper relaxed some. "Second, how do you feel about being promoted to a floor manager position?"

The harpy's glimmering eyes widened, making her look like a deer in the headlights before she answered the question with one of her own. "Is this a joke? De, please, you know I can never tell when you're kidding or serious."

A deadpan stare was the Furie's response. Would NO ONE let Delia be nice?! She sighed, and shook her head. "I'm nothing but sincere. We need more help around here, and I'd rather move you up than go through the challenges of a new hire for management."

Harper snorted, "Challenges? You mean the half you don't kill?"

Delia wasn't going to touch that but yeah, admittedly, she had killed more new hires than she kept or fired. "ANYWAY. You in, or no?"

"Ohmygosh, ohmygosh! Yes!! Thank you!" Harper bounced in her seat as she answered.

Bouncy was so NOT Delia's thing, but she tried to refrain from rolling her eyes so the kid could have her moment. "Cool. Find me a replacement DJ I can tolerate and then we'll get you trained. Now, on to the third thing." Harp was still bouncing; gods help the demoness, she had to move this meeting along. "I have something I need your help with, a surprise for Justus when he gets here." Delia checked the time on her phone. "We should have a little over an hour before his arrival."

"OHMYGOSH!! OHMYGOSH, OHMYGOSH!!!! I finally get to meet the infamous Justus?! And, of course I'll help!!"

The amount of excitement coming off of the girl was nauseating, but Delia trudged ahead with the details of the surprise.

# CHAPTER 20

Justus checked his watch, he was running a little late. His Sydney security firm had been a bit of a three-ring circus since Hannah pulled her stunt and dropped off the face of the earth. The half-breed had a sneaking suspicion that she'd fled to another realm, but he had his private investigators searching. She'd turn up somewhere, eventually.

After signing off on payroll and touching base with a few VIP clients, he shot Delia a text to let her know he'd arrive at the club shortly.

Tying up the last of the loose ends, he noticed his mate never replied. The half-breed assumed she was busy with some fresh dumpster fire at Hell's Rejects. He traced over to his local flat to check things were as they should be. He couldn't wait to bring his woman over for a visit. She'd never been to Australia, or anywhere other than the States, for that matter. He'd remedy that. She'd lived to work for far too long. Now it was time to simply live, and partake in all of the wonders of the many realms. They had so much to experience together and he couldn't wait to watch the world through her eyes.

Content that his apartment was safe and sound, he traced to the club's office. Empty. Justus stepped over to the surveillance monitors, scanning for his one and only. It was barely 5 pm, not a packed house yet, so she should be easy enough to locate.

Unable to find her on the screens, he exited and jogged down the stairs to let their mate bond draw him to her. He strode through the hall of private rooms and felt a tap on his arm from behind. "Not interested," he grunted dismissively without looking back, and continued walking. A tiny female with crazy green hair jumped in front of him, a huge smile plastered on her face. "I said 'NOT interested', now move along." His angel side attempted to keep the grumble out of his tone, while still making it abundantly clear that the girl needed to get out of his face.

"You're Justus, right?!" The bouncy girl asked, as she held out her hand in salutation. Justus nodded with a grunt, crossing his arms over his broad chest. He stared at the female as she lowered her offered hand and continued, "I'm Harper, the boss-lady asked me to usher you to a place to wait on her."

Justus relaxed, relieved the little one wasn't hitting on him. "My apologies, then. Show me the way," he swept his arm out in invitation for her to lead.

"Sure! Right this way!"

The half-breed was rather surprised when Harper headed toward the dancers' portion of the club. It seemed odd that Delia would wish him to wait in a sea of mostly naked women. Sounded like a blood bath in the works. But if that's what his fated mate wanted, then he'd enjoy the brawl as it unfolded.

His brow furrowed when they turned the corner into the vast room and it was empty. Perplexed much? Why yes, yes he was. As a rule, the area was never without spectators. Yet, there he stood, in open, deserted space. Had the wicked little Furie already killed all of the dancers? He pondered the possibility for a moment.

"Where the hell is everyone?" Justus asked, as he peered around the expanse.

Harper giggled and shrugged her shoulders. "Never know what'll happen around this place, ya know?!" The girl ushered him to a red velvet, high-back, armless chair that sat front and center, facing the main stage. "Delia said to 'plant your ass here'. Soooo, there ya go!" The light-bright turned and trotted over to the DJ booth as he tentatively sat down.

Overhead lights began to spin and change colors as a disco ball lowered above the stage.

Justus was at a loss for words as to why he was in this scenario. Was Delia testing him? Curious how he'd react to what she assumed would be dancers tempting him? His mind was all over the place, entertaining all manner of theories. The one thing he knew for sure? He was not intrigued. He'd never frequented strip clubs, and wasn't about to start now.

Justus rose from his seated position, prepared to jet when Adrenalize by In This Moment began playing on the surround sound speakers. At the same time, Harper, in a rather entertaining announcer's voice, boasted through the mic, "Now, for your viewing pleasure, please welcome the one, the only Roooyyaaaall Hiiiiighnesss. The Queen of Furie mayhem! The Mistress of Wickedness! Heeeeeere she is! Ms. Delia to bring the sensual Payne!"

The half-breed could have been knocked over with a feather. Ice blue eyes widened and his jaw dropped as he turned to the stage to see his sinfully sexy mate emerging from behind the shimmering curtain. He dead weighted it back into the chair as she strutted across the stage in a black lace bustier. A perfectly short, black tutu and thigh high fishnet stockings had Justus biting his lip, shook. His mind instantly fixated on having her black, five-inch heels locked behind his back...or better yet, wrapped around his neck.

The Furie was the gothic Barbie that wet dreams were made of. Silken, ebony locks cascaded down to the beautifully sculpted ass that peeked from beneath her skirt. Her makeup, little more than smokey eyeliner, had her glittering greys popping against the darkness. And those glossy, onyx lips... He knew exactly where they needed to be.

She'd never needed any make-up, in his opinion, but she knew how to highlight his favorite features.

Elbows planted on his spread knees, Justus sat forward with hands clasped in front of him, itching to touch his temptress. He hadn't a clue why he'd been granted this treat of epic proportions, but he was definitely riveted now. He couldn't tear his eyes away from the seductive show. The Furie was a ravishing sight to behold, he'd never seen her dance in this way but she was a natural.

Singing along with the music, Delia provocatively pranced her way around the stage, making use of each and every floor-to-ceiling pole. All four of them. At one point, she was hanging upside down, with only her locked ankles holding her in place. Graceful fingers skimmed along her tantalizing curves, drawing his eye to her alluring 'assets'. To say the dark goddess was testing Justus' restraint would be a ridiculous understatement.

A mental note was made to have a pole installed at the castle.

Justus was beyond tempted to snatch her from that stage. She deserved to be traced home where he would show the wench how overly aroused she'd made him. The beast trapped in his slacks was about to explode, but he could not halt her performance prematurely. That would be utter blasphemy.

The song wound down and Justus let out a long, low whistle. Finally, he could take his female somewhere private and devour her. But that thought ended when Chris Isaak's Wicked Game began playing.

Justus locked eyes with the vixen as she sauntered slowly toward him, lowering the side zipper of her corset. His gold gaze observed hungrily as it opened and dropped to the floor. An eyeful of perky, bouncing breasts were strutting toward him and his hands were itching to feel them.

*Did he just lick his lips?* Damn right he did. His mate was beyond delicious and gods help her when he got her alone.

Delia ripped the skirt off as she descended the three stairs to the floor, showcasing a black, rhinestone studded thong. Before she reached Justus' chair, she seductively twirled and bent over to display her heavenly bare backside.

The half-breed's fists clenched, his jaw ticked. This female would surely be his ultimate demise. She was the definition of erotic. His femme fatale.

On one particular sway of her hips, Delia was within arms' reach. Justus took the opportunity and yanked her into his lap with a growl, "You're playing with fire, woman." He ground his aching shaft against her firmly.

A sensually wicked laugh softly aired, her finger raised and traced the half-breed's pouty lips. "I'm well aware, gorgeous." Sitting up, she playfully bit his stubbled chin and stood, swatting his hands away. "No touching allowed, sir."

"The fuck it isn't," he snarled, grabbing her hips again. "This belongs to me. I touch when I want." He released her with a corrupt grin and watched as she bent at the hip.

His thirsty eyes drank in her scenery as the demoness trailed her fingertips up her flawless calf. Breasts bobbed, begging to be tasted, while her claws skimmed along her shapely thigh and over her hips. Fingers veered inward to highlight the Furie's toned stomach.

Answering his prayers, his sultry minx finally pranced back over to him and climbed into his lap, straddling his tree trunk thighs. Delia brushed against the prisoner in his pants while she shamelessly nibbled at his lips and unbuttoned his shirt.

Justus' hands snaked around and groped the generous globes of her ass with a groan, "You're killin' me, wench." Her scent had overtaken his senses, the heat and dampness of her thonged sex against him became nearly more than he could tolerate without throwing her to the ground to have his way with her.

Voluptuous lips kissed and nipped along the line of his jaw, down his neck, and to the mate mark at his shoulder. Chills spread over him, landing a throbbing heat directly on his engorged rod. The naughty Furie lined up her fangs with the scar and pierced him, sending electric bolts of desire hurtling down his spine.

*Game over.* It was leave now or... He quickly glanced around. Harper was gone. They were alone, and the doors into the space were closed.

Worked for him.

Justus fisted a thick mass of ebony hair and yanked Delia's head back to meet his glowing glare. "You knew what you were doing with that bite, Dove," he growled. She grinned; her onyx gaze enraptured. She knew exactly. Jus drew her lips to his and plunged his tongue deep between the seam.

As mouths wrestled for dominance, Justus reached down between them, unfastening his slacks to free the caged brute trapped there. He bit Delia's tongue and indulgently suckled the blood from it as he hooked his finger under her thong, ripping it free. His hands moved to her hips, raising her enough to align them and then slammed her forcefully upon his aching shaft.

Jus nearly blacked out from the abrupt ecstasy.

Delia yelped against his mouth as her slippery walls promptly made way for his girth and welcomed him into the depths of euphoria. Their breathless kiss broke when the demoness leaned back, relishing in the rush of his punishing pace. With each rise and subsequent impalement, Delia's claws sunk progressively deeper into his shoulder as she held on for support.

Jus pummeled into her relentlessly, his angle hitting her sweet spot with precision.

Their rhythm slowed when Justus dipped his head to capture a beaded nipple between his teeth. The suckling and biting tossed the demoness over the cliff, causing her back to bow as the waves of a climax overtook her. Sweet honey washed over Justus' cock and spilled down his sack.

Heady moans and whimpers added to their carnal symphony.

As aftershocks dissipated, Delia sat up and purred in his ear, "Your turn, baby." The wicked vixen speared her fangs into Jus' mate mark; this time with true purpose.

He saw stars.

A sensual electricity ripped through his body and, as if flipping a switch, the half-breed bucked into an extraordinary release of his own. The demoness' bite held firm as she rode out his explosions, keeping him firmly anchored deep within her.

When their movement slowed, Jus' hands released her hips and moved to her back, lightly brushing her oversensitive skin with gentle fingers. Delia unsheathed from his shoulder and languidly kissed her way up his neck. "See, good mates get nice surprises," she rasped at his ear.

Powerful arms wrapped tightly around her while her face remained buried in the crook of his neck. Panting turned to steadier breaths as they sat, locked together.

Justus could honestly say that was the best surprise he'd EVER received. He pleaded to the gods to let it happen again, and soon. He could certainly celebrate this mated life if it continued this way. His mate was unparalleled in every aspect. *Except cooking. But no one is perfect, yeah?*

"Beauty, you take my breath away. You are truly exceptional."

Delia leaned up and bit his chin, then brushed over his kiss swollen lips. "As are you, baby." She winked at him and kissed the tip of his nose. "Now take me home to clean up so I can get back to work."

# CHAPTER 21

*Two months later*

"Do you want it in a sippy cup, too, honey?" Delia snarked to the brunette in the 'Bride to Be' tiara, when she ordered up a Sex on the Beach from the bar.

It was another packed night at Hell's Rejects and the Furie had been slinging bottles for a while. Every time she thought she had new hires well trained and decent schedules on a lock, some shit would go down. Mostly because of her temper, but hey, baby steps. Tonight, the bar manager had been a no-show.

The little twit giggled, apparently believing Delia was kidding around with her. "I know, right?! It's such a girlle drink."

De rolled her eyes and turned to grab a bottle of peach schnapps. Quickly mixing her drink, Delia set it, rather harshly, in front of the giddy female. "Good luck with that," the demoness told her, pointing to the tiara. "Drink's on the house."

De's eyes widened as the words left her mouth. *What the fuck?!* WHY would she say something so out of character to the girl?! And comping her drink?! Who gave two fucks if the marriage sank or swam?!

*Fucking hell*. Delia thought she had multiple personalities before, but this was getting out of hand. At least she didn't smile at the twit. THAT would have been too much for the demoness to handle. If she started going around being 'sweet', she might have to return to the Underworld to escape the embarrassment!

"If you scream at me one more gods-damned time," she yelled over the loud music to another waiting patron, this one a runt male, "you'll be leaving with a broken jaw. Got it?!" Ah, there it was. Her dazzling personality was fully onboard again.

The shaggy, dark haired kid grunted his acknowledgment and piped down. Purposely being a bitch, Delia made him wait longer, even though he was at the front of her line. She pointed to the guy behind him and handed him the Stella he'd patiently ordered.

The demoness looked back to the runt. "Whatcha want?!"

"Jack and coke, please," he politely called out.

Delia chuckled to herself; he'd decided to go the 'nice' route. Clever boy. "Coming up," she mumbled, turning to pour. When she set the glass in front of him, he took it from her hand, making skin on skin contact with her. Her molars ground as anger increased. "That's $8.50, and a big fucking tip for your attitude earlier." He laughed; she glared. "Not fucking kidding, small fry," she barked out.

Should have up-charged him for touching her to begin with. She generally dodged males pretty expertly, but when it was super busy it could be impossible to avoid getting touched here and there.

"Fine," he sneered and held out a twenty to the demoness, "just give me five back."

She snatched the bill from him. "Don't think so, prick, move along." He cut his hazel eyes at her and huffed. Then, after a moment's pause, he turned and disappeared into the crowd. *Smart move, asshat*.

Checking her phone, Delia groaned. She'd been slinging bottles for over six hours.

The Furie took one more drink order, then scanned the crowd; it was leveling out. FINALLY. She'd done enough peopling for now and was definitely over it. Delia ducked out from behind the bar and hightailed it up to the office.

The demoness and Justus had fallen back into their old routine of working far too much. Jus was trying to keep his business soaring while also on the hunt for Hannah. Delia kept busy putting out fires left and right at the club. As a result, their time alone together had been spotty, at best. It was really doing a number on the demoness. Her mental stability as precarious as ever. Turned out she was no longer a loaner, but one half of a bonded pair. She rather liked that fact. If only they had more time to spend with one another.

Things had to change.

The office door flew open. "This is ridiculous! We have got to get a better handle on staffing!"

"Do I look like I'm in the mood for this bullshit?" Delia snarked, lit joint hanging from the corner of her mouth. She sat up on the couch where she'd been laying, going over P&L reports.

"You fired or 'disposed of' three servers and two dancers last week, what did you expect would happen?" Rez asked, in his usual smartass tone, as he closed the door behind him and leaned against it.

Delia's manicured brow quirked. "I expected you to hire more. I mean, what am I paying you for?!"

"Everything, apparently." It was his deadpan stare that really got under her skin.

"Thin ice, asshole. Thin. Ice." Setting down the file, she stood, glaring at him. Arms crossed, Delia took a hard drag on the joint. On the unhurried exhale, "Consider your next words carefully."

Rez sighed heavily, stuffing his hands into his front, jeans pockets. He glanced down at his shoes before responding, light bouncing off of his cleanly shaven head. Meeting her gaze again, with a less combative stare this time, he stated more calmly, "Listen, I've moved around half the staff to try and cover the holes, but it's not working. You've got to handle the hires, maybe then you won't dispose of them so easily."

He actually had a point. Most of the ones she'd had an issue with were the ones he had brought on. "Okay, I can do that soon. I assume we have plenty of applications in the 'call back' file for me to choose from?" De asked, trying to calm her own temper.

"Yeah, boss." He nodded toward the locked file cabinet in the far corner. "Locked up tight in the top drawer."

"Cool." The demoness sat back down, kicking up her bare feet onto the coffee table. "Do I need to be interviewing for a new GM while I'm at it?" she asked, taking another toke. Her face was stone cold serious, even though they both knew she was kidding. She'd lose her mind without him around to pick up the slack. Rez had been with her since she opened and knew everything about everything in the place.

"Go for it," he grumbled. "We both know no one else can put up with your shit show full time." He smirked, then added, "I almost feel sorry for Justus... ALMOST. But, from what I can tell, he deserves the fuckery you dish out. You two are so dysfunctional, you're perfect together." He did not mean that as a compliment, and they both knew it.

An amused grin played on the Furie's lips. "Aww, that's the sweetest thing you've ever said, hoss," she fawned, dripping with sarcasm. "Now, fuck off!" Delia picked the reports up again. "Meeting adjourned, motherfucker!" And gave him the ever ready middle finger salute.

"Fuck you, too, boss," he grumbled, as he turned and walked out the door.

Rolling her eyes, Delia checked the clock overhead. It was coming up on 3 am. She decided she'd leave Rez to the trainwreck staffing issue and go crawl in bed with her ridiculously sexy mate. That'd teach her second in command to cop an attitude with her, she thought as she tossed the file and traced home.

The following morning, Delia awoke to an empty bed. Livid, she slammed her hand down in the spot Justus should have been laying. They weren't exactly operating in the same time zones but DAMNIT! She really had just wanted to cuddle for a few minutes!

Violently kicking off the red satin sheets, she grouched from the bed and tossed on a tank top and boy shorts. De could hear Jus on a call and traced downstairs to see him pacing their extravagant kitchen. The demoness stood at the entrance, daggers shooting from her eyes. Jus mentioned going into the main office and the bitch switch flipped…mixed with her inner toddler. The thought of her, yet again, losing his undivided attention made her mental.

The Furie stepped into her mate's path with narrowed eyes, poking a stiff finger into his hard chest, "Oh no you're not!" Her head vehemently shook side to side; tousled, ebony locks flying all over the place.

Jus scowled at her, shaking his head, as well, for her to shut up and sidestepped her. The half-breed walked across the expansive room, continuing his call. Delia traced, tossing herself to the mosaic floor in front of him and kicked out to halt his forward progress. When he pinned her with a furious glare, she snapped her fangs at him. Arms outstretched, sharp claws clacking on the tile, Delia dared Jus to do anything other than pay attention to her.

That marked the moment the female had her demon card revoked and officially became THAT BITCH-- acting like a needy, over-possessive, lovesick moron. She should kick her own ass. Yet, in that moment, she didn't care how she looked or sounded. Her only thoughts were of having him to herself.

---

Frankly, it was difficult to hide a grin as Justus witnessed this peculiar display. His female certainly kept him on his toes! Predicting her behavior was always a losing contest. If anyone had told him that one day, the one and only, Delia Payne, would be sprawled out on the ground, pitching a fit like a petulant child, he would have laughed at the absurdity…yet, here they were.

"Jaymes, I'll call you back. A situation has developed and I need to see to it." Justus ended the call and set his phone on the marble countertop. He peered down at his ridiculously adorable mate. Delia's dark mane was strewn about the floor; her piercing grey eyes never leaving his.

Squatting down on his haunches, he scooped her up into his arms and lifted her. "Dove. You okay?" He asked, with a deep chuckle, as he dipped his head and nipped her plump, bottom lip.

Delia slung her arms around his neck and pouted, "I never see you and when I do, you're working."

He couldn't help but notice her little feet kicking back and forth as she searched his face for sympathy. There was none to be found, but there was a twinge of the same longing reflected in his eyes. She actually worked more than he did, so a fair amount of their absence was indeed *her* fault. "You truly miss me that much? Fine. Prove it. You've got one hour to pack a bag and get the club situated before WE leave for a getaway. Can you manage that?"

Skeptical eyes glared at him. "I don't care to go across the world to watch you work. I've got my own shit to do."

"What I need to take care of at the office can be managed in less than an hour. Then I'm all yours. My apartment overlooks the beach and we can go sightseeing."

The demoness scrunched her nose. "The beach? Gross! All that gritty sand, just like being in Hell again." She shook her head, uninterested.

"De. Have you ever been to a beach? Ever felt the ocean waves crashing around you?" He knew the answer.

"No."

"Then your first time will be with me, and I'm willing to bet that you'll feel differently once you are there. If not, we'll go somewhere else. Deal?" Jus gave a wink and a nod, encouraging her answer.

The Furie's mood lifted and she pulled his head down for a kiss. "Deal."

# CHAPTER 22

The couple materialized in the living area of Justus' Sydney residence. Delia's wandering gaze popped as she spun around, allowing the backpack on her shoulder to fall to the pale, hardwood floor. "Jus, this is not an apartment. It's a damn penthouse. Get your terminology right, dude!"

Floor to ceiling windows surrounded the contemporary space, which overlooked a stunning Bondi Beach. Soft earth tones of the decor, highlighted by natural light, complimented the exquisite architecture. The open floor plan included a large, entertainer's kitchen and spacious, private terraces on each side of the home.

Justus grinned and shrugged, "It's a place to live. I don't get caught up in what to call it."

He took her hand as she continued peering around in awe, and walked her to the grand master bedroom. This space decorated in darker earth tones. Delia could peek a portion of the marble en-suite and a cavernous dressing room. The entire place was quite remarkable.

"Put your things where you'd like and relax out on the deck while I get business squared away. I'll be back before you know it." Dipping his head to kiss her goodbye, a loud slap resounded as Delia's open hand met his face.

"Seriously?! You can't stay five minutes to show me around and let me settle!?"

A large hand flew out and she felt a tight grip around her throat as a hardy growl rumbled from the half-breed. "Stop antagonizing, De. I told you that I had to go in to the office before we got here." He caught her hand as she attempted to slap him again.

Jus slammed her against the wall; his oversized body pinning her. Arresting need flooded the demoness. The aroma of dark chocolate and cherries quickly filled the room. "If I start in with you now, then I'll never make it to the office. You know that. Now, STOP, wench." Delia snapped her fangs at him and he crushed his lips to hers, kissing her senseless.

"I'll be back soon," he breathlessly grumbled, straightening to adjust his suddenly ultra snug jeans, and disappeared.

Delia hissed and stomped her way back through the penthouse, retrieving her bag and returning to put her things away. Once done with that, she took a better look at the bathroom. It was wall to wall white tile and marble. A clawfoot tub, big enough for a few of her, sat in the far corner. She'd definitely be taking advantage of that while she was here, and planned on wrangling her mate in with her, too.

The Furie meandered into the closet/dressing room next, which was easily the size of a small bedroom. Fingers fondled Jus' hanging suits as she walked past them. His scent lingered heavy and made her long for him all the more. *Asshole.* Leaving her alone in a foreign land as soon as they arrived. With a huff, she exited the area and sulked off to the kitchen.

Rummaging through cabinets, she found some chips to snack on and moved on to the massive, double-wide refrigerator. Ah, yes, Satan Sake a plenty, just as she was hoping. Delia snatched a bottle and strode out onto the beach view terrace.

The first thing that caught her attention was the smell of saltwater on the breeze. She hated to admit it, but it was delightful, and seemed to be unclenching her nerves. The sound of the crashing waves was the next immediate awareness that grabbed her.

Delia looked out over the balcony. The calming chaos of the churning water below was lovely, further decompressing her. *Okay, fine, Justus was right*. It was quite peaceful out here, with all of its commotion.

She took a seat at the large, rectangular, glass table that was centered in the space. Twisting the cap off her brew, she leaned back, propping her bare feet up on the chair across from her. The sun shone directly above, warming her.

De took a giant swig from her bottle and then closed her eyes. Absorbing all of the peaceful sounds around her, she soon drifted off to slumberland.

In exactly forty-two minutes, Justus was leaving the meeting with his client. He materialized in the kitchen of the beach home, half expecting the place to be wrecked in another of his mate's temper tantrums, but much to his delight, all was as he'd left it.

He spotted Delia out on the deck. She appeared to be wholly relaxed, with her midnight mane surfing on the wind as she rested in a chair. His features brightened, observing his Furie finally content for a moment.

Justus grabbed several brews and crept out to join his female. When he neared, De's tired eyes cracked open. Shielding her from the sun, he leaned over her and kissed her hello. "You've found the best spot on the floor, yeah?" He asked with a grin, while he took a seat beside her. "I've spent more time out here than inside. It's quite soothing. Wouldn't you agree?"

Still waking up, Delia lazily turned her head and glimpsed at him. "Yeah, baby. You were right, I like it here. Still not sure about that whole sand sitch, though."

Justus chuckled. "We will make our way down there when you're good and ready to. You can check it out and tell me what you think. I promise it is nothing like the Hell coal you're used to." He reached over and tucked a lock of wayward hair behind her ear. "I wouldn't put you through that, Dove."

Delia nodded her head and looked to the ocean. "So, other than the beach, what's fun to do around here?"

"You name it, love, and it's probably nearby. There's parks and cliffs to explore. Luna Park also has rides. There are zoos and animal sanctuaries." That got her attention; she smiled over at him. "Also, we have the iconic Sydney Opera House just down the way." Her lip curled on that mention. Noted, not interested in that landmark. "Tons of restaurants and shops within walking distance, too. Actually, if I could persuade you to go flying with me tonight, there is a witch's shop we can pop into for a cloaking tonic."

The Furie sat bolt upright at that notion and spun to face him fully. "Flying? Like, by way of your wings? With me…in your arms??"

Jus had never seen his mate so excited about something that didn't involve sex, drugs, or music. And torture, always torture got that reaction. He had to admit, it made his tattered heart swell that just the mention of him flying her around was the magic mood amplifier. *Triple noted.* "Yes, Dove, with me, by way of my wings." A thrilled grin tugged at his lips.

His mate flew into his lap, nearly knocking over the table and their drinks in the process. Delia peppered his face with sweet kisses, then bit his chin and sat back, locking gazes with him. "Baby, I can't think of anything I'd rather do." Her brow furrowed, then she smiled that rare smile he so seldom saw. "Well, other than the obvious…other thing." The wicked little minx squirmed in his lap, ensuring the beast in his pants was fully awakened.

Justus traced her inside and demonstrated how to thoroughly work her over and keep her sated.

---

The tink of a bell above the door sounded when the couple walked in to The Double Whammy shop, hand-in-hand. It was as good a name as any for a witch's boutique.

A kind voice called out to greet them from a hidden room, "Take a look 'round. I'll be out in a moment!"

The couple did as they were told and wandered about, looking at all manner of gifts and souvenirs. There were crystals of every shape and color, candles, spell and wiccan history books. Figurines, oracle cards of every variety, artwork, spell pouches and potions, clothing and furniture.

"Oh my stars! Justus! You didn't tell me you were stopping by! And who, pray tell, is this beautiful creature on your arm?" An older lady, donned with a thick mass of ginger locks bound high atop her head, ambled over to them and patted Jus' arm.

"Ah, hello, Ms. Lola." Justus hugged Delia tight against his side. "Please meet my fated mate, the exquisite and somewhat infamous, Delia Payne."

Delia smiled and extended her hand. "Nice to me you, Ms. Lola." *See, the demoness could pull off manners when the mood struck her.*

"Oh for Goddess' sake, child!" Lola pulled Delia in for a hug. The demoness' eyes bugged out as she looked to Justus. Hugging strangers was *not* her thing, but she let it slide this time, given they needed something from the witch. It's generally a good practice not to offend or piss them off. "We're all family around here. And I do believe I've heard your name mentioned before. Either way, welcome to my little shop, doll." Finally, she released Delia from her embrace and prattled on. "... everything is marked and those prices are non-negotiable, as Justus here will tell you, but I've never had a complaint. No matter your needs, I'll make sure they're met. What are you kids in the market for today, hmm?"

Delia attached herself to Jus and let him do the talking. "We need two cloaking tonics. I'm taking my woman flying tonight and best if we do not have an audience for that."

Ms. Lola nodded her head. "Yes, yes. The less eyes on that the better, I agree." The witch walked behind the counter and disappeared behind the wall for a few minutes. She came back with two blue, velvet pouches, and set them on the counter. "These will do the job. Mix the ingredients and drink. Easy peasy, ya see. It'll give you approximately six hours of invisibility. Now, don't forget to split the dragon's blood in each pouch between you, so that you can see one another. Otherwise...*awkward*." The witch chuckled and pushed the bags toward them. "Anything else I can help you with while you're here?"

"No ma'am. This'll do it." Justus picked up the satchels and placed five Benjamins on the counter. "Have a nice evenin', Ms. Lola. We'll see you around."

"Yes, thank you, and nice to meet you," Delia added as they turned to leave. *See? Manners*.

"Now, you two lovebirds don't be a stranger! Take care," Ms. Lola called out as she disappeared behind her wall again.

---

The couple walked back to the penthouse and put on their swimsuits. They had several hours before sunset and Delia was ready to experience the beach. She still felt rather nervous, but was ready nonetheless.

They made their way down the stairs and stayed on the patio for a few moments while Delia took in the scene from the ground floor. Biting her lip piercing, as she often did when she was anxious, the demoness finally took that last step out onto the sand.

She stood there for a brief time, a death grip on Jus' hand as she let her toes wiggle into the grainy substance. Delia grinned up at her mate. "It's finer and softer than the coal."

"I know, love. I wouldn't have subjected you to it otherwise," Jus reassured her, kissing the top of her head. "Come on, let's walk." He gave her hand a faint tug and they moved toward the water.

It was a warm and gorgeous, partly sunny day with a light breeze and the waves not harsh at all when they stepped into the surf. Grey eyes grew large as the water rolled out, pulling the sand from beneath, tickling Delia's feet. She smiled up at Jus with a childlike expression of wonderment. "Woah. That's hella cool."

Justus peered down at his mate with complete reverence. For most, this would have been only a new, pleasurable experience…but Delia? She'd had to face many past demons to step off that ledge, onto the sand. He wanted to scoop her up into his arms and tell her how proud he was, but he couldn't. She needed to continue moving forward of her own volition to fully get past any remaining fears that may arise. That and she'd likely deck him for making a big deal of it. The demoness was peculiar about how she was perceived, especially in public. She had a very strong, personal brand: SHOW NO WEAKNESS.

The couple continued deeper into the surf. Delia laughed and shrieked as the cool water splashed up her deliciously inked body. Justus chuckled when she jumped on his back and pointed to the depths before them, "Carry us out, my trusty steed!"

He playfully bit the arm wrapped around his neck. "As you wish, Furie." Justus traversed the waves and carried them out until they were chest deep. He brought Delia around his side to face him in a hug. "There's my brave beauty," he told her as he kissed her.

In return, she nipped his lip. "Whatever. It's only water. Hardly a big deal." But her glistening gaze told another story as she splashed him. Since the demoness felt safe with him, she'd allowed more of her fears to surface at times. All of those emotions, she'd viewed as weak, were no longer under heavy lock and key. Justus was honored and felt grateful to be granted these occasional peeks behind the curtain.

They spent a solid hour playing and floating out there. Possibly some inappropriate PDA was had as well, but given how deep the water and few people around the private beach, they hardly cared about being seen.

After they returned to shore, Justus attempted to teach his mate the joys of skimboarding. The half-breed apparently forgot to take into account her mischievous demeanor. Delia's intent was purely sinister as she feigned interest in his lessons.

He stepped away to release his little dove into the surf on her own. The Furie zeroed in on a water nymph down the beach who had been watching them with far too much interest. The demoness, board in hand, ran a few feet before tossing the toy at the water's edge and jumping on it. Not to ride it, but to launch it. With accuracy far better than she could have hoped for, the skimboard shot from beneath her feet and careened straight into the side of the head of the gawker.

Hands over her mouth, covering a gigantic smile, Delia spun around. She winked at her Jussy and cackled, "OOOOPS!" as blood sprayed from the other female's scalp. The board had sliced clean into her skull. Luckily, there were no human onlookers as the nymph shrieked in horror and dove into the ocean, disappearing below the waves.

"Nice sport, baby," she laughed. "I could really get into this skimboarding shit!"

Laughing, Justus tackled the naughty Furie; the waves cushioning their landing. Delia came up sputtering and still laughing, Jus tossed her over his shoulder and deposited them both onto the beach blanket away from the water. "Always have to push the envelope, don't you, wench?" He asked, shaking his head, attempting to hide his amused grin.

"Umm, hey, bud. It's your fault! YOU told me to have fun…" And she did.

The happy couple laid there for a while, chatting and relaxing, before Justus noticed the time. "Are you hungry, Dove? I can order us some food before we get ready to go out."

"Yeah. That sounds good. I'm gonna stay down here a few more minutes though, okay?

"Of course. Take your time. I'll only be upstairs if you need me." He kissed her a few times and then left her to her own devices.

Propped up on her elbows, Delia watched, nearly hypnotized, as water swept in and out.

After several random passersby broke her trance, she went back down to the shore. The sand in the surf fascinated Delia for numerous reasons. It reminded her of so many things. As she sat in the chaos of the rolling waves, her mind went in countless directions.

Tiny granules of sand slipped through her fingers as water rushed by then receded again, over and over and… It captivated her.

The sand called forth memories of the dungeon. The coal dust that had coated her. Molested her. Tormented her. Made her feel dirty and worthless. However, playing in the surf soothed those images. Much as Justus did, this made her feel cleansed; redeemed. A part of something much bigger than her menial existence in Hell. She couldn't explain why the ocean comforted her, but, strangely, it did.

She felt her handsome mate's gaze on her and glanced up at him on the balcony. Sunglasses hid his eyes, but she knew that behind those shades were icy blue orbs trained hungrily on her. If she were a betting demoness, and she was, she would say, most likely, there were glowing gold flecks swimming in them, too.

She would have won that bet.

Delia took a moment to truly take in her mate.

Justus was her ocean. All encompassing, with his strength and might, yet also soothing and healing.

Dominant and commanding, yet calming and comforting.

From now to eternity, she wanted nothing more than to swim in his depths. To be carried away by his waves to the place where nothing mattered but the love they had for one another. The place where their hearts and souls merged and they became one.

Her favorite place: anywhere that she could be at one with him.

# CHAPTER 23

"I can do it. I'm not a moron, ya know." Delia smacked his hand away.

After a bout of mattress olympics and a shower, the couple had enjoyed a nice dinner, ordered in from a local bistro. Now they stood at the kitchen's immense bar, mixing the contents of Lola's pouches.

"De, I know you're not a moron." Jus raised his hands in surrender. "But you were about to knock over the oil of nightshade."

The demoness looked to see the blue bottle by her elbow, precariously set on the edge of the counter, and sneered, "I knew it was there." *No, she didn't*. Delia picked it up and added it to the mixture in a small tea cup. "Don't forget to split the dragon's blood," she instructed, though he was already in the middle of doing so.

"I'm on it, bossy." He would have smacked her rear for that, but she figured he was afraid it'd cause her to spill the concoction she was working on. "Keep up the attitude, wench, and I'll dunk your ass in the middle of the ocean while we're out."

Grey eyes cut to him. "If I go down, you go down, asshole."

Her brow waggled as the double entendre set in.

"Noted, you wicked vixen," Justus chuckled, stirring the contents of his cup. "Down the hatch?"

Lifting her cup, she nodded, "Let's do it, baby." Both quickly drank the entire, less than tasty mixtures and then stood staring at one another. "Wonder how long it takes to kick in…" Given they could both see the other, hard to say when it worked.

"Should be immediate," Justus shrugged. "Ah, yeah, it worked," he told her as he pointed to their non-reflection in the glass windows.

"Sweet! Time to fly, mate of mine!" Delia excitedly grabbed his hand. "How're we gonna do this?"

Hugging her to him, Justus traced them to The Gap, an ocean cliff nearby. "Like this," the half-breed answered, releasing the demoness to remove his t-shirt. "It'll be easier to catch flight from here."

Delia looked over the lip of the steep ledge. "At least we'll have a horrendous landing on those sharp rocks if anything goes wrong," she snickered, but quickly lost that thought when she heard the *WHOOSH* of her mate's wings making their debut and spun around.

The Furie walked over to Justus as he extended them in a stretch and shook them out. Merciful gods, they were unbelievably magnificent. With a wingspan of over twelve feet, it was difficult to be anything other than awestruck.

The satiny sheen of the raven feathers caught the light of the full moon above, causing them to glisten as he flexed. Delia couldn't help but reach out to touch them.

---

A shiver cascading down his body, Justus groaned with pleasure as his mate's hands brushed along the elegant appendages. "Dove, if you continue petting me, we'll never make it off this cliff," he rasped, before picking her up, kissing her senseless.

Moaning against his lips, Delia agreed. "Point made, angel." After making one more pass of her hand, she ceased fondling his wings. "Let's get high, baby." She winked up at him and bit his chin.

"My Furie gets what she wants," he winked back. The half-breed kept Delia hugged tight to him as he walked over to the cliff's edge and fell forward. The demoness shrieked with exhilaration into the crook of his neck as they plummeted. His wings soon caught the wind, halting their descent, and they began their sail over the ocean.

Once Delia relaxed, she unglued her face from his neck, and Justus felt her gasp. "WOOOW, baby," she crooned, absorbing the view around them.

Cradled safely in his arms, the demoness peered down to the dark ocean, which must have been dozens of stories below. Tiny wave crests caught the moonlight, causing them to glow before they disappeared.

They could not have chosen a better night for this adventure. The ocean was calm and the sky clear. Stars above were on full display as they soared.

Jus stopped and hovered over the endless sea, allowing his mate to take in the full majesty of the landscape. The half-breed couldn't help but stare at his mate in wonder. Flushed cheeks highlighted Delia's natural beauty. Moonlight bounced off of her long, ebony locks as they drifted on the wind. The mesmerized smile that she did not realize she was wearing, melted his mending heart.

The angel's grip tightened. Not for fear of her falling, but because he needed to feel her more snugly against him. Without a shadow of a doubt, he knew in that moment that he would hand over his life in sacrifice if she ever deemed it necessary for her wellbeing and happiness. There was nothing he wouldn't do for such a magnificent creature.

He cleared the lump in his throat and whispered against her ear, "That view doesn't hold a candle to you, beauty, my most treasured gem."

Shimmering eyes lifted to meet his gaze. Delia's petite hand cupped his jaw, stroking the stubble adoringly. "My savior. Always making me mushy," she grinned. "You are my sun, my stars, my moon. Nothing of any realm could ever compete with how glorious you are in my eyes."

Justus' breath hitched at her heartfelt declaration. She, actually both of them, so rarely spoke of their true feelings. Times like these were quite monumental. It took all of his determination to keep them hovering as his lips crushed to hers, taking full possession of her thoughts.

Nipping at her, Justus asked the question he'd been holding for months. "Will you marry me, Dove? Be my wife, my mate in every sense?" His voice sincere, and full of love. If this wasn't the perfect time for a proposal, he didn't know when would be.

Delia leaned back slightly to catch his expression, her vibrant greys bled to black as they grew wide and misted. She opened her mouth to respond several times but nothing came out. Justus hoped that was a good sign.

Icy blue hues began to radiate a celestial gold as he stared at her. The full moon backdrop highlighted his beloved in a soft, angelic glow, making him wish he could cocoon and protect her from the many evils that plagued her; past, present, and future.

"I-I...uh, I'd love nothing more than to be your wife, Jussy!" She finally managed. Those words were music to his ears. He planted another mind scrambling kiss on her and squeezed her tight.

"I'm assuming you don't expect me to wear a hideous white dress and walk down an aisle, true?" She asked through a panting chuckle.

A genuine laugh escaped Justus before he kissed the tip of her nose. "Love, I would never ask you to be someone you're not. I'm remarkably aware that *that* is not your style." Justus winked at her and kissed her forehead. "I was thinking more along the lines of marriage by way of the old Demoni gods' tradition. How does that sound?" It was not for the faint hearted. It would be a harrowing, private ceremony that one had to be fully committed to.

The Furie stammered again, and it was the most adorable thing he'd ever witnessed. His mouthy, often crass, spitfire couldn't find the words to express how she felt, but he could read the emotion etched in her features. She wanted this as much as he did. "It sounds fucking amazing!" Delia eventually yelled excitedly. "Yes, baby! YES!"

Turning her in his arms, he hugged her to him as she locked her legs around his waist. "I can't accurately convey how happy you've made me with that answer, Dove," his voice cracked as he nuzzled into her neck. "I love you more than I ever thought possible. And soon, we'll be as one."

Justus felt moisture on his face and wondered if it had begun to drizzle. He had been too distracted to notice anything other than his female. But no, turned out that he, for the first time that he could recall, was crying tears of joy.

A sweet kiss met his temple. Delia whispered softly then, her voice barely intact, "Take me back to the beach house, baby. I need you and your wings in bed, minus these clothes."

# CHAPTER 24

Terribly groggy and perfectly sore in all the right places from the previous night's festivities, Delia curled closer into her husband-to-be in bed. A dreary, overcast day on the other side of the windows encouraged them to take their time getting up. Justus groaned tiredly as his arms wound around his mate and kissed the top of her head. No words were needed; they continued to doze in and out of sleep, blissfully intertwined.

After a while, faint, continuous chirping from her cell phone roused Delia from her peaceful snooze. Rolling to the edge of the bed, a hand blindly felt for the device as her eyes adjusted. It wasn't there.

The demoness got to her feet and followed the sound of the alerts, which led her to the kitchen. Rubbing her eyes to clear the sleep, she scanned the counters and saw nothing. The phone went off again and it was coming from above. *What in the monkey's arsehole was it doing up there?!*

Delia hopped up on the counter to stand, reaching over the top of the cabinets, and felt around until she found it. Irritated by the hunt, she jumped down and stormed into the bedroom.

"Why the fuck did you hide my phone, asshole?!" She yelled at Justus, throwing a pillow at his head. "You could've at least turned the damn thing off beforehand!"

Jus cracked an angry eye and threw the pillow back at her. "I haven't touched your phone, wench! What the hell are you going on about?!" He sat up, scrubbing a hand over his face. "If I didn't want you to have it, I'd have thrown it in the ocean!"

"So, it was the fucking phone fairy? Are those common around here?" She rolled her eyes, debating throwing something more substantial at him. "I sure as hell didn't put it on top of the kitchen cabinets!"

Half asleep, Jus glared at her, confusion all over his face. "Cabinets? Wha-... No! I didn't put it there! Did you get drunk or high after I passed out and do stupid shit? Because that is what it's sounding like." The half-breed rose from the bed and stormed into the bathroom, barking, "You know you're insane, yeah? Fucking nutball."

Jaw hanging wide, Delia glared through the open door where she could no longer see him. Obviously, she knew she could be a bit bonkers at times, but she'd damn well remember putting her phone in such on odd place. "Listen, prick! I hadn't left the bed since we got in it last night; it wasn't ME!"

Justus slammed the bathroom door closed. The demoness plopped on the bed and woke her phone.

Great. Twelve texts and three voicemails, all from Rez and Harper. Surprise, surprise. Another shit fest.

Delia put her phone on speaker and listened to the most recent message from her second in command, "I'm serious, De! If you don't come and deal with this asshat, I'm gonna kill him!"

Huh? Which asshat might he be referring to??

On to the next voicemail, again, from Rez. Jus emerged from the closet, dressed and highly annoyed as he, too, listened. "De! Answer your fucking phone or Marc is going to lose his head. He is outright refusing delivery unless you meet with him first. And the vault is basically dry at this point!"

Ah, yes, Marc the extracurricular entrepreneur who supplied all the fantabulous drug vault goodies. Also, a giant drama queen.

Delia flung herself back into the blankets as Justus stood before her, arms crossed, glowering. This would be what one would call a 'no win sitch'. The demoness laid there, thumbing through the texts that basically said the same as the voice messages.

Jus piped up, "Tell me you aren't considering going in."

*Rut roh.* He was *not* going to be happy.

Delia didn't bother meeting his venomous eyes when she answered, "Uhh, that's a huge chunk of my revenue. Of course I am, I have to."

"Unbelievable! You literally throw a tantrum over my working and here you are, leaving our holiday to go entertain a drug dealer! Explain to me how this makes sense?! It's not as if anyone will DIE without them...actually, quite the opposite!" Jus paced back and forth, his hand spearing through his short hair as he shot her death stares.

The inner churnings of Delia's Furie traits were trying to burst free. Her light eyes had already bled to black, and her porcelain skin had a slight red tinge to it. The points above her temples swelled, as her horns threatened to break through. But this was not the time nor the place for her to erupt. She went to great lengths to control her temper. A new thing for her, admittedly.

Deep breaths and repeating mental chants began, to attempt to calm herself and avoid any bloodshed.

Jus wasn't making it easier as he rambled on, "It's not like you need to work! Between the two of us, we have plenty of money. Just let Rez handle it!"

This was the problem. Justus didn't see her club as anything more than ridiculous and utterly expendable. What he failed to understand was that it was the only thing that had ever been *HERS*. She'd built it from the ground up. Its success was solely because of her...and Rez, because he'd always supported her.

Before Justus, she'd had nothing but Hell's Rejects. How was she to simply walk away from it because she had a mate now? He wasn't going to shut down his company for her. Not to mention, if they both left their jobs, they'd kill each other from boredom at some point. There was only so much togetherness that could be tolerated. There had to be more to keep them both level and happy.

Getting up, she sneered, "I'll handle it," and pulled on clothes that were hanging over a nearby chair. "You can come with me, or you can stay here. Your choice." Delia's fiery gaze met his as she waited on him to decide.

"I'm going," he growled, when he brushed past her to grab his phone from the bedside table.

"Fine. Don't start any shit with anyone there and we'll be back in no time." De grabbed his hand and traced to her office.

---

"Are you gods-damned kidding me, Rez?!" Delia shoved past her second in command after she and Justus materialized.

The demoness fired up a blunt before she flew through an adjoining door where the visibly irritated pusher was waiting in a side office. "What the fuck is the problem, Marc?" Could be heard by anyone within a three-block radius.

In the main office, Rez and Justus had been left unsupervised. Rarely a good occurrence, given the two men barely tolerated one another on a nice day.

Arms crossed, Jus leaned his backside against the desk and scowled at the other male. "Can't manage to give her a few days off? Have to fuck shit up?" A hint of his Aussie accent coming through with his ire.

"Fuck you, man," Rez growled from across the room, arms also crossed, as he stood staring at the security monitors. "The guy is a prick who always prefers Delia. Nothing I said or did would've made him happy." He briefly sneered over his shoulder to Jus. "And, for the record, I have to listen to HER shit, not yours. So, again, fuck off."

You could cut the testosterone swirling in the air with a knife.

Justus slowly straightened, mentally reminding himself 'you can't kill him' as he attempted to reel in his anger. He knew if he ripped the guy's head off, Delia would go berserk. "Listen, Cue Ball," he taunted, knowing the smug, bald bastard hated that nickname. "She's my concern, therefore, yeah, you're going to hear from me. She pays you an exorbitant amount of money and more than a few side perks. The least you could do is properly take care of business in her absence." His tone was level, but the aggression behind it was by no means subtle.

"Excuse me? You think..." Rez trailed off with a groan, turning to face the room when he heard Delia storm through the side door to rejoin them.

The demoness had sent her business associate out of the back exit after they easily came to an agreement regarding pricing and product. The guy was a fucking tool. There was no reason she'd needed to come back in for such an issue.

Delia came to a halt, making a triangle out of her and the two males. The hostility in the room was palpable. The demoness took a hard pull on the blunt as she traded glances with the two of them. She spoke wearily on the exhale, "Why do I feel like I just walked into a lit powder keg? I have no patience for your bullshit, too."

Both men silently stared at each other. Waiting for a response, De glanced at her mate with suspicion and then to her friend.

After a few moments, Justus chimed in, tearing his glare away from Rez. His icy gaze landed on Delia. "I was simply querying the demon, here, about his incompetence." Justus smirked with satisfaction when Rez immediately ignited. He enjoyed pissing the other male off, possibly a little too much.

"FUCK. THIS!" Rez snarled in Justus' direction, then looked to his boss, throwing his hands up. "De, I'm done! I bust my ass around this place with insane loads of overtime and I'm done. You can thank your mate!" The demon's chin hitched toward Justus as his fists balled at his sides. "Maybe he'll take my place so you don't have to work around the clock." And with that, he disappeared.

Delia pinched the bridge of her nose and hit the blunt hard. Vehement eyes cut to her mate. Justus couldn't help the amused grin that spread across on his lips.

"Seriously?!" She seethed. "Get the fuck out! No telling what other fucking fires I need to put out around here." She angrily strode to the door and opened it, turning back to Jus, "Eventually, I'll get to come home and deal with your ass, too."

"Oh, come on! What's the big deal?!" Justus couldn't keep his chuckle subdued.

A half full bottle of liquor came sailing through the air in response. Destination: his head. He sidestepped, missing the collision and dropped the shit eating grin he'd been wearing.

"It's a big deal because he is my best friend! When I had nothing and no one, HE had my back! How about you show him a little gratitude instead of being such a prick! Now. GET. THE. FUCK. OUT OF MY FACE!"

"Okay, I'm leaving." He supposed she did possibly have a point. Justus hadn't a clue what Delia had been through since fleeing Hell. "I'll be back later, with dinner," he added before he ghosted.

---

*Little more than a year after Delia's escape from Hell*

*"Listen, honey, you've got the body for it. Just get out there and shake it around. You'll have tips flying in from the get-go," Chastity, a veteran stripper, told Delia on her first night at The Kitty Kat Club.*

*The demoness was petrified to strip, or possibly be touched by strange men, but she wasn't exactly cut out for much in the way of working in this new world. She'd bombed so many interviews it was laughable. Her personality left a lot to be desired and her limited talents couldn't exactly be utilized: torture and killing. No help wanted ads for that sort of thing in the newspaper.*

*To this point, she'd mostly stolen what she needed, but that got old. She wanted to make money to buy a place of her own. She was finished sleeping in abandoned houses and apartments.*

*"Here, smoke this. It'll calm the nerves," Chastity told her as she passed a joint. "We all get by the best way we can, ya know." The attractive female shrugged her shoulders as if she understood what Delia was going through.*

Pfft, as if.

*"Mmhmm." The demoness attempted a half-assed smile as she accepted the lit gift. De took a drag, and so began her love of weed and all the drugs that would follow.*

*Horrible Coping Mechanisms 101. Delia excelled in that course.*

*The Furie cringed when she peered down at the costume they had given her to wear. She wasn't sure how it qualified as clothing with so little fabric. It was a school girl outfit.* Gag. *A tiny, plaid skirt and a sleeveless, cropped, white, button-down shirt that tied in a knot between her breasts. Her own red, lace bra and matching thong was worn beneath, peeking through.*

*Nightmare. This was a nightmare. She'd almost rather go back to her dungeon than take the stage next.*

*She bit down hard on her lip piercings while her hands fidgeted anxiously. The demoness was approximately two seconds away from bolting when she heard her name announced over the house speakers.*

*Chastity gave her a nudge from behind and there she was, out on the stage, surrounded by countless strange men cheering and waving money in the air. Delia retreated to the Wonderland in her mind. The same place she'd go to when she had been raped and tortured in the Underworld. It allowed her to turn off everything and go on autopilot. That was the only way she, and the spectators, would survive this career choice.*

*That was the last thing Delia remembered until someone was setting her on her feet outside, in the alley. When her faculties came back online, she looked down her body. Blood was spattered and smeared all over her and her underwear had money hanging from everywhere possible.*

*Delia combed her brain for hints of what went down but drew a total blank.*

*The owner of the place came bursting through the rear exit, yelling, but his words made no sense to her. Russian, perhaps?*

*A thick fog rolled in. That's when she noticed the overgrown, bald bouncer who'd delivered her to this spot. He shoved the owner back inside, accompanied with a few threats. The demoness' mind was all over the place while she stood there like an invalid, passively absorbing the happenings. She was nothing more than a spectator of her life that evening, it seemed.*

*The big guy walked toward her and the fog followed him. But then, it wasn't fog at all, was it? No, it was scentless smoke. It surrounded them when he stood before her.*

*The Furie reached out, her hand slowly waving through the whitish-grey vapors, causing them to separate and then come back together. "You're a smoke demon," she said quietly, as her gaze lifted to meet his.*

*"And you're a newby to this realm who has no business working in a human establishment. You're sporting Lucifer's brand." He pointed to it in full view. "You're going to get innocents killed. In fact, it's a miracle you didn't kill anyone tonight. What were you thinking?"*

*It was a proper question, Delia supposed, given she'd chosen to space out and hope for the best on that stage. The bouncer stood there, staring at her with inquisitive amber eyes.*

*A dancer took a look past the door and yelled, "Rez! Hellloooo?! We need our Bloody Mary back!" The two demons watched as the woman peered around, looking for them, then turned and went back inside.*

*"That's me, I'm Rez," the large male grinned. "And they can't see or hear us while we're in the smoke."*

*"Ah, cool." Delia nodded her head in understanding. "Sounds like my name is 'Bloody Mary'." Her eyes rolled hard on that one. "What, uh… What did I do to earn that name, huh?" She was afraid to ask, but she needed to know how much damage she'd done. Although, it sounded like she still had a job since they were looking for her to return.*

*"What? You don't remember? How-how could you forget? It only just happened." Delia could read the confusion on him as she rolled her shoulders with no answer. "Exactly what type of demon are you, female? You don't exhibit any clear markers I can distinguish…" His hand rubbed his jaw as he looked her over, not in a sexual way, but more as a puzzle to figure out.*

*Delia frowned. Once upon a time it would have been unmistakable what she was. "Furie. I'm a Furie," she said with a dejected sigh.*

*"Seriously?! Wow. Now that's impressive and makes it even more of a miracle that no one was killed." He examined her a little more reverently. "You've truly mastered suppressing your genetics."*

*The demoness lowered her gaze. "Not by choice. One might say they were beaten into submission, over a long period of time." Was that her voice? When did she become so small…*

*"Oh. Damn." Rez's hand touched her shoulder softly, causing her to jump. "Shit!" He swore under his breath and jerked his hand back. "I'm sorry. I reckon I better understand your reactions on the stage now."*

*Tear filled, shimmering slate eyes raised to his. "What happened? How bad was it?"*

*"Don't get me wrong, it was entertaining as hell," Rez laughed. "It just wasn't something we see around here. The dancers let security handle the people who act up, but you took it into your own hands to teach them a lesson." He yanked his shirt over his head and handed it to Delia when she began to tremble.*

*The thought of those men putting their hands on her made Delia want to vomit. She was almost too distracted by her own disgust to notice Rez's massive muscles covered in beautiful artwork. But she followed the narrative of his ink as she pulled on his shirt. It was toasty warm and she had not noticed until that point how cold she'd been.*

*"Anyway, yeah, so one guy grabbed your leg and you punched him, breaking his nose. Then, his friend attempted to fondle your ass when you turned and you put him in a headlock and wailed on him, too." Smoke swirled heavily as he threw his head back, laughing huskily. "Luckily, you calmed some when I broke up the scuffle and tossed you over my shoulder to get you out of there. You seemed like you were teetering on the edge of a volatile meltdown, if I'm being honest." Rez peered down at her, with what appeared to be a twinge of pity.*

*"Don't look at me like that," Delia warned.*

*"Like what? I'm not looking at you any sort of way, other than respectfully." His gaze stayed on hers. "You were fantastic. Anyone watching, other than the owner, got a kick out of it. And I can guarantee, after a start like that, no one will mess with you again." He smiled and*

*winked at her, attempting to encourage her, she assumed, as she unconsciously ran her hands up and down her arms, trying to warm herself.*

*"I don't know if I can do that, again," she told him truthfully. What if she killed a human next time? She didn't know much about this world but she did know that rule. Immortals had to stay unknowns. If they went around killing humans that was the fastest way to be discovered for what they truly were. "Clearly, I'm not cut out to be here." Here or anywhere, apparently. If killing herself wouldn't land her right back in Lucifer's lap for eternity, then she would have offed herself long ago.*

*She was nothing now, and barely even passed for a demon. She had no home, no money, no mate, no friends or contacts. She was miserably alone in a world that wasn't for her.*

*"Nonsense," Rez scoffed. "You'll be the most popular dancer in this place." His bald head nodded decidedly. "You only need to get cleaned up. Where do you live? I can escort you home so that you can shower, if you'd like. Count all those bills you've earned." His smile was wide now. "There were guys still stuffing your garter as I toted you out. I may have 'accidentally' elbowed one of them in the jaw."*

*It dawned on Delia that she had been standing here, half naked, talking to this guy and she wasn't reacting or self-conscious. He'd picked her up in the middle of her losing her shit and she'd let him.*

*She searched his face and scrutinized his body language, scanning for anything that triggered her. Usually, simply being near a male triggered her in some way, but he didn't. She felt comfortable in his presence; not scared, disgusted, nor enraged. He felt familiar and kind. And while he was an impressive male, in build and stature, she didn't feel any sexual tension or even attraction between them.*

*Rez reminded her of Justus, in a way, when they'd first worked together, back in Hell. He brought a calmness to her chaos and it felt like they'd known each other for far longer than they actually had.*

*"Uh, well, I'm staying back there." She pointed to an abandoned apartment building, two blocks down the street. "Showering there isn't an option, but I can use the one in the dancer's lounge. Honestly, it's half the reason I wanted to work here." Delia smirked and rolled a lazy shoulder. "Priorities, ya know."*

*Rez shook his head and crossed his arms. "Yeah, no. That won't do.*

*Listen, I have an extra room at my apartment. You're welcome to use it until you get on your feet. I even cook." He gave her a goofy grin and nodded his head slowly. "This is where you say 'that sounds great!' And take me up on the offer."*

*Staring up at him, debating whether this was a good idea or not, Delia responded, "You saw what I did on that stage. Understand that is just a drop in the bucket of what I'm capable of if you fuck with me."*

*"I wouldn't expect anything less. You* ARE *a Furie, after all. And you have my word, I will not 'fuck with you'." His dark brows raised as he awaited her response.*

*"Okay." Delia's periwinkle locks bounced around her shoulders as she nodded her agreement.*

*"And maybe a 'thank you'?" Rez smirked, amused.*

*A solid punch connected with his shoulder as Delia's lip began to curl at the unfamiliar word use. "Right. Thanks."*

*Over the next three years, they fell into a close, sibling type relationship. Rez watched over Delia, appointing himself as her personal bodyguard. She continued to dance, and eventually bartend, at The Kitty Kat Club. Once she'd saved enough to buy and fix up her own establishment, the smoke demon never left her side. She soon built that business into one of the most renowned and infamous underground clubs in NOLA.*

# CHAPTER 25

Justus ended up at his office in Sydney after concluding that he might as well catch up on the business side while Delia was pissed at him. He scanned half-heartedly over contracts and noted meeting requests, but he couldn't shake the earlier argument over the misplacement of his mate's phone. The more he thought about it, the more it grated on him. Something felt…wrong. Whether Delia was off kilter or not, even Justus didn't think she'd put the device in such a peculiar place.

He popped open his laptop and pulled up the security app for his beach home. Justus rewound the video feeds to the evening before. Luckily, he'd forgotten to turn off the camera in the master bedroom and he couldn't help but grin when their mattress olympics flew by on the monitor. *Damn they looked good together.*

Readjusting his pants that were becoming too tight in the crotch, Justus moved on. He stopped the scan when he noted her phone on the bedside table. It was well before they'd gone out flying.

Delia had actually left it there after dinner, before she showered, and never picked it up again. Going forward on a slower examination of the feeds, Justus swore under his breath when he saw the phone seemingly move of its own volition from the bedroom. When it reached the kitchen, Hannah fully materialized, waived to the camera, then tossed the phone atop the cabinets. She *wanted* to be seen.

The half breed slammed his fist on the desk, infuriated. He knew Hannah wasn't an angel, even though she'd attempted to carry that line the entire time he'd known her, but this was ridiculous. This went far beyond simple jealousy and infatuation. The fact that the dark fae would send his mate back to Hell for potentially an eternity of torture and then taunt them in this manner… That meant this chick had far greater mental problems than he could have ever fathomed.

Justus picked up the office landline and buzzed his secretary. "Good afternoon, Mr. Azrael, I wasn't aware you were here. What may I help you with?" Lura, an elven maiden, responded. Elves were generally pleasant and extremely helpful; he needed to hire more of them.

"I'm only in briefly, Lura, thank you. I see several hellhounds have contacted us. Reach out to them and have those who are available come here for a meeting in an hour." Justus had to get this Hannah situation resolved sooner rather than later, and hellhounds were excellent trackers.

"Yes, sir. I'm on it."

Returning the phone to its cradle, Justus went back to the security feeds. Obviously, it was time to change the code and passwords to something that Hannah couldn't hack. He'd taught that bitch too well, obviously. Over the next forty-five minutes, he reworked the configuration and installed some fun little booby traps that would fry her system the next time she decided to attempt spying on him.

The intercom buzzed before Lura spoke, "Your guests have arrived, Mr. Azrael. They are waiting in the conference room."

"Thanks, I'll be over in a minute," Justus replied, as he wrapped things up on his laptop and shut it down. He grabbed his phone and traced to join the assembled males.

Chatter in the room ceased immediately when he materialized at the head of a grand, oak table, large enough to sit thirty. Standing before them, Jus noted all of the familiar faces of those who had put their lives in jeopardy to help himself and Delia escape Hell. The half-breed found himself disappointed that Blayde was not in attendance.

"Please, take a seat," Justus said, indicating all of the empty chairs. As the males did so, he continued, "First, I'd like to formally thank you for your assistance in the Underworld. Myself and my fated mate, Delia, owe you a huge debt of gratitude."

"Nah, man, it's all good."

"Don't mention it, brotha."

"It was our honor, sir."

"It was the least we could do."

"Are you serious?! You're Justus freakin' Azrael, dude!"

Overlapping responses from all of the hounds had Justus shaking his head and raising his hand to quiet them. This was not up for debate. They truly owed the beasts their lives. "Regardless, fellas, you've always got a friend in us. Delia and I likely wouldn't be here without you." He had to quieten them again, as the chatter started back. "Okay, okay, enough of that. It is what it is. Now, you requested this meeting; please tell me how we can be of assistance to you."

Luckily, Glok rose from his seat. It appeared they had appointed him the mouthpiece and Jus wouldn't have to struggle through all seven of them answering at once. "Mr. Azrael..."

"Justus. Please, call me Justus."

"Yes, sir," Glok continued, pushing his light brown hair out of his line of sight, "Justus. Some of us aren't as familiar with living in this realm as others. We wondered if you might have job and living quarters recommendations you can share." The tall, slender fella stood rather stiffly with his hands clasped behind his back as he met the half-breed's sympathetic gaze.

Justus could tell he was a proud male that wasn't entirely comfortable yet in this realm. It couldn't have been easy coming to him for help, even though they were told to do just that before Jus left Hell. "As a matter of fact, guys, we've planned for this day." He grabbed a piece of note paper from the table beside him and scribbled an address on it. "My residence in New Orleans has a separate wing for guests," Justus told them, as he pierced a finger on his fang, then smudged a drop of blood on the paper. "You lot are welcome to stay until you find a place of your own. When we're done here, my secretary, Lura, will get you all set up on payroll. I already have a job lined up and waiting for each of you."

Excited commotion and whispers of disbelief sparked amongst the hounds. Grinning, Justus stood and handed the paper to Glok. "Trace to our home and give this to the butler, Myrin. He'll show you around your wing of the castle and see you to your rooms."

"Sir...I mean, Justus. Thank you so much! I'm not sure we can accept all of this, though. We don't want to be a nuisance to you and Miss Delia." The sheer gratefulness exuding from the hound was all Justus needed to see.

"Don't be silly. It was Delia's suggestion, anyway. And the place is far bigger than we need. Trust me, you won't bother us at all. We'll likely barely notice you're there." Justus winked and clapped Glok on the back. "Sincerely, we owe you fellas this and much more. Please, be our guest and treat it as your own home."

Glok stared at the paper, at a loss for words, as Jus continued speaking to the whole group. "Okay, now, down to business!" Everyone jumped to attention and sat back down. "Your first assignment is to track down my ex-office manager, Hannah. She is the person responsible for returning Delia to Hell."

Thundering growls escalated as that information sunk in. Never hurts to have loyal beasts on your side, Justus thought as he let them get the emotions out of their systems.

The rumbles died down and he continued, "As of last night, Hannah has also taken to harassing the Furie, which means she is getting sloppy about keeping her whereabouts secret. Find Hannah and report that location back to me. I will handle the rest." Justus checked the clock hanging on the wall behind him. It was well past dinner time in NOLA.

Wrapping things up, he told the hounds, "Lura has a file on Hannah, including a blood sample. Anything further you need, either Lura or Myrin can assist you if you can't get myself or Delia. De's number is on that paper, also. Any questions?"

---

Another bustling night at Hell's Rejects and Delia was taking the time to schmooze a large party of VIPs with Harper. The finicky lot were still getting used to the new, young Co-GM. It was understandable, given the high stakes games they played, but irritated Delia, nonetheless. When they felt comfortable with the little harpy, Delia could be away from the club more often, but she'd have to give a little extra attention now to gain that freedom later.

Once everyone was a bit more relaxed with Harp, De went downstairs to the back hallways near the private rooms. There, she conducted a quick meeting with all five of the on-duty managers.

Ten minutes later, while they were wrapping up, Ranger, the night's head of security, sent an alert to the demoness' earpiece.

The managers dispersed. Delia activated the comm and sat a little straighter on the corner bench she occupied as she responded, "What's doing, Ranger?"

"Boss, we just pulled an Incubus off the main stage. He was attempting to assist Cressida with her dancing." Delia pulled the stretchy band from her wrist and began winding it around her raven hair. No one touched her girls without consent. She tightened the binding of hair as she listened. "He says he knows you and to find you."

Unless it pertained to a high-roller, no one around the club got special treatment. The demoness barked, "What's the moron's name?"

"Jalin Gollach," he answered, irritation evident in the vampire's voice.

Ah yes, the mayor's son, Delia thought with a smirk. The mayor she'd bought long ago and kept snuggly in her back pocket. Giant pussy of a man, really. She'd already informed the city official that if his kid caused any more grief at her establishment then he would be treated as everyone else; a swift ass-kicking and a permanent ban from the club.

Delia chuckled, "Sure, I know the pissant. And he'll get the same treatment as any other clown. Haul his dumbass to room 5, I'm on my way."

Laughing, Ranger replied, "En route. Ponytail up?" Everyone in the club knew that Delia's ponytail meant she was on the way to inflict pain…and enjoy it immensely.

"You fucking know it," Delia answered, amused, as she entered the 'disciplinary' room.

She flipped the light switch and rows of fluorescents flickered to life overhead. It was a 15 by 20-foot room with no windows. Graffiti painted the cement block walls; some lewd images, others violent. Boot heels click-clacked across the cement floor when she walked to a hidden panel and opened it. The demoness retrieved a pair of pliers and some pruning shears. The compartment closed behind her as she walked over to a metal chair that was bolted to the floor and placed the toys on a stainless-steel surgical cart a few feet from it.

The Furie was yanking on the binds attached to the chair when Ranger and the young predator strode through the door. Delia straightened and turned to face the two males. Arms folded across her chest, she smirked. "Jalin." Narrowed black eyes promised nightmares for the light haired, bougie guy. He was lanky, and easily a good foot taller than the owner, but young and dumb. "You're like a leech that can't be shook, huh?" Delia asked, not pausing for his answer. She continued as Ranger shoved him further into the room and shut the heavy door, barring the exit. "Didn't I tell you the last time you put your grubby mitts on a dancer that it was your last warning?"

Mustard-colored eyes were five-alarm panicked. It appeared that Jalin had figured out that daddy's name wasn't going to save him this time, and began to stutter, "But..but…my-my dad will have you arrested! He'll have this place shut down for good!"

Delia folded over with laughter, then threw her head back in a howling laugh, raven hair flying this way and that. In a split second, she traced to the youngster and tightened her hand around his neck. Effortlessly, she tossed him a car length away, into the chair. The demoness had him shackled at the wrists and waist before Jalin had a clue what had happened.

When the gravity of his situation registered, he kicked out at the Furie's shins. Clucking her tongue, she traced again, binding his feet to the chair legs. As Delia stood, she slipped on a pair of brass knuckles she'd had in her back pocket, and drilled her weaponized fist into his jaw.

Lights out.

The demoness turned to face a snickering Ranger and curtsied. It wasn't terribly uncommon that she got a little silly and giddy when she was able to rough someone up.

Spinning back to the kid, she grabbed smelling salts from the cart and shoved it up his nostrils. Immediately, he regained consciousness and began wheezing and coughing as he bucked in the seat.

Delia put the brass knuckles back in her pocket as she stood staring at the loopy, flailing detainee. She waited to say anything until his eyes got a little clarity about them. Once it appeared a light bulb had come on, she snapped her fingers to grab his attention and spoke over his groans. "Stay with me, punk." Fingers snapped again and Jalin raised his steadying gaze to her. "What. Did. I. Tell. You. Would. Happen. Next. Time?" A devilish grin tweaked Delia's lips when she saw the answer register on his face.

"My-my fingers and-and my…my eyes," a pathetic whine in his voice.

Where in the fuck did all these deplorable males come from?! She wondered, as she stared at him, disgusted. Throughout her countless tortures and rapes in Hell, Delia was never as useless and whiny as most of these asshats who caused trouble around her club. If she culled this fleshbag, she'd be doing the immortal world a service.

A slow, threatening nod confirmed to the male his answer was correct, then he truly started the stage show. "My father will kill you!" He screamed as she picked up the shears and grabbed his right hand. Jalin's index finger went under attack as the blades clamped down where the finger met palm. "No! NO!" He yelled, beginning to hyperventilate; subdued limbs strained to break free. "He'll kill you and everyone you love! And he-he'll burn down your bar!"

Jalin was grasping at straws big time with that one, Delia thought with a chuckle, as she clipped his finger off. She always did adore the crunch one got when snapping through bone.

Blood curdling screams of agony exploded from the spoiled brat. Delia bounced around like a boxer in the ring, cackling with laughter. She never, ever tired of hearing that particular melody.

Bending down, she retrieved the severed digit from the floor and held it up in front of Jalin. A crimson stream dripped down the demoness' forearm. "One down, nine to go, twatwaffle. Ya ready?"

He bucked in the chair and shook his head in the negative. Delia reached out with the bloody finger and used it to wipe a tear from his cheek, causing him to screech like a little bitch. The demoness nearly fell over from the glee of it all.

Suddenly, the Furie straightened, goosebumps spreading over her entire body. Justus had just arrived. Delia could feel his presence down to her bones and shivered.

"It's your lucky day, assface," she informed the Incubus as she leaned back and blasted a kick to his chest. The snap of his sternum was loud in the small room. Delia continued speaking over Jalin's blood choked cries, "Ranger will finish with you, even though I was really starting to have fun."

Ignoring the gibberish the kid was spewing, the demoness turned. She motioned with a bloody hand to Ranger, who was propped against the closed door. "He's all yours. Rough him up a bit more. Maybe take another finger, then dump him in his daddy's lap."

"You got it, boss."

Delia ghosted and materialized in her office, expecting to see Justus. Instead, there was a large bouquet of wilted wildflowers sitting on her desk. "What the fu..." her voice trailed off when Jus walked through the door. De faced him with a disappointed smirk. "You really think some ugly ass flowers will help you out at this point?"

"What?" He peered around to see what she was referring to and scoffed. "If I'm sending flowers, you can bet your sweet ass they wouldn't look like THAT."

"Fuck!" Delia turned back to the sickly arrangement and plucked the card from the sad petals. When she raised her gaze back to Justus, it was dark and seething. "Your fucking girlfriend sent them."

Thick brows furrowed, Justus glared at the Furie. "Excuse me? What does the damn card say?" The demoness handed it over, to read for himself.

*Dearest Delia,*
*Trouble in paradise already?*
*What did you think would happen? Happily ever after?*
*It's adorable that you believe you can keep him satisfied.*
*Sorry, that's not working out for you.*
*No worries, I'll pick up the pieces.*
*-H*
*P.S. How was your visit in Hell?*

Justus scrubbed a hand over his face, his lip curling over his fangs as anger built. "She hacked into the security system at the beach house. She was watching us there, and she's the one who hid your phone." His head quirked back and forth, his neck cracking and fangs dipping far past his lips. "I'll kill her," he hissed.

"The fuck you will! That bitch is MINE," De retorted, snatching the card back from him. "Have there been any leads on her yet?"

"That was one of the things I came to discuss. I've enlisted the hellhounds. A small pack of them are going to stay with us until they get used to this plane. I've already put them on Hannah's trail."

"It's about fucking time they showed up. Is Blayde in the pack?" Yes, she had a soft spot for that particular beast. Bouncy or not, he'd done the impossible for her.

"No." Jus appeared slightly disappointed, himself. "But I heard he's doing well. He already had a place to live before their Hell stunt. So, he's okay."

At least he hadn't been killed or imprisoned! "Oh. Good."

"I've changed the security configurations in Sydney. Hannah won't be able to stalk or get in, at least not that way again. We'll get her soon, Dove. She's getting careless now." Jus pulled his ornery mate to him for a hug. "And she was NEVER my girlfriend, just so we're clear."

"Fuck buddy, then," Delia muttered against his chest.

"Dead. Dead is what she's going to be. I do not, nor have I ever felt anything for her. You know that is the truth, love." He kissed the top of her head and squeezed her tighter. "You've always been the one, Delia Payne."

*WHY* couldn't she stay made at this half-breed?! Delia wrapped her arms around him and gave his pec a love bite through his shirt. "I know," she grumbled. "You ready to get to work now? I need you on security, since you ran off Rez." She was completely serious; his actions had consequences. "Until he comes back, you work for me, jackass." It was this or kill him, and she really didn't want to do that.

A growl rumbled around, deep in his chest. The bastard knew he owed her! "Dinner first?" He asked, with a hint of stubbornness.

Delia lifted her gaze to his, wearing a shit eating grin and bit his chin. "Sure, why not, you're buying."

# CHAPTER 26

Half asleep, Delia stumbled down to the kitchen to grab a cup of fresh coffee. She'd smelled it brewing while she laid in bed, dreading movement, but eventually the aroma coaxed her to her feet. It'd been weeks since Rez walked, and the demoness and Justus had been working around the clock to keep both their businesses running smoothly in his absence.

The Furie trudged down the halls, descended the grand staircase, and meandered through the dining room to the kitchen. Entirely too many males were gathered in the space, shooting the shit.

"Mornin', Miss Delia!" Gunnar, one of the hellhounds, greeted her with a huge smile.

De cut her eyes at him and kept heading for the mammoth coffeepot. For the most part, she was happy to have the hounds there, but they could certainly push the limits of her less-than-zero patience before noon.

"Dude!" Rhun whisper-shouted to his auburn-haired pack mate. "She told you NOT to talk to her in the mornings before she's had her coffee!" He was the sensitive one in the bunch, and seemingly, the only one who actually followed directions. Rhun was the equivalent of a big teddy bear; a large, burly guy with a mouse brown mop top. He sort of reminded Delia of a taller, thicker version of that Peeta guy from The Hunger Games movie.

Gunnar frowned, his sapphire blue eyes lowering. "Sorry, Miss De," he said remorsefully, before rebounding back to his normal happy-go-lucky self and returned to conversation with the others.

Delia rolled her eyes, shaking her head, as she snatched a mug from the cabinet and then the coffeepot. Justus stepped up behind her, sweeping her hair around her shoulder, and kissed along the column of her neck as she poured the go-go juice. "Good morning, Grumpy."

The amusement in his voice was enough to make her snap, but she grunted her displeasure instead. *Was it truly that difficult to simply pretend she didn't exist until she'd leaded up?!*

"The fellas have gotten some good intel on Hannah. We're getting close, Dove."

De nodded faintly as she sipped the liquid gold from her Mad Hatter cup. The dark fae had been playing hide-and-go-seek with them, leaving breadcrumbs in her wake as she jumped from realm to realm. "Keep on her, guys," Delia grumbled, as she turned away from the counter, nearly bumping into Jus and spilling her coffee. "Dude," she growled, glowering up at him. "Do you fuckin' mind?" Jus grinned, and stepped out of her path. "Better," she muttered when she walked past him. The Furie threw up a middle finger to all the males as she exited the kitchen.

Entirely too much togetherness for morning time.

Dodging housekeepers scurrying around, completing their chores, Delia made a quick hustle upstairs to the music room. Closing herself into the therapeutic chamber, she walked along the wall of hanging guitars, brushing her fingers over their curvy lines until she decided on one.

A mahogany Gibson Montana Hummingbird was freed from its hanger, and then Delia planted herself in her beloved lounger. After placing her half full mug on the coffee table, she curled up with her legs folded beneath and began to stroke and pluck at the strings. Eerily beautiful notes stung the air as she let her heart lead the tempo.

The exhaustion of work, combined with the sadness of missing her two best friends, on top of the anxiety and impatience of finding Hannah, kept the chords low and morose. Delia had called and texted Rez umpteen times, but he'd refused to respond. Zaylee had moved a month ago to Los Angeles to tattoo in some big, fancy shop and was staying as busy as Delia had been. It felt like forever since they'd been able to chat or catch up.

A knock at the door brought her attention up to see Justus stick his head through the crack. "I come in peace. And with fresh coffee." He pushed through the entrance, grinning. "I intercepted Myrin. You're welcome." He brought over the silver carafe and refilled her mug. "I reminded him the studio is off limits to him and anyone else when you're occupying it. Except me, of course." Jus winked at her and kissed her forehead. Setting the pot on the table, he seated beside her on the adjoined sofa. "What's wrong, Dove?"

Delia's gaze went back to the strings as she continued to fondle them. "Why do you ask questions that you know the answer to?"

"To give you the option to discuss, should you wish to." Jus' thick fingers gently combed through her tangled mass of hair, causing goosebumps to ripple all along her body.

When had she EVER been the 'talk about your feelings' type?? "Nope." The acoustic was speaking for her just fine.

"Okay." Jus inched closer and kissed her bare shoulder; his scruff tickling her. "Would you prefer I leave you be?"

"Nope." His touch did more for her than any instrument in this room ever could. "It's nice to have you to myself for a few minutes." Delia turned her head, smirking sadly as their gazes met, and kissed him softly. She missed him, too, not just her friends. They'd had no quality time since Rez left and the hounds moved in. "I love you, Jussy," she whispered, lightly nipping the tip of his nose.

His icy blues widened when she actually said the L word.

Though she still strummed the guitar, Jus pulled the demoness into his lap and leaned back into the cushions. "I love you, too, Dove," he replied, kissing along her neck, compelling her to squirm and lean into him more. "Do you reckon you're talented enough to continue playing that thing while I play *you*?"

The underlying growl in his tone, accompanied by the growing appendage that jabbed into her lower back had Delia heating up instantly. Not that it took much effort where Justus was concerned.

She groaned as she watched his skillful hands slide over her hips and in between her thighs, parting them. "Considering I just broke a string, I'm gonna say 'NO'."

Inquisitive fingers dallied with the hem of her boy shorts before dipping beneath to sample the heat and moisture building. With an outstretched arm, Delia blindly set the guitar on the floor. It was only getting in the way of progress at this point.

"Good girl," Justus rasped, his long fangs hooking and ripping free the strap of her tank top before grazing down her shoulder, only to return back to her neck. "Let's see how well I can make you sing, beauty."

Delia settled back against his chest and freely let him manipulate her instrument however he pleased. Her sharpening claws lightly traced over his occupied arms, earning her an approving growl from her mate.

One meaty hand abandoned her thigh and began its slow climb up her abdomen, dipping beneath her tank, and continuing on to capture a pebbled nipple that had been straining through the fabric. Delia's legs scissored when hot chills swept over her and took up residence between her thighs, causing her sex to clinch, in need of more of him.

Banging at the door, along with both of their phones going off simultaneously, had the couple barking in unison, "FUCK OFF!"

More knocking and a muffled voice, "Sorry! It's an emergency!"

"You have got to be fucking kidding me!!" Delia roared, while Jus growled profanities under his breath.

Justus turned her in his lap and kissed the demoness so deeply and desperately that she nearly melded into him. When he released her, they remained for a moment, foreheads pressed together, he quietly promised her, "We will finish this soon, Dove."

Nodding in agreement, she sighed, "Damn straight we will, baby."

They stood and straightened their clothes before storming to the door to find out what all the fuss was about. Yanking it open, they found the hounds, Mach and Vaij, on the other side. Vaij spoke immediately, "Sorry to interrupt, but your Sydney penthouse is on fire." His jet black hair looked as if he'd been yanking at it.

A chorus of swearing from the couple broke out before Jus instructed the males, "We'll get changed and meet you there in a few minutes."

"Yes, sir! We'll gather the others and head there now," Mach answered, his luxurious, curly locks bouncing around his shoulders as he nodded in agreement.

---

Fireys buzzed around the once magnificent residence, working tirelessly to extinguish what was left of the smoldering beach home. Across the street, Justus, Delia, and the hounds listened to a report from the fire chief. "Preliminary findings indicate that the fire started in the master bedroom and spread quickly throughout, exacerbated by an accelerant. I'm afraid the residence is a total loss." The chief was interrupted by the communication radio clipped to his chest strap. "Sorry, mates, I've got to get back over there. The investigator will contact you soon. Terribly sorry," he told the group, stepping away.

Justus, nearly quaking with anger, pulled a livid Delia in tight and hugged her. The hounds paced around them, plotting. "We'll rebuild, Dove," Jus told her, kissing the top of her head. "After we kill her."

Hannah. They all knew who was responsible for this. "Hey, guys." The hounds stepped closer. "Get to tracking. She's got to be close and watching." No sooner had the words left his mouth, the hair on the back of his neck stood on end. The hounds felt it, too, and instinctively formed a protective circle around the couple, their eyes and senses wandering, seeking out the dark fae.

"She's there," Ghem growled, his emerald green eyes glittering as he gave a faint nod to a building a block away. No one made a move. "She's in all black, standing on the roof, hidden in the shadows." The wiry lad turned his back to her location as he continued speaking quietly. "Jian, see if you can get to her before she realizes we're onto her."

Standing an even six feet tall and built like a cross country runner, Jian was the stealthiest member of the pack. The cotton haired male was the best shot at getting to her. If Justus or Delia traced, so would Hannah. It had to be one of the hounds. "Okay. I'll double back and sneak in. Glok, give me a twenty second lead and then follow," Jian kept his calculating, honey-brown gaze on the fire crew as he spoke.

"I've got your six, bud," Glok, too, made it a point to keep his attention averted from Hannah's position when he replied. "Fall out."

Jian walked leisurely in the opposite direction of Hannah; Glok followed shortly thereafter. Justus, Delia and the rest of the pack held their positions on the sidewalk, seemingly watching the cleanup of what was once a beautiful home.

Delia constricted her arms around Justus' hips; he could feel her elongated claws nicking his jeans. Sterling greys raised to his frigid blues, inky blackness threatening to overtake her color. She, no doubt, fought to control the reaction for the sake of all of the gawkers around them. "She is still mine to take. Don't forget that," she reminded her mate.

"I know, love." Jus kissed her forehead, there was no way he would take that away from her. His soon-to-be wife deserved that, and so much more.

"We'll be rid of her soon." His head swung around when a faint yelp was heard. It wasn't loud enough for humans to detect from that range, but their group definitely took notice. Within seconds, two flashes of fire disappeared as quickly as they'd been seen up on the roof where Hannah had been. "Fuck," Jus and Delia both hissed.

"Sounded like Jian took a hit, but they're following her now," Rhun informed the couple. "We'll catch up with them and inform you when we have her."

"Thanks, guys," Justus called when the remaining hounds took off at a run to find a shadow to shift and trace from. "So close, yet so far," he told Delia with an angry sigh. The Furie looked as though she was about to combust. "Listen, I'll take care of things here. You go back home and get ready for work. I'll find you when there is anything to report."

"Sounds good. The last place I need to be right now is in the middle of this crowd of mortals. Find me soon, baby." Delia raised up on her toes and bit his chin before kissing him goodbye.

# CHAPTER 27

"Yeah, NO. You can't roll over, Harp. Dig deep and bring out that inner boss-babe and throw down the hammer! I promise, you show that calamitous Harpy side only once and those guys will never even consider crossing you again." Delia sat in front of the drug vault, auditing its contents, as she counseled the young, apprehensive GM. The demoness knew the girl had it in her to run Hell's Rejects with a vengeance; she simply had to believe in herself.

"I guess, but I don't want to hurt anyone, especially on accident," Harp admitted, her vibrant yellow eyes full of uncertainty.

Delia snorted, "Gotta break a few eggs to make an omelet." Or at least that's a saying she'd heard, but she truly didn't know shit-all about cooking.

"But, Do, I could kill someone." The Harpy's head lowered with regrets of the past, while today's neon pink hair obscured her weary features.

Delia didn't know the how or why of it, but apparently the girl had hurt someone at some point. Therefore, she worked dutifully to bury her power. Such a shame, in Delia's opinion. "Look, kiddo. The gods wouldn't have given you phenomenal abilities if they didn't expect you to use them. I get you're unsure, but the only way to master your proficiency is to employ those skills and practice." The demoness stared assuredly from her chair, hoping the girl would hear her words and open up to the possibility. "Come on, now. How many asshats do you think I've killed or maimed around this joint?" She couldn't help but chuckle. "It's just part of the territory." Delia was determined to draw out Harper's full potential, if it was the last thing she did.

"I'm not like you, though. I don't enjoy hurting others. It makes me sick just thinking about it." She wouldn't meet Delia's eyes, instead she watched her hands toy with the hem of her tie-dyed tee.

*Crying damn shame.* An absolute waste, Delia mused. With a scoff, she pointed out, "You'll get there, kid. You're a HARPY. You were built to kick ass and wreak havoc on those who deserve it. Look on the bright side, you're a seasoned pro at thieving!" It wasn't much in the way of harpy traits but it was something. They coveted the valuables of others, especially food. Any day Harper was working, you could count on the fact that no one would be able to find their snacks or meals in the break room. There was a reason Delia kept her food locked tight in the adjoined apartment. The demoness may not live there anymore, but it still came in handy.

Harper laughed, the worry in her gaze lifting, "That doesn't exactly gain me any friends, but yeah, I am good at that."

A buzz from the security station's intercom in De's neighboring office, broke up their powwow. "What now?!" She grumbled, as she locked the vault and they went to see what was up. De activated the two way on the desk and instructed whomever was on the other side, "Speak."

"Devlins are in the kitchen and dancer's lounge."

"Fuck me sideways," Delia hissed, then barked, "So kill them! I'll be down in a minute." Devlins were Hell's equivalent of rats in your house, only much more destructive. They could be kind of cute, but wreaked havoc and were a diabolically evil pain in the ass. She hadn't seen any in quite a while, and guessed that the recent hurricane must have stirred them up.

Turning to Harper, Delia grinned and waggled her dark brows. "Let's go tear some shit up!"

"I-I can't. I can't hurt them, De," Harper confessed, chewing on her lip nervously.

"So, what would you do if I wasn't here?" Delia was on the edge of punching the girl just to see if it would bring the harpy out to play, but didn't. This time.

"Call an exterminator?"

Delia rolled her darkening eyes. "Just hold down the fort. But know this, one day, you're going to show everyone the badass that I KNOW lives in there." She poked at the harpy's sternum. "Go ahead and start preparing. It'll happen one way or the other." Shaking her head, the demoness traced to the kitchen.

The scene she was met by was absolute pandemonium. Pots, pans, plates, utensils and glasses were all flying. Food painted the walls, floors, and counters. Flashes of dark scarlet ricocheted this way and that in the massive, industrial space. “Come here, you little bastards!” Delia snarled as she traced, dodging debris missiles, to catch one of the devlins. The Furie materialized on the other side of the kitchen, by the stoves, holding one of the hairless, fire-brick-colored monstrosities up by the scruff of its neck.

Glowing red eyes the size of golf balls darted back and forth as a mouth full of fang-like, serrated teeth snapped aimlessly, furiously trying to take a chunk out of Delia. Grubby hands at the end of all four legs waved around wildly, attempting to grip on to anything. The long, slender tail wound around De’s wrist, stinging her with venom it secreted.

She gave it a good shake to rattle its pea sized brain and stun it into submission. “Cut it out, dude!” She shook it again, harder, for good measure.

The demoness had no clue why she was trying to reason with the mutated raccoon-looking demon. They should be killed on sight, but she always gave the first catch an opportunity to make amends. The thing continued having a go at her, though, spewing taunts and threats in the old Demoni language. Delia’s claws sharpened and lengthened, impaling its thick neck. The devlin let out an ear piercing shriek as blood trickled down De’s arm. When it still refused to behave, the Furie crushed the thing with a firm grip that popped its wretched head clean off.

Delia dropped the twitching body to the floor to rest beside its putrid noggin. She grabbed a wayward dish towel that hung from an empty pot rack above her head and wiped blood and venom from her hand and arm. Her irritated gaze perused the wrecked cooking area as the workers went about cleaning. Yelling over the ruckus, Delia asked, “Where’d the other one go?” Shrugs and mumbles of “I don’t know” were the useless responses she got. Great. Not a headache she wanted.

The boss-lady stormed out of the kitchen, only to slam into Ranger in the hall, as he was returning from the dancer’s lounge. Bouncing off of the vampire built like a Mack truck, she inquired with a hiss, “Seen a devlin running around here recently?”

“Yes’m,” Rang grinned as he answered, pushing wavy, caramel locks from his face. “I cornered one in the dressing room and it jumped out the window. I traced to catch it, but I didn’t have a clear view and I missed. Sorry.”

“Shit happens. They’re slippery assholes. Hopefully it won’t come back.”

Delia was glad it was gone, although dead would have been better. "Make sure the dock door stays closed, will ya?"

"Yes'm. I'll remind everyone." Ranger gave her a mock salute and cut through the kitchen to go check said door.

The demoness traced back to her office, where she found Rez sitting on the couch, lacing up his shitkickers. She didn't know whether to scream with joy or stab him.

Planting her feet and crossing her arms, she glared at him. "Look what the cat dragged in."

"Well, I heard you have a vermin problem," he replied with a snarky smirk.

"Did ya, now?"

"Just because I've not been here, doesn't mean I haven't been keeping tabs." Rez finished with his boots and stood; he was dressed in security detail.

"Well, it's about gods-damned time you showed up. Finally get your phone fixed? Or did you only forget how to use it where I was concerned?" Her tone was even, but her irritation was evident.

Rez chuckled, "Good to see you, too, De. Did you miss me? Or have you enjoyed working around the clock?" His thick arms flexed as he crossed them. "You know, like you've had me doing for months on end."

Once upon a time, she would have attacked him, but she was truly just happy to have him back. Her gaze held his as she debated her words "Listen, ASSHOLE." There it was; she was still DELIA. She wasn't going to kiss his ass. "What you did was NOT cool. You know if you were anyone else, you wouldn't be allowed back after that antic." Her temper was rising.

Rez took a measured breath before responding. "Maybe not, but since your mate showed up in town, the majority of work around here has fallen on me. Now you know how back breaking it's been, yeah? I need sleep and down time, too, damnit!"

The demoness chewed her lip piercing for a moment. He did have a point, as much as she didn't want to admit it. She'd worked far less since Justus became a thing. She'd been wrapped up in their bubble, but now she realized what she'd put Rez through. The Furie had been severely neglecting her long-time friend and her work duties.

"You're right." Delia couldn't help but be amused when Rez's jaw literally dropped. "Yeah, you heard me correctly. And I'll likely never say that again, so I hope you took a mental snapshot." She sighed heavily. "Things will be better; I'll do better. And I've already made pretty good strides with getting the VIPs to trust Harp. We'll get there."

"Perfect. I'm glad you've finally come to your senses." The smoke demon smiled smugly.

"Dude." Black began to swirl in her dove greys as she pinned his amber gaze. "Lose the fucking attitude already. You won."

A devious grin widened on his mug. "But it's fun poking you when you're trying to act civilized."

"Whatever." Delia rolled her eyes until they nearly dislodged. "Get your ass to work. I've got to sleep so I can track down a dark fae that's been begging to be crucified. I've had basically no rest since you left. Time to catch up."

"And that was how I felt for months," Rez sneered. "Hard pill to swallow, isn't it, boss?"

Yep, she'd even missed the asshole's scathing attitude. "All that down time didn't fix your personality, huh?" She narrowed her gaze at him, willing herself not to smile.

Flipping her off, Rez flashed the demoness a snarly smirk.

"We're done here." She traced to him and punched him forcefully in the gut, garnering a grunt out of him. He grinned. They were back. "I'm going home to curl up with my man and you can take care of all the shit-tastic fun around here." She turned to grab her things from the desk and added, "Don't even think about calling me to come in."

"Before you go, we need to discuss 'your man'."

Cutting him off immediately, Delia snarled, "FUCK. NO. That is not something we're doing right now." She stepped up to him and stabbed him with a stiff finger in the chest. He began to growl and she continued, "Don't you growl at me! It's a convo we WILL have, but not tonight! You two males are going to be the death of me. Y'all better learn to get along or we're ALL gonna be miserable!"

Shaking his head, he thumped her forehead. She punched him again. "You're mental, woman. I've tried tolerating the guy but he insists on being impossible to like."

"Seriously?! Bye, jackass!" She punched him a final time before disappearing.

# CHAPTER 28

It was nearly 3:00 a.m. NOLA time. Justus was still vibing in the Sydney zone, so he was starving for dinner when he arrived home. After changing into some comfy gym shorts, he traced to the kitchen and rummaged through the refrigerator to find something light but filling.

Mission accomplished, he pulled up to the table with his plate and dug in.

He felt her presence before he heard or saw her. Delia had just arrived home, as well. Jus couldn't stop the grin tugging at his lips as he continued eating. He knew she'd be along to find him shortly.

And just like clockwork, a few minutes later, he heard her little feet flying down the grand staircase.

His head turned to the demoness when she strolled into the kitchen wearing his *Metallica – And Justice For All* t-shirt. A growing smile brightened his features, he loved seeing her in his stuff; even if it hung down to her knees. "There's my Dove," he crooned as she neared.

"Hey, baby," Delia whispered near his ear as she stepped up behind him and loosely wrapped her arms around his thick neck. Her head poked over his shoulder, midnight strands of soft hair tickling his arm as it brushed against it. "Why're you eating a diet burger?"

"What the fu-..." Confused, Justus stared down at his tossed platter of lettuce, tomato, onion, cheeses, bacon, and croutons. He chuckled when he realized her meaning. Bringing his gaze back to her, he bit her forearm playfully. "It's called a salad, crackhead."

"TahMAYtoe, TahMAHtoe." She nipped his jaw with her fangs and shrugged. "And I'm only a crackhead if you're the crack."

Justus pulled her around to the side and pushed his chair back a bit to slide the demoness into his lap. "I'll be anything you want me to be, beauty," he testified with a voice full of gravel, as he kissed up the slender column of her neck.

"Sex slave?" she rasped, leaning back in his arm, giving him better access. His other greedy hand trailed up her exposed thigh, he groaned with carnal need when the demoness shivered and her scent filled his senses.

"Mmmhmmm." A growing erection jabbed into her hip, demonstrating he was well equipped for just such a title. "Use me and abuse me, wicked Furie." Sharp fangs left welts in their wake as they lightly raked along her shoulder to find and blissfully torment the mate mark there. Tracing the mark's borders, Delia squirmed wantonly, her hip putting exquisite friction on the rock-hard appendage pressed between them.

Both of their phones erupted with calls and texts.

"NOPE. Fucking cockblockers can wait!" Delia leaned to the table and knocked the phones out of reach. "Let's move this party before the bastards show up looking for us."

"Couldn't agree more," Jus grated. His arms held her tight and he traced them to their uninhabited guest house that sat a few of acres away from the castle. It would take anyone but the hounds a hot minute to find them there. And if it were the hounds with news on Hannah, he'd take this time with his mate over another scavenger hunt. They'd dispatch that bitch in due time.

They materialized in the dark interior. Justus tossed the demoness onto her back on the metallic silver, Victorian bed. At the same time, he willed on the nearby lamp and a soft light filled the space. Golden eyes zoned in on the glorious female displayed like a rare jewel on the plush, sapphire duvet.

He stood bedside and grabbed her ankles, yanking her butt to the edge of the mattress. Dropping to his knees, Jus lifted her right leg and draped it over his shoulder, scraping his fangs along her inner thigh.

He repeated the action with her other leg and her moans were an aphrodisiac like none other.

Dark chocolate and cherries bombarded his senses as her scent filled the room. The massive erection in his shorts struggled to burst free of its confinement.

Slowly inching the oversized t-shirt up her toned legs and over her hips, Justus revealed the black, satin thong the demoness was wearing and his mouth watered. "This is far better than any diet burger," Jus groaned, as his hungry gaze raised to hers.

Delia propped up on her elbows, staring down at him ravenously. "Less calories, too." The wicked smile that dotted the Furie's full lips with those words was nearly his complete undoing. The half-breed all but lost his load before getting to the good stuff.

Tearing his gaze away, Jus dipped his head. He kissed and nipped up her thigh to the flimsy fabric of her underwear and ripped them free with his teeth.

Yanking her shirt off, Delia fell back from her propped position when his mouth went to work on her drenched sex. The Furie's fingers made their way to his head and tangled in his hair. Jus' skilled tongue flicked and sucked her bundle of nerves until her breathing became labored.

One of his hands moved from her hip to explore between her silken folds while the other hand moved up her toned stomach to find and torment her breasts.

The moans and curses became louder when he slid one, then two fingers, deep into her tight, slippery depths. Delectable honey coated his fingers and lips, driving him mental with need for the alluring vixen as he continued to ravage her.

Thick fingers curled to stroke the hidden sweet spot within, while his mouth worked her sensitive clit into a frenzy. The demoness writhed against him, the sharp tips of her claws nicking his scalp.

After paying proper homage to her pebbled nipples, his hand trailed back down her quivering stomach. With his forearm, Justus pinned the Furie's hips down as they undulated frantically while she neared her release.

He added a third finger to her dripping entrance, at the same time he growled against her flesh, producing the perfect vibration to send her over the edge. Delia erupted and it took everything in him to keep from joining her as she bucked and hissed her approval.

When the demoness unwound and went lax, Jus took the opportunity to release her. The half-breed lapped at her divine juices as he shoved his shorts down his thighs.

Jaw clenched tight, struggling with control, Jus rose and plunged his over-engorged length into his version of heaven. Delia cried out as her tight walls expanded to accommodate his thick mass and euphoria overtook him. His mind completely shorted out when her drenched sex clenched around him.

Delia stared up at her beautiful mate through lowered lashes as the half-breed powerfully thrust into her. All of his inked, flexing muscles put on quite the erotic show.

He was the drug she so desperately craved.

Her body, still humming from the toe curling, body shattering orgasm minutes ago, was priming for another as the angle he was working was right on the money spot. Delia's claws shredded the bed covers as the impending release edged.

Eyes slammed shut, Jus' head fell back. His jaw ticked as he ground his molars with the effort of holding onto control. He had a vice grip on her thighs, holding her steady while her ankles locked behind his head. About the only thing the Furie still had on the bed was her head and shoulders.

She knew Jus was close to his own explosion, and loved the fact that she affected him in the same way he affected her.

Faster than the demoness registered, Justus traced them onto the bed. Him on his back and her seated fully atop him. The devilish smile that spread across her flushed features caused him to growl. She knew he much preferred to watch her riding him when he exploded.

She adjusted slightly, bringing her legs around so that she was steadied on her knees. The Furie's hips began moving and she ground down on his shaft, then rose and reseated.

Justus filled her completely, and the sublime pressure rearranging her guts was making her slightly dizzy.

Slender fingers snuck behind the Furie's back and down to his sack to fondle and tease him to madness. Cupping and then gently tugging, she voraciously watched his eyes momentarily roll back with the pleasure.

Large hands clamped Delia's hips. Jus lifted her high enough to roughly slam her back down on his cock with a force that made Delia see stars. Onyx eyes rolled back in her head, her fangs sinking into her bottom lip.

Justus was the flawless embodiment of what she could only assume a sex god would be.

Delia felt her already enlarged fangs begin to swell further, her gaze popped wide.

Mating venom leaked down her chin. "Baby..." she whimpered, staring down at him with slight panic and confusion.

Justus froze, letting go of her hips. "What's wrong, Dove?! Did I hurt you!??" His swirling gold gaze searched her face for answers when she didn't immediately answer.

"Wh-why are my fangs doing this?!" She fully bared them and Jus' eyes widened when he noticed the venom dripping. "That's only supposed to happen until you're marked, right?!"

A sinful grin played on her gorgeous mate's lips. "I'm not sure, beauty, but you can mark me every damn day if you want." He nodded encouragement. "Do it, love. Mark me again."

Delia smiled deviously; she'd always been an overachiever. Planting her palms on Justus' chest, her hips began to rock again, languid rolls triggering Jus to return to his punishing pace.

Once they were back on a gluttonous rhythm, her body tensed for another release. Just as the pinnacle crested, her body fell onto his. Throbbing fangs speared deep into his chest, just above his heart where Lucifer's brand had been.

Roars echoed as Justus continued wrecking her slippery depths. The venom pumped into his body while Delia writhed through her orgasm, oblivious to everything but their union.

Erotic fireworks exploded in her core. Electric chills flooding her system convinced her they must have died and were now floating in an euphoric ether, never to be seen or heard from again.

Then she felt Jus join with his own volcanic eruption. There was no mistaking the convulsions of his length, pulsating deep within her; rope after rope of his seed filling her.

Groans and moans lessened as her glorious mate emptied. Things eventually slowed to a halt, leaving them entangled and struggling for precious oxygen. After a short bit, Delia corralled enough brain power to direct her fangs to disengage from his flesh.

Jus grunted as they left him and hugged her tighter against him. "Thank the gods we ignored our phones," he panted, his voice all sexy and raw.

"Yeah, fuck 'em and all their stupid urgency," Delia's voice barely registered as she spoke against his sweat and blood slicked pec.

A forked tongue flicked out to collect the intoxicating concoction and she purred like a lion. The high her mate gave her was boundless. It went beyond descriptive words. She floated in the clouds with her body set on a heavy, erotic, tingling thrum. If she could bottle and sell the sensation, they'd be billionaires a hundred times over.

"Agreed. We will be sleeping here tonight." Jus kissed the top of her head. The Furie couldn't help but grin with satisfaction. "If anyone dares to hunt us down, it may be their last action in life." Delia lazily nodded in agreement against his chest.

Justus grabbed the thick comforter and tossed it over them. He tucked it around the demoness to keep her warm, now that they were cooling down. "I love you, Dove," he murmured, streaming his fingers through her tousled mane.

"L-word you, too, baby," somehow made it out of her mouth before she passed out.

---

Late the next morning, loud banging on the door brought the couple out of their dead-to-the-world slumber. Sleep deprivation had been an issue of late. "Just a damn minute," Justus grumbled sleepily, rolling up against his mate. He looped an arm around her waist, pulling her back flush against him.

Ignoring the morning wood, or trying to, he nuzzled through her messy locks to kiss her neck. "We've been found."

Squinting against the blinding sunlight that forced its way in through parted blinds, Delia's head turned and she nipped the tip of his nose. "Surprised we got as much time as we did." She wiggled her firm ass against the lead pipe molesting her. An electric bolt of need shot through Jus. His irresistible mate was testing his restraint and he was about to break. "We need to find a secret hideaway and threaten the hounds with a miserable death if they even think about finding us."

"Done, beauty." Hell, he'd agree to just about anything at this point. They never had any time alone. "High priority task on the books. Another beach house, eh?" Justus gave her a brief squeeze and bit her shoulder softly.

Dull claws lightly brushed up and down his forearm, causing shivers to creep down his spine. Delia purred, glancing over her shoulder with an excited grin. "Definitely a beach house."

Both of them growled when the doorbell rang…and rang…and rang. Someone apparently had a death wish.

Furiously tossing the sheets away, the couple got up and yanked on the clothes they'd worn the previous night. A quick smooch, then they traced to the front porch, meeting the offending party waiting there.

Justus' icy blues narrowed on Vaij. The hound seemed wholly unconcerned about his intrusion on them as he stood there, arms crossed, with an apathetic look. "Did you suppose we wanted to be found when we left our house with our phones sitting on the table?"

Vaij smirked and shrugged. "Hell if I know, dude, but you told us to get you details on Hannah as soon as we got them. I'm here to do that." Smug bastard, Justus thought, as Vaij stared expectantly at the couple. He owed the hound a lot, but his patience ran thin with the guy. They possibly had too many personality traits in common. "Shall I continue? Or would you like for one of us to try again another day?" *Arrogant ass.*

Delia snorted under her breath and turned, burying her face in the half-breed's chest. The other male appeared confused by the demoness' reaction. But Justus knew exactly what was tickling his mate. The same thing happened when he and Rez interacted. De fancied seeing how far others could push Justus before he snapped. And Jus knew, if this was anyone else speaking to the Furie with that amount of sneer, she'd rip their tongue out. But the hounds damn near worshipped the ground she walked on, and he'd yet to figure that one out.

Delia hated males, as a rule, but she had some sort of connection with the beasts. Not sexual, obviously, but more along the lines of a protective and adoring, older sibling type bond. Well, as adoring as was possible for a Furie demon. And the hounds seemed to feel the exact same toward her.

Jus had to admit it was rather mind blowing to see his mate interact so closely with them and not once had she harmed a hair on their heads. Now *that* was the miracle of it all.

"Continue, asshole," Justus instructed Vaij.

Vaij quirked an ebony brow. Cough. "Takes one to know one." Cough. "We foun-…" Delia snorted again, breaking Vaij's train of thought, making his words trail off. He cocked his head at her and inquired, "You okay, De?"

"Mmhm," Delia hummed, keeping her face hidden. She, undoubtedly, was doing her level best to refrain from bursting into laughter. *Mischievous wench.*

Lime green eyes glowed with curiosity as Vaij cranked his head to the other side. After a beat, he straightened and continued the report. "We found where Hannah is living. She's over at the parallel universe, Releiney. And, get this, the bitch is staying in a carbon copy of your beach house. You know, the one she just burned down." He smirked his disgust. "Issues, dude… This chick has volumes." The hound shook his head as if to say, 'WOW'. "Anyway, Mach and Jian are laying out on the beach, keeping a close eye on her place. Or making an excuse to take a nap, it's anyone's guess." Vaij smirked again, a deep dimple in his cheek making itself known.

Delia had turned around quick when Vaij mentioned Hannah's name, and they'd both soaked in every word the hound said. Finally, they had her nailed down to a single location.

"She's there? NOW?" Vaij nodded. Justus looked down at Delia as she raised her gaze to his. The Furie's eyes were an inky well of darkness. She, most likely, was already contemplating tactics for the fun day ahead. Jus looked back to Vaij. "Meet us in the kitchen in thirty. We'll be ready to go."

They needed a hound to get to the hidden realm. Without one of the beasts, they'd need a witch who could provide a portal. Luckily, hellhounds were easy to come by these days.

"Sure." The hound ghosted.

The thrilled couple traced to shower and gear up.

# CHAPTER 29

"Happy Torture Day, bitches!" Delia cheered when she and Jus joined Vaij and Gunnar in the kitchen. The hounds chuckled and whooped, giving her high fives. Vaij had apparently gotten a haircut in the short time they'd been separated, and was sporting a short, spiked mohawk. Delia punched his shoulder as she walked past him to the table. "I approve of the new look, fella."

Vaij grinned and shrugged, "I had time to kill."

Delia noticed Jus looking back and forth between her and the hound, perplexed. Vaij was always sweet to De and an ass to everyone else; just like her mate. They were two peas in a pod.

"Good use of time, then," she told Vaij as she snatched her phone from the table and shoved it in one of the pockets of her black, tactical pants.

She strolled over to the corner, floor-to-ceiling cabinet, and pulled the door wide open to reveal a vault. The demoness placed her hand on the biometric panel, the lock popping open after it recognized her prints. Dove-greys lit up when she opened the door that stood taller than herself, and got a gander at all of the fun weapons. It was a Furie's wonderland.

"You guys want anything?" She asked, as she pulled out poison tipped throwing stars and tucked them into hidden sheaths on the side of her shitkickers.

"No, Dove, this is your party. We're only here for security," Justus answered for all three of the males. Vaij and Gunnar nodded in agreement, as they stood back, letting her do her thing.

The demoness tossed a seductive smile over her shoulder to her mate. "Smart AND sexy. Now *that's* a winning combo, soon-to-be hubby."

Gunnar and Vaij both groaned.

Gunnar whined, "Come on, you two. Please don't get all lovey dovey. We heard enough of that last night."

"Yeah, no thanks to you jerks," Justus scoffed. "And get used to it if you're going to live here. It's a common thing, ya know?! You guys need to go find some nymphs to saddle up. Get your own sex lives and stop interrupting ours!"

Vaij rolled his neon eyes. "Dude, we're doing the job *YOU* gave us. Don't bitch if the intel comes at inopportune times."

Delia had to see this exchange. She spun on her heel just in time to catch Justus' fist make contact with the hound's jaw. Vaij took it like a champ, too. De lost it. The demoness folded over and howled with laughter as Justus' feral growl reverberated around the room.

Straightening from the blow, Vaij's neck cracked as he readjusted his jaw. The hound glared up the two-inch height difference to Jus and smiled like a psychopath. "Thanks, Daddy."

"Enough!" De squawked through snort-chuckles. "This is MY day, assholes! Fight *after* I murder that twat."

The guys obliged, reluctantly, and went to separate corners as she turned back to the toys. She pulled a cross-shoulder harness over her dark tank top and buckled it securely beneath her breasts. Next, she retrieved two Luciferian daggers, sculpted from dragon's teeth with perfectly gripped black pearl handles, and placed them in the chest holsters under her arms.

Brass knuckles and cuffs went into her pants pocket, short blades on her belt clips, and lastly, she concealed a small pair of ultra-sharp pruning shears. That should do, Delia thought, as she stared into the safe one last time. Nope, still needed smelling salts. De grabbed a few packs and tucked them away.

The demoness closed things up and trotted over to her mate, jumping on him. He caught her in his arms as she wound her arms and legs around him and laid a giant, loud smooch right on his juicy lips.

"Seriously! Come oooooonn!!" Gunnar. Such a baby. Vaij simply turned his back to them.

Delia turned her head and stuck her forked tongue out at the ginger hound, teasing. "You should see the things I do to him when you're not around."

"NO, he shouldn't!" Justus snapped, popping her ass.

"NO, I definitely shouldn't," Gunnar agreed, shaking his head.

"Y'all are so serious today, geez! Fine." Delia may have been slightly delirious from the death scenarios running through her mind. Torture days were simply glorious! "Hounds, assume the position and let's get this joyride underway!"

"Yes, ma'am!" They chuffed in unison. Shreds of jeans hit the air like popped confetti when they shifted. Seconds later, two flaming beasts stood before the couple, shaking out their coats, red eyes glowing like laser pointers.

Delia grabbed their duffel bag and climbed aboard Vaij, the flames heatless as she moved through them and settled.

For the most part, all of the hounds looked quite similar in beast form, but they all had their distinct markings or battle scars that differentiated one from another. Vaij had a chunk missing from his left ear tip, and the other ear had a thick scar that ran the length of it.

Gunnar nodded to Justus and he mounted the beast's back. Gunnar's identifying mark was on his chest; a large, oblong patch of scarred skin. Delia didn't know the story, but given they couldn't be burned, she assumed he must have been splashed with toxic blood or maybe an acid of some sort.

The demoness met her mate's gaze with a million-megawatt smile and announced, "Hellhound Express for the WIN!"

---

The group materialized on the dark, three-story roof of the apartment building across the street from Hannah's penthouse.

Vaij was correct. The dark fae had a property that was indistinguishable to Justus' Sydney home. Every, single, last detail...duplicated

Jus and Delia's boots hit the blacktop. De tossed the duffel containing fresh clothes to the hounds, and averted her eyes as they shifted back to human form and dressed.

The couple walked to the ledge and surveyed their target. "This is some weird shit, man," the demoness chuckled, leaning into her mate. This world was an exact replica of Earth, only opposite time. So while it was coming up on noon at home, it was nearing midnight here.

Delia had never been to this realm before, or any other, for that matter. Justus planned to change that and show her any and every plane she wished to visit.

"It IS weird seeing my beach house, given it just burned to the ground," Justus admitted, staring at the immaculate architecture. He pulled a sophisticated scanner from his pocket to detect the type of security system Hannah had on the place. He would be shocked if she didn't have one.

While he waited for the results, he pulled Delia tight into his side and rested his scruffy cheek atop her head. His eyes closed when her scent filled his nostrils. "Dove. I beg you not to push the limits when we get in there. You know how potent her blood is."

"We've had this convo, baby. I'm highly tolerant. I'll be fine."

"Damnit, Delia. It still affects you and the longer you're exposed, it could overtake you."

"If I pass out, it'll be long after she's immobilized. Then you finish her." Her tone gave away the fact she was enjoying just the thoughts of the upcoming event.

"If you pass out, I'll beat your ass when you recover," he growled.

"Don't you threaten me with a good time, Mister. I'll damn well take you up on it," she chuckled, hip bumping him.

Jus smacked her perky backside. "De. Please. Don't take it too far." His voice was full bore, no-nonsense.

She gave him a mock salute and a wink. "Roger that, commander." She cleared her throat and feigned a mic check, tapping on her closed fist before she spoke into it. "Tower, this is Ghostrider, requesting a flyby." Her lips twitched with a smile begging to burst free.

Justus growled; he knew exactly what that meant. *Smartass, little hellcat*. The demoness had zero intentions of playing it safe. His female would be the death of his sanity.

Vaij and Gunnar stepped up on either side of the couple. Gunnar peered at the ocean front property and inquired, "What's the plan, boss?"

"Awaiting intel on her setup. Once I have that, I'll disable it and we're in, once Hannah shows." Justus had never been more grateful to be a security architect and hacker. "The show is Delia's after that. We are only here to keep things in check. Under NO circumstances do you step in between her and Hannah." His mate grinned up at him. "Understood?" That didn't mean Justus couldn't intervene.

The hounds answered in unison, "Understood."

Vaij yipped high and sharp, three times in quick succession. Seconds later, they saw Jian and Mach jog up from the beach ahead. "They should have a report of recent movements."

The scanner beeped. Justus flipped open the screen and snickered. "The self-righteous twat has the equivalent of any run of the mill, basic shit. She truly thought we'd never find her here."

While the others laughed about it, Jus typed in a few lines of malicious code that obliterated Hannah's system, but would still make it appear to be behaving properly to the dark fae. "Done," he announced, as he put the scanner away and removed a small jar of oil from another pocket.

Justus held out the potion to the group standing in front of him. "Someone drip this around the perimeter of the building when she enters the penthouse. Once that's done, we'll have a mirage up. No one will be able to see or hear what we're doing."

"Nice. I'll do it," Mach volunteered in his resonant, bass drum voice, accepting the jar. "See ya down there," he told them as he turned and jogged off. Jian fell in behind him to go with, while the rest held their positions and watched the residence, waiting.

Justus knew Delia was about to burst with anticipation. She was nearly vibrating off the ground with anxious energy. They couldn't invade the premises before Hannah arrived, though. If they did, the dark fae would pick up their scents before she'd even unlocked the door and ghost.

No way were they losing her this time.

The stakeout lasted nearly an hour before Hannah showed up. They watched as she pulled her white SUV into the immaculate three-car garage. When the door lowered, Justus looked down to Delia, who was sitting on the detonation button.

Her inked, porcelain flesh was now a pale crimson. He noticed her fangs were already dipping past her lips, and her claws elongated and razor tipped, ready to strike. Silky, raven hair drifted on the breeze and tickled his chest and arms.

Jus leaned down and kissed her temple while she glared at the penthouse. "Ponytail up, Dove. It's showtime as soon as we get the signal," he reminded her when the penthouse illuminated as Hannah entered.

The demoness nodded, pulling a band from her wrist and bound her thick mass into a high pony.

Everyone snapped to attention when they heard Jian's yips. Delia bounced on her toes; an epically evil smile spread across her beautiful face. "I'm in first, give me ten seconds and join the party, if you want," she instructed.

Justus took her face into his hands and went nose to nose with her for a brief moment, then kissed her goodbye. "Go get her, Furie." A good smack on the ass and his breathtaking, boss-bitch mate disappeared.

---

Wine glass in hand, Hannah stepped out onto the large balcony that overlooked the beach. Delia materialized on the opposite end, immediately casting a poison-tipped throwing star.

Hannah shrieked, dropping her glass to shatter on the ground. De's projectile had found its mark, impaling the back of her neck, barely missing her spine.

Given the dark fae's noxious blood, the poison tips wouldn't incapacitate her, but they would at least slow her slightly and prevent her from tracing. That was all that Delia was concerned about. The bitch wasn't allowed to run again.

Hannah struggled about as she wrestled the star from muscle and flesh. Black blood trickled down the back of her white, flowy blouse. She turned to face Delia with a hiss.

The demoness smiled and gave a cutesy wave as she pulled a chair from the table and had a seat; the same exact table set Justus had in Sydney. Thick knots began to protrude just above Delia's temples; her skin tone becoming a deeper red now.

Rather quickly, she got the response from Hannah she wanted, PANIC. The fae had just realized she couldn't trace. Delia winked at the twit as she leaned back in the chair, intertwining her fingers. Resting her hands over her stomach, Delia flashed an ominous grin. The Furie couldn't wait to see what tricks her captive would play to attempt survival.

Justus, Mach, and Jian appeared on the patio. They kept their distance and stayed silent behind Delia. Hannah looked to the males then back to the

Furie. In a very unoriginal move, the dark fae turned and jumped over the balcony.

Chuckling, De jogged to the railing, looking over to find that Vaij had Hannah in a choke hold. He smiled up at her, giving a thumbs up.

"Haul her dumbass back up here!" Delia yelled down, then turned to the penthouse and started for the door. "Come on, guys. Let's enjoy Jussy's place one last time." They fell in behind her, and followed her inside. "Look familiar, baby?" She asked Jus over her shoulder, as they walked through the open living area.

Justus scoffed. "Identical." He glowered at all of the furnishings as he scanned the area. "I trust you to make her pay sufficiently, Dove." His icy hues nailed her inky orbs and she gave him a curt nod before she opened the refrigerator to look for a tasty beverage.

"Score!" The bitch really did have an exact replica of their old place. "Jussy! All your faves are in here." Delia grabbed a few bottles of Satan Sake and a container of red grapes. She turned back to the fellas, kicking the door closed, and set the items on the kitchen island.

She looked to Mach and Jian as she handed a bottle to Jus and popped the cap off of hers. "You pups look around and take anything that tickles your balls because letting all of this burn to the ground for a second time will just be wasteful." Neither the demoness nor Jus would take anything for themselves. Everything in the place reeked of the bitch's foul scent.

"Yes'm." Jian began to wander.

"Sure thing, De." Mach went the opposite direction, toward the bedroom.

Taking a long swig of her drink, Delia and Justus stared at one another. "Love, please know your limits and adhere to them," he spoke softly and quietly, so no one else heard his plea.

Delia lowered her bottle with a salacious grin. "I don't have limits. You know this, baby." Her dark brows waggled playfully.

Their attention shifted to the front entrance when Vaij slung it open. He tossed Hannah inside, slamming the door behind them. "Hot potato," he sneered. "She's all yours. I'm going to wash off her blood." Inky streaks were smudged on his shirt, arms, and hands.

Vaij strode hastily to the guest bathroom and water was heard running from the sink. The hounds were highly tolerant to the toxic fluid, as well, but no need risking unwanted side effects.

Hannah hobbled to the sofa and sat on the arm. Apparently, when she'd jumped, her reflexes failed and she'd wrenched her ankle. Her mess of blonde hair had matted, black tangles from her struggles.

Delia dropped her bottle to the counter and walked over, removing a small blade from her belt. "Oh dear," she said, in a faux concerned tone as she stepped up beside the fae. "What do we have here?" Delia fisted a handful of that dirty mane. Hannah grabbed her forearm with one hand and swung with the other, landing a desperate punch to Delia's ribs. In return, the demoness' blade raised and cut off the chunk of nasty hair, then quickly grabbed another, using it to jerk Hannah's head up. "Tsk, tsk, tsk. I hope you have more fight than that, sweetheart." She allowed Hannah to punch her again, while the fae's scant claws sliced into her arm.

The demoness smiled malevolently when she felt her horns erupt and emerge, curling up and over her skull. Damn, it was nice to have all of her Furie traits back in full force!

The hounds quickly returned to witness the showdown, taking up residence by the bar with Justus. Her mate popped the cap on another bottle. Apparently, he'd already downed the first, Delia noticed, as she ignored Hannah's pitiable blows. When she looked back down, crimson blood was dripping from her elbow onto the bitch's light, ruffled shirt. It was quite a beautiful sight, actually.

"Brace yourself, this is going to hurt," Delia told the fae in a sing-song voice, before she plunged the blade into her kidney.

"You cunt!" Hannah dropped the demoness' arm and fell to the sofa cushions, scrambling to remove the blade.

Delia walked over to the guys, picked up her drink and chugged it. "Anyone bored yet?" She asked, as she nonchalantly walked to the fridge and grabbed another bottle.

"No, love, we're good." Jus tossed her a wet hand towel. "Wipe her blood from your hand."

Delia shrugged and did as instructed. "Hardly see how it matters. I'm about to be covered in a whole lot more of it." She tossed the dirty cloth to the sink and walked back to Hannah, who was sitting on the floor, her back against the far wall.

Crouching in front of her, the Furie asked secretively, "How ya feeling?"

"Fuck you," the fae screeched as she swung the blade she'd managed to remove from her back.

The demoness batted away the fae's arm, and headbutted her with those magnificent, hard-as-steel, ebony horns. Delia heard the crack of bones and cackled with delight. The blade dropped to the floor, forgotten.

De had put a pretty decent dent in the top of Hannah's forehead. Oily fluid dribbled in streams down the fae's heavily painted features and dripped from her chin.

Delia turned to Justus while Hannah braced her head in her hands, cursing. "Jussy, she's making a mess on your beautiful floor." Jus simply grinned back her, letting her continue with her game. "Oh, okay. I'll make her clean it up," the Furie asserted as she snatched another handful of dirty, blonde hair, using it to shove the fae's head to the floor, thrashing it around, mopping up some of the blood.

Floundering, Hannah screamed, "I can't believe you, Justus!"

Unhanding the fae, De turned to Jus and stood. "Well, *THIS*, I have to hear. Don't you, Jussy?"

"Sure, why not," he answered, uncaring.

Grabbing her drink from the island, Delia leaned against it, facing Hannah. "Go ahead, princess. Elaborate for us."

Doing her best to compose herself, somewhat, Hannah sat up against the wall. She pushed the matted hair from her face and wiped blood away with her forearms. After a couple of steadying breaths, she looked to Justus and gave her last-ditch-effort speech. "J, I'm so-..."

"Call him 'J' again and it'll be at the cost of your tongue," Delia warned, her onyx gaze boiling as she glared.

Hannah narrowed her eyes, but looked back to Jus and continued, "I'm sorry I burned your home. I was...frustrated. I don't understand why you'd be with someone like *HER*." She cut her disgusted gaze to Delia, whom smiled proudly, then back to Justus. "I only needed you to choose me, to marry me. Father vowed if I wed one with royal blood, such as yourself, then he'd relinquish his realm. The Night Nexus would be ours to rule."

Delia yawned. "Is she done yet?"

"We can hope," Vaij popped off. "Can I have a grape?" He asked, grabbing a water from the cabinet.

"Sure, man. Anything here is yours for the taking," Delia grabbed another brew and snapped the top. "Right, Hannah?"

"Justus," the fae wholly ignored the others, "...please, think about it. You could be a king!"

Delia had pulled her pony around and was braiding it when Justus broke her concentration, yanking his shirt over his head. "You're just showing off, now, baby," she purred, gawking at his flawlessly muscular structure.

The half breed leaned into the overhead light and pointed to the mate marks on his chest and shoulder. His lip began to curl over a fang when he replied to Hannah, "NOT. INTERESTED."

Silver, bloodshot eyes widened as Hannah got a good look-see at the double whammy displayed. "That's disgusting what she did to you," she sneered.

Justus pulled his shirt back on and recrossed his arms. "No one cares what you think, bitch. Delia is my mate and I love her. Nothing you say or do will change that."

"J..."

Delia traced, materializing on her knees, straddling Hannah's outstretched legs, dagger in hand. She grabbed the fae by the jaw and wrenched it open, producing a loud crack as it popped out of the socket. Hannah tried to fight but De slid up on her, pinning the fae's arms with her knees and headbutted her again.

Hannah cried out, and Delia ripped her tongue clean from her mouth. "Well, would ya look at that! I didn't need the blade after all." De tossed the useless muscle over her shoulder. "I told you not to call him that again."

A dark river flowed from the gaping mouth as Hannah cried and writhed in pain. Delia leaned in and licked the length of the fae's bloody cheek.

"DELIA!!!" She heard her name yelled a few times. Like she cared.

"I hate to tell you this, but you taste like shit," De whispered in Hannah's ear, as she bucked beneath the demoness' legs, choking on her own fluids. Delia rolled off of the fae and sat with her legs folded beneath her, facing Hannah's side. The fae slumped over and De righted her. "You're so lazy. Would you sit up, already."

Hannah stared frantically at the pruning shears that Delia produced next. The dark fae scrambled away on her ass but, once again, De brought her back. This time, by her shoulder, and with enough force to dislocate it.

Hannah swung out with her other hand, claws gouging into Delia's cheek. The demoness felt warm streams racing down her face to jump from her jaw onto her clothes.

"Enjoy that, did ya?" Delia asked, slowly hyperextending the wrist that offended, allowing the fae to feel each tendon snap, one by one. Hannah wailed in pain. Such a baby. "Then you're gonna LOVE what's next."

Suddenly, De was holding Jus' hand. She arched a brow and smirked as she examined Hannah wearing her mate's identity. "Hey, baby..." the demoness called out to the true Justus.

"Yeah, babe?"

"You seeing this shit?"

"Afraid so."

"Tell cute Hannah, here, if this ploy is going to work in her favor."

Jus snorted under his breath. "That would be a *hard* NO."

"Exactly." Delia stabbed the shears deep into the pretender's crotch, with a twist for good measure.

Hannah morphed back to her form, curling into a ball, crying.

The guys went apeshit in their theatrics, yelling and grunting. When De glanced over her shoulder, most of them were doubled over, holding their junk. *Weirdos.*

De turned back to her captive. "Silly males," she scoffed, rolling her obsidian eyes.

While the dark fae screamed through gurgling chokes and kicked wildly, the Furie snipped off each of Hannah's fingers. "You're awfully squirmy," Delia remarked, picking up her dagger and stabbing it deep into the fae's pink, legging covered thigh a few times. Then did the same to the other side, rendering the Dolly knock-off basically an invalid.

"Will someone bring my drink?" Delia asked, looking to the guys.

Vaij opened a new bottle and brought it over, handing it off. "It's probably time to start wrapping this up, De." Concern lined his voice.

Black and red blood mixed on Delia's hands, arms and clothes. She peered down at the mess after taking a huge gulp and snapped, "It'll be wrapped up when I'm ready." She set the bottle behind her and shooed Vaij away. "Hannah, here, doesn't deserve a quick, tasteful death. Do you, princess?"

The dark fae was a sight to see, covered in what was mostly her own blood, her mouth stuck in a permanent yawn, and arms and legs rendered useless. The demoness yanked those dead legs and got Hannah flat on her back.

If looks could kill, then Hannah would be winning. She glared at Delia with all the hate and disgust one could possibly harness.

"Hey, baby. Will you grab me the cleaver out of the rack?"

Hannah flailed and gurgled, producing noises that were probably supposed to be screams. Delia patted her shoulder and assured her, "Shhhhhh. It'll be okay. No worries." That didn't stop the fae from having her come apart, though. *Go figure.*

Delia picked up the severed fingers and crammed them all into the cavernous pie-hole. Hannah choked more severely, thrashing her head back and forth. "It's okay, you can pass out." Delia continued patting her arm with faux comforting. "I'll bring you back around so you don't miss the really good stuff."

"Dove." Justus stepped up with the large butcher's knife. He squatted down and leaned into Delia, whispering, "You are covered in her blood. Please, finish her and let's get you cleaned up."

Leaning away, Delia grinned at him. "Do I appear impaired? No. I don't." She snatched the cleaver from him with a black, sticky hand. "I got this."

Justus returned to the others to watch, swearing.

"See. Even he can't save you now, princess." Delia smiled maniacally at the hot mess. Hannah was fading fast, given her airway was drowned out. "Oh goodness. Is oxygen hard to come by? Here, let me help." De dipped her head and ripped a chunk out of the fae's neck with her lethal fangs. The demoness spit out the disgusting flesh and took a swig from her drink while Hannah sputtered further, making ungodly noises. "There. Bonus air hole!"

A chorus of yelling curses from the males rattled her eardrums. They were quite dramatic.

Chuckling like a rabid clown, Delia put her face inches above Hannah's. "Ready for the finale?" The light left the dark fae's eyes. *Unacceptable.* The bitch had to at least see the big blade fall before she checked out.

De turned to the peanut gallery, a wee bit dizzy. They didn't need to know that, though. "Someone toss me a stick of smelling salts." *Oh wait, she had that, didn't she*?! "Never mind," she mumbled, nearly falling over as she leaned to the side, fishing it out of a pocket.

De snapped the small ammonia stick in half and removed it from the wrapper. She shoved half up Hannah's sniffer; immediately reviving her. The demoness took a good whiff of the other half, decently clearing her emerging brain fog.

Hannah laid there gurgling on her putrid blood with wide, frantic, bloodshot eyes. What little of her body she could control, twitched and jumped wildly. The dark fae pleadingly shook her head as Delia raised the meat cleaver.

"It's time to say farewell, princess," the demoness told her in a sing-song, baby-talk voice.

The grotesque thud and crunch as the thick blade plowed through Hannah's sternum caused Delia to break into hysterical laughter.

Hannah went limp, passing out. The blade rose and fell several more times; inky jets of dark oil splattering all over Delia, the walls, and everything else within at least a ten-foot radius. The demoness was completely unhinged.

The guys were full on losing their minds but she paid them little attention as she played in the dark fae's innards.

The Furie dropped the cleaver and straddled Hannah to slide her hands into the sternal opening and yanked it wide apart, making it appear the fae had small wings protruding from her chest. Delia plucked Hannah's heart free and crushed it in her hand.

She was well on her way to unpacking all of the fun treats in the meat suit as dizziness swept over her like a tidal wave and she wobbled. Next thing she knew, she'd face-planted beside Hannah and Justus was scooping her up.

# CHAPTER 30

"Delia Payne, you are the most stubborn, bullheaded wench in existence!" Justus berated the blood drenched Furie in his arms and traced her to the master shower. He knew she'd pull some shit like this. Hopefully they could get home and he could heal her before she slipped into a coma.

"I'm fiiiiiiiiine. Everythin' is fiiiiiiine," Delia slurred as he set her down on the corner bench and cranked up the hot jets, dousing her while he removed her clothes. "HELLOOO. You gettin' nakey, too, sexy?"

Ignoring the question, Justus left her for a moment to retrieve their clothes from the duffel bag on the kitchen island. "Vaij, stand by and prepare to transport us in a few minutes. She's in rough shape, and worsening."

"I'm ready when you are," Vaij told him as he went and stood by the bedroom door, shifting into hellhound form.

"The rest of you, cut the gas lines and torch the place when we're all clear," Justus instructed Jian, Mach, and Gunnar, before he traced back to the bathroom.

"Bloody hell!" Delia was on her hands and knees in the shower, retching up thick, dark liquid. Her soaked, midnight hair, slipping from its binding, was tangled around her shoulders. Justus peeled off his shirt as he knelt down to remove the remaining toxins that adhered to De's pale skin. There was no color, save for the beautiful tattoos. "Love, how's that wonderful tolerance you've been spouting about working for ya right about now?" He couldn't help but make the remark, he was infuriated and terrified at the same time.

When the heaving calmed, Delia hoarsely grumbled, "You're such an asshole."

"And you are a bigger one for pulling that stunt," Justus turned off the water and grabbed a towel to dry them. Gently wiping her down, Delia managed to pull herself back onto the bench, then swatted him away. "Fine, do it yourself, obstinate chit."

"It hurts, jackass! My fucking skin is on fire! *EVERYTHING* is on fire!" What was meant to be yelling was barely audible, her vocal cords were completely wrecked from the corrosive blood.

Justus sighed and cautiously helped her dress. "I know, Dove. We'll get you home and healed soon. Vaij is waiting outside the door, as soon as you're ready."

He pulled on his own clean clothes and the demoness attempted to stand. Justus caught her before she took a nosedive into the tile and cradled her. "Aaand that is why I'll be holding you during transport."

Incoherent words hissed from his mate's lips when he carried her out. As Jus climbed aboard the hound's back, with her secure in his arms, there was no doubt in his mind that Delia was in indescribable pain. Otherwise, she wouldn't be making a peep. Justus had never met anyone who could handle pain like his mate.

If she was complaining, things were hella bad.

"The castle. Quickly," Jus directed Vaij.

Molecules scattered and the trio materialized next to the oversized, master king in the couple's bedroom. Vaij ghosted after Justus disembarked, a barely coherent Delia in his arms.

He gingerly placed his fading mate on the bed and carefully removed her clothes. She was beat to hell and not healing at all. Deep gouges from Hannah's claws on her gaunt face and forearm were seeping blood and pus. Large, fist sized bruises covered her ribs on the right side, where she'd allowed Hannah to punch, undefended.

"Damn you, Furie," Justus grumbled, straightening and removing his t-shirt, "You can't ever do anything the easy way."

After a few steadying breaths, he flexed his back and ebony wings erupted. Jus shook them out, then climbed into bed with his now unconscious female. He pulled her between his legs to lay back against his chest. "Time to get you fixed up, Dove."

The half breed flinched slightly when he plucked a silky feather from the dense left wing. Next, his fangs tore open his wrist and brought it up to Delia's mouth, allowing his healing life force to flow into her. Instinctually, the demoness' forked tongue sluggishly lapped at the wound. When she faded away again, he vigilantly trickled his blood over the gaping injuries on her face and arm.

Finally, he picked up the feather and dipped the quill into his quickly healing wrist punctures, coating it in the crimson antidote, and etched ancient healing symbols into Delia's flesh; two on her shoulders and three on her abdomen.

Satisfied with his applications, he rolled onto his side, bringing Delia in tight against him, and swaddled her with his immense wings. A soft glow emanated as his efforts went to work.

Countless hours went by before Delia showed signs of life again. Justus knew she had rejoined the land of the living when her graceful fingers sifted through his feathers, eliciting quiet moans from them both. "Welcome back, Dove," he told her groggily, as his arms tightened around her and he kissed the top of her head. The healing process had drained them both, thoroughly.

"Hey, baby," was the hoarse response, as her other hand joined in the attempt to pet all of the luscious feathers. Justus shivered with pleasure as electric chills spread over him. "How long have I been out?"

With the jet lag of jumping realms, combined with the exhaustion of taking care of his Furie, Justus hadn't a clue what day it was, let alone what time it could possibly be. "Not sure. I reckon we'll figure it out together when we manage to leave this bed." He was fighting the urge to return to slumberland as her fingers brushed over him. "Which I am in no rush to do. How're you feeling?"

"Umm..." She twitched and stretched against him; his body reacting in a way he didn't have the energy to entertain. "Stiff and sore." SAME, Justus thought. "And mildly braindead."

"As to be expected, when you behave like a screwball." His wing lifted, giving him the leeway to pop her bare backside a good one.

Delia purred, of course. "I'm alive; she's dead. And I had fun. Those are the only facts that matter." She wiggled her ass against the hardening appendage between them. She knew how to distract him. "Now we don't have to constantly be on alert, Jussy. We can wed and do whatever we want."

He did love the sound of that. "As a matter of fact," a wing pointed to the bureau in the corner, "I don't see any reason why we can't marry this week. I was able to collect the ceremonial daggers from Ms. Lola while I was in Sydney, after the fire." Delia whipped her head around to gawk up at him. Her stunning, steel greys wavered as tears welled. She looked back to the chest of drawers when one escaped and cascaded down her flushed cheek. Justus hugged her tightly, kissing her temple. "Or we can wait. Your choice, love."

---

"No. Now." Delia sat up and turned to face him, swatting away rogue tears. Gods how she hated to cry. "I want to do it NOW." Only the thought of wedding him renewed her energy.

"Really?" Gold flashed in his icy blues as he, too, sat up. "I would love nothing more but are you sure that you're healed well enough?"

The ceremony was daunting, and would zap their remaining strength, but she couldn't care less. She wanted to be his wife. She'd already waited too long. "I will never be too weak to marry you, Justus Azrael." Her voice cracked with emotion, and she dove onto him, laying him out on his back, smothering him with a passionate kiss.

This was all a fantastical dream come true for her.

Psyched, she raised her head and stared into his radiant gaze. Their eyes, full of an insatiable, burning need to be as one.

"Now," he agreed with a throat full of grit.

Delia rolled off of him, allowing him to go retrieve the blades from the drawer. He rejoined her and placed the leather pouch beside them as he crawled back into bed. Jus sat against the headboard and pulled her into his lap to straddle him.

The demoness opened the bag and unveiled the most beautiful weapons she'd ever laid eyes upon. The sacred blades were fashioned from dragon glass; an opaque, deep purple that was as smooth as silk and sharp enough to cut through titanium like warm butter.

The pearl handles were lined with stunning black diamonds. Emerald, Demoni wedding symbols adorned the hilts and glimmered in the light. "Wow, baby," she crooned. "You outdid yourself with these." Delia could barely peel her eyes away from them.

"I'm glad you approve, Dove," he told her as his fingers threaded through the black mane that fringed her enchanting features. "Only the best for my Furie. You deserve nothing less."

Delia placed the daggers on the bed and met Jus' gaze, taking his face in her hands. "I don't know about that but I do know I wouldn't be here or alive if it weren't for you." Her voice was weak and unsteady but she was determined to do this. "Now that we are together and you're mine..." Justus gently wiped an absconding tear from her cheek. "There is to be no more dwelling on the bullshit that we had to traverse to get here. This is our beginning." The demoness kissed him tenderly, certain he had to feel every ounce of immeasurable love and devotion she held for him in that moment.

When she raised her gaze back to his soulful eyes, her heart nearly swelled to bursting. "I would be honored to become your wife. Now."

Golden eyes flared. "And I, your husband, my precious mate. But you know when that moment comes in the ritual, I will loathe hurting you." His thumb brushed along her kiss swollen lips as he searched her face for signs of doubt, then kissed her as if their lives would end if he didn't.

Delia wrapped her arms around his neck, her hips beginning to grind against his swollen shaft. She was well past ready to begin this ceremony; to feel him possess her in every way imaginable.

Large hands gripped her, lifting to line them up to join. Delia's groan mixed with his growls as he lowered her onto his engorged length. She was already dripping wet and the descent felt heavenly. Slowly rocking, she fully seated herself and their breathless kiss broke. She could feel his racing heart deep within her; her rhythm matching.

Struggling through his emotions, Justus spoke hoarsely in the ancient Demoni language. His teary gaze held his mate's as he promised to protect, defend, cherish and honor her. To love her for the rest of their days and beyond.

Delia repeated the words back to him as tears freely flowed from onyx eyes.

Justus took the first blade and handed it to his Furie. She unwound her arms from him and sat straighter; a heady moan escaping her with the action.

Jus picked up the second blade and continued in the old language, "Blood of my blood."

Delia gave him a slight nod, assuring him she was ready, before repeating the words. They each sliced across their own palms. The demoness watched in fascination as crimson streams dripped onto their stomachs and ran down to mingle with their joined bodies. When her gaze rose, she wore a weepy smile.

The half-breed had to clear his throat before continuing. "Blood of my mate's beating heart," they spoke in unison; neither voice free of cracks. It didn't escape them that both had, at one point, physically taken the other's heart and obliterated it.

Here and now, they were healing those wrongs.

As if already operating as one, they lined up their daggers against the other's chest. Slightly off from the sternum and between the third and fourth ribs, blades attentively penetrated flesh. To activate the binding symbols, they only needed to nick the other's beating heart with the tip of the dagger.

When that was accomplished, the blades were carefully removed and dropped to the bed, forgotten.

Justus hugged his mate to him; their bodies flush against one another. A blinding illumination emitted the moment their wounds met and breath left them as their bodies and souls fused as one. The magnitude of the bond shocked their systems, causing them to gasp for air before settling into an otherworldly comfort and calm.

Their spirits embraced above them in peace and harmony before reentering their physical forms.

As a bolt of oneness catapulted through them, they could hear a chorus of the ancient Demoni choir warbling, "As there was once two, there is forevermore only one. Wed for all eternity." The blazing light evaporated and the ritual was complete.

The couple moaned as their bodies began to move again, blood mingling in the sex somehow amplifying the sensations.

In a matter of moments, with hips working against each other, Justus and Delia climaxed as one. His roar joined her screams and they rode out epically rising and cresting waves together, leaving them an exhausted mess of entangled limbs.

Delia slumped into her husband's chest, kissing away the delectable crimson life force around the healing wound as Jus leaned back against the headboard. After several minutes, and they'd regained some of their faculties, Justus remarked in a hazy voice, "That was quite different from the ceremonies witnessed in Hell… and, dare I say, remarkably more intense." He squeezed Delia tight and kissed the top of her head.

"Mmmm," the demoness hummed. "So much better. Probably something to do with that angel DNA of yours."

"Possibly…" Sable wings enveloped Delia, their gossamer feathers tucking her in as she gave way to the relentless exhaustion and passed out. "Or perhaps because our love is stronger than anything Hell has ever witnessed..." Justus whispered affectionately, before joining her.

# CHAPTER 31

"Holy shit, you're alive! We haven't seen you guys in like three days!" Rhun, always keeping tabs on them.

Lime eyes rolled. "Nah, we knew you were alive. We're not deaf." Vaij quipped, always the smartass voice of truth. His candor pulling laughter from the others in attendance.

Justus and Delia strolled through the kitchen, hand in hand, to the coffee pot, ridiculous smiles plastered across their faces. "Not only are we alive, we're wed!" the proud husband gushed.

Cheers of congratulations echoed through the room as the hounds converged on them for a flurry of high fives and fist bumps.

Vaij stepped up to Delia, hugging her like she was his most valuable sibling, then quietly told her, "I'm happy for you, De. Perfect pairing if I ever saw one."

Wide eyes watched the exchange, waiting for the demoness to put Vaij through the wall. Instead, she beamed with pride and acted like it was the most normal thing in the world to her.

Justus' jaw hit the floor as he pulled Delia into his side and bent to her ear, "Is my Furie still in there somewhere?" The hounds wandered back to the table and bar, letting the newlyweds have their space.

Delia laughed and smacked his rock-hard abs. "Don't worry, she's all here, baby." Meeting his bewildered gaze, she shrugged. "I have a soft spot for some of the pups. No way to explain it, but I kinda like having them around."

"As long as you don't go around hugging all the males that walk by..."

"EWWWWW, GROSS. Justus Azrael, stop talking shit!" This time she decked him, nearly breaking her hand, then doubled over in laughter.

"I'm just sayin'. I've never seen you voluntarily let anyone but me touch you, much less hug you! It's baffling." Jus smirked down at her, a grin attempting to take its place. "But, if my wife is happy, then I'm happy. Just don't make a habit of it or it could turn tragic for them."

Delia winked her understanding and bit his chin. "Save for special occasions, yeah? All safe then?"

"That'll do," he growled, lifting her to sit on the counter. Jus poured them each a large thermos of coffee, then stood between her legs, large hands caressing her thighs. "I'll come find you at the club tonight when I'm done at the office. We can have dinner together. Plan?"

As if she could turn him down. "Definite plan. I can't wait, Hubby." Delia booped his nose with a chuckle. Who knew she could be *this* joyful?! "Wait. YOU are dinner, correct?" Dark brows waggled with mischief.

"I'm anything you want me to be, Dove," Justus growled softly against her lips before nipping them. "Now I must go, before I take you back to bed." He kissed her goodbye and grabbed his coffee. "You have no idea how difficult it is to leave you."

The demoness smiled wickedly. "Oh yes I do, remember." They had a deep emotional grid on one another since the ritual, and could literally feel the emotions of the other if they put their mind to it. And they were learning to communicate telepathically.

"Right." Justus grinned. "That's going to take some getting used to. But I love it. And I love you, Wifey." He kissed her again; the hounds grumbling in the background about PDA.

"I love you, too, Jussy." That L word had become much easier for her to use, it seemed. "Now go, before the hounds start a riot." She nipped the tip of his nose and he disappeared.

The demoness took possession of her thermos, full of liquid gold, and hopped off the counter. "Okay pups, I'm outta here, too. Who's on my security team tonight?"

"Me." Glok.

Jian raised his hand. "Me, too, boss."

"Cool. See the rest of ya when I see ya. Night!" *Yes, she knew it was late morning.*

Delia materialized in her office. Nice and empty. Although, it looked like someone recently had a frat party in there. She set her coffee on the desk and went to the bank of monitors, hitting the security comms button.

A few chirps and she heard, "What?" Rez, ever the endearing pain in the ass.

"Come say that to my face," she answered, keeping her good mood under wraps.

"Oh. Well, what?" She heard a slight bit of happiness.

"Bitch, say 'what' one more time and I'm leaving. Now would *you* rather go home instead?" Gods how she loved bickering with him. No matter the reason or just for fun.

"You know the answer to that." Yeah, he was definitely happy.

"Then get yo tail out tha door, punkass!"

"On it." Rez appeared by the sofa, grabbing his duffel. "I heard you got to play in the dark fae's blood. Have fun?" He neared her, looking her over as if she were an alien. "What's up with you?"

"What's THAT mean?! Nothing's up with me… except I'm married now." She flashed him a giant Cheshire Cat smile. "We did the Demoni ritual and everything."

"Woah. Damn, so it's like done, DONE! Shit. I did not see that one coming. Good on ya, De. Congrats." He thumped her forehead.

She punched his shoulder. "Right. So, you and Jus gotta learn to play nice. PERIOD. I'mma ride both of your asses til y'all figure it out, too." They'd end up friends even if she had to crack some necks a few times. And she would.

"That's a tall order, Captain Crazypants." Rez tossed his earpiece on the desk. "We'll see." He almost grinned. "Congrats, again, De. You deserve to be happy, even if it's with that guy." The demon chuckled, fully aware he was pushing buttons.

Rolling eyes behind her brain, Delia sneered, "Just get the fuck outta here, asshole." A thump popped her forehead again and he ghosted.

Chirps sounded from the boss-lady's ear comm. Activating it, she struggled from the floor, stretching. She'd been inventorying the vault so long that her backside was dead asleep. "What's up?"

"Check the cameras. Pickpocket, rear bar."

Delia didn't recognize the voice, but returned to her office to have a gander. "On it." Scrolling back the footage on that monitor, she slowly scanned, looking for the troublemaker. It wasn't hard to find him quickly. Turned out he was a decent sized guy. All the better, she thought. *Ponytail up*.

Grabbing a bottle of brew from the mini-fridge, she traced down to an unoccupied private room and walked into the hall to the rear bar. She leisurely strode through the small crowd and stood a few feet behind the offender.

Watching. Waiting. His scent caught her attention, and the demoness perked up, a grin tugging at her lips. She'd been around nearly a millennium, and had spent most of her life in Hell with demons, so she knew damn well what one smelled like. This should be eventful, she mused.

After several minutes, the thug struck again. This time the victim was some drunk chick leaning all over the guy beside her. The thief unzipped the purse the idiot had left hanging from her bar stool. Delia watched as the guy slyly removed the female's wallet and shoved it in the front of his jeans; his long button down covering it.

The sneak meandered to the other end of the bar, and casually ordered a drink. Delia took that opportunity to sidle up to him as he waited. She nudged his arm and spoke over the loud rock music when he looked down at her with interest. "Hey man, wanna play a game of poker?" She did her absolute best to appear friendly, and apparently, she'd pulled it off.

The slender male, with a dark buzz cut, bent down closer to her ear to reply, "Hey there, sexy. I'll play any game ya like." Between his weak voice and arrogant smile, Delia had to stifle a gag. And a punch.

Her patience fading fast, the Furie grabbed his shirttail and pulled him toward the room she'd previously emerged from. "Come on, we'll play my favorite game," she yelled over her shoulder.

He followed her eagerly; his big, brown eyes nearly glowing with anticipation. Delia stopped at the door and pointed him into the suite. The demon wasted no time getting his knickers through the entrance. Delia followed him, shutting and locking the door behind her. When she turned to face him, she punched him square in the nose. Blood gushed freely from his face, decorating the tan, tile floor.

"WHAT THE FUCK?!" He roared, as he bent over slightly, hands clinging to his crumpled feature.

The Furie dealt him a solid kidney punch, followed immediately by a knee to his temple. She felt the bone crunching on impact. Delia laughed as the guy cursed and backed away from her; clearly in shock from the assault and her strength. There weren't many Furie demons around these days.

"You raided my customers, assclown," the boss informed him as she pulled a dagger from her boot and whipped it at him. The whiner bellowed when the poison tipped blade pierced the top of his skull, burying deep into the grey matter. *Ouch.* That was going to leave a mark.

Hissing and moaning in agony, the demon fell to his knees, then flat on his face. The poison was frying his brain and quickly racing through his bloodstream.

Delia strolled over to stand before him. He weakly grabbed at her leg, and she kicked out of it. In turn, she kicked him in the ribs. The sound of fracturing bones causing her to giggle.

Hands planted on hips, De stared down at him as he instinctively curled into the fetal position. The sweet sound of his cries was music to her ears.

Damn, she was almost giddy, although slightly disappointed he hadn't put up more of a fight. He was a damn disgrace to demons everywhere.

The demoness kicked him in the face; his head whipped back, neck popping out of alignment. "Before you pass out, let me officially ban you from my club. Step foot in here again, and you'll no longer possess a head. Got it?!" She didn't actually expect a response. In fact, he likely hadn't a clue what she'd said. That poison burned like a son-of-a-whore!

Skipping over to the wall intercom system, she pressed the red button, allowing her to speak into security's ear. "Clean up on aisle 5!"

"Good, you're done," Ranger answered. "There's a guy out here, says he's here about the bar manager position."

"I didn't have anyone on the books to interview." The boss-lady checked her phone, it was just after five in the afternoon. "Tell him to make an appointment. Preferably with Rez."

"Uh, he heard all that." Ranger nervously cleared his throat. "And he said, 'get your cranky booty out here', that you know him."

The fuck?! Delia didn't know ANY male that would dare speak that way to her, especially through her crew. Time to spill some more blood.

Leaving the small room, she fumed and nearly ripped the door off the hinges. The Furie turned the long corner and saw the ballsy guy in question.

Grey eyes widened and her hands flew to her mouth when he made a beeline toward her.

"Hey, Miss Delia!" Blayde called out as he neared. When he reached her, he put a giant bear hug on her and swung her around.

All of the witnessing staff and patrons stopped dead in their tracks and stared. Anyone who'd ever seen the demoness, much less knew her, knew she didn't tolerate such antics. Many ran away, dodging what they feared was coming in retaliation.

However, the Furie not only allowed it, she laughed, leaving all onlookers speechless. Seriously though, if the pup could remove Lucifer's permanent brand from her hip, then a hug was nothing! And…he was kinda her favorite. *Don't tell Vaij, though*. No need for them to start competing over the title.

The hound put her feet back on the ground and stepped away. "Blayde! Where the hell have you been? You should be living at the castle with the pack!" The crowd cautiously went back to what they were doing.

A giant grin spread on his face, dimples blaring. "Nah, I've had my own apartment down in The Quarter for years. But I'd love to visit." He batted his long, pale eyelashes at the demoness.

"It's a revolving door around there these days. Pop by anytime. Everyone would love to see you. Especially Justus." She waved him to follow her as she turned and spoke loudly over her shoulder, "Let's take this where it's quieter!"

Up the stairs and down the hall, they entered the office. "Have a seat," Delia motioned him to the couch, while she sat on the arm of the recliner. "Are you actually here for the job?"

"Sure am!" He beamed. "I heard through the grapevine you guys were on the hunt. Annnd since I know the owner, I figured I should check into the position."

Delia quirked a brow at him. "How many years have you spent behind the bar? Managerial experience?"

The pup gave her a cutesy wink. "Over three decades pouring the juice and coming up on twelve years managerial." He flashed her his pearly whites.

"Hmm. You know you sound too good to be true, yeah?" There was no stopping the grin that crept free. "But given you kinda saved my life, I think I'd be pretty rude not to give you a chance, huh?"

Nodding profusely, Blayde affirmed, “Yes, ma’am! Can’t go wrong! I promise you won’t regret it.”

“Okay, pup. How about this, you kick ass around here for two months and I’ll bump you to a floor manager, as well.” Gods knew they could sure use some stable help!

“SWEET! I’ll knock your socks off, Miss Delia. Just wait and see!” The kid was nearly levitating off the sofa in his excitement.

Laughing, Delia nodded. “Okay, hound, you’re on. I’m logging you in to start tomorrow night. That work for you?”

“Heck yeah! Thank you so much!”

Delia narrowed a stare at him and smirked. “Come on, now. You pulled my ass out of Hell. Literally. A job is the least I can do… Hey, guess what?!” The demoness stood, unable to remain seated to deliver the following exciting news.

The tall pup also stood, feeding off of Delia’s exhilarated emotions. “What? What?!”

“Jus and I got married! Old Demoni ritual and all!” She bounced on her toes, biting her lip piercing. “Can you believe it?!”

“Holy cow! Congratulations, Miss Delia!”

“For fuck’s sake, Blay, call me DE!” A huge smile decorated her features.

“De! Congrats, DE! Now I HAVE to visit soon. WOW. That’s so awesome!” Blayde jogged over and hugged

her again, and again, she allowed it.

“I know, right?!” Delia wondered if she would always be this delighted to speak of her wedding and her husband. She hoped so, because he was the single most important thing in her life.

Her sun, moon, and stars.

# EPILOGUE

They were having an epic jam fest on Christmas Eve night, all sitting around the studio in the castle, playing different instruments. Delia was saddled up to her cello, Justus at the piano, Vaij on bass, Rez on drums, and Gunnar on electric guitar. The rest of the hounds chattered about, drinks in hand, cutting up.

All, except for Blayde, who was low man on the manager totem pole, so he and Harper were running the club.

Myrin knocked on the door, and it swung it open.

"Theeere's my baaaaby!!!" Delia squealed. *Yes, squealed*. A huge, tri-color American Bully came galloping through the room, eyes only for his mama. He jumped up in her lap, knocking them both to the floor. His lack of personal space boundaries had him pinning her down as he cleaned her face. Delia cackled and half-heartedly shoved at his 120 pounds. "I missed you, too, big boy! Now let mama up, silly clown!"

After seeing how much Delia connected with the hellhounds, Justus wondered if his wifey might like an actual dog as a pet. One of his employees happened to be fostering the large canine, so Jus had brought him home about a month ago to meet Delia. Moose never left. *Yes, that's his name.* Although they called him just about every endearing term under the sun instead of his 'name'.

"The party can start now, putas!" Zaylee danced her voluptuous ass through the door, holding a bottle of tequila in one hand and vodka in the other. "Who missed me?!" The tattoo artist had been able to visit frequently of late, and was considering moving back to the swamp.

Delia was thrilled to have her bestie around more often. Zay was also going to tattoo the newlywed's wedding bands while she was in the area for the holidays.

"You know we've all missed the beautiful Latina!" Justus rose from his bench to give her a hug. He took the bottles and added them to the liquor collection at the bar.

Struggling to remove herself from beneath Moose's enormous paws, Delia crawled from the floor, straightening her clothes. "Bitch, you know I missed you." She hugged Zay, smacking her plump booty. "Get your drink on, babe! Then I better see you dancing and having fun." The succubus did as instructed and chatted it up with the hounds as she made her way to the bar.

Delia climbed into Jus' lap after he reseated at the piano. She looped her arm around his back and nipped his jaw before kissing it. Moose ran over, nudging her legs with his big ole snout, and the Furie rubbed his floppy ears lovingly as she leaned into Justus and looked over the room. She finally had the cherished, dysfunctionally-functional family she never knew she wanted or needed.

Justus squeezed her tight, kissing her temple. He knew exactly why the demoness was getting emotional. Telepathically, he whispered into her mind, "Yes, Dove. You do deserve all of this happiness. Merry Christmas, wifey."

# PLAYLIST

The Devil in I - Slipknot
Vicious - Halestorm
I Hate You I Love You- Gnash ft. Olivia O'Brien
Nightmare - Halsey
Popular Monster - Falling in Reverse
Dark Side - Bishop Briggs
Wasted on You - Evanescence
Hurts - James Arthur
Toxic - Sofia Karlberg
Under Your Scars - Godsmack
Always Been You - Shawn Mendes
Addicted - Zayn
Adrenalize - In This Moment
Wicked Game - Chris Isaak
Fire - Two Feet
Bodies - Drowning Pool
All of Me - John Legend
Him & I - G-Eazy ft. Halsey

Hell's Rejects Series

Book 2

Spring 2022

# Hell's Hound

# ABOUT THE AUTHOR

Dara Kenny was born, raised, and currently lives in southeast USA. She can usually be found at her home with a house full of rescue dogs, but when granted the opportunity, she loves to vacation and travel with her hubby. Dara dreams of living on the beach one day; she might possibly be part mermaid. The jury is still out on that.

After fifteen years of sitting on the board of a pit bull rescue, Dara reluctantly retired due to the toll the heartache and stress were having on her mind and health. Unsure what to do with herself, she began creative writing as a hobby and quickly fell in love with it. One thing led to another, and Dara took the leap and decided to publish her first novel.

And here we are. Knee deep in pages of paranormal romance fun! Sex, gore and F bombs galore!

Dara's REALLY awesome, too... so come hang out with her on her social media pages!

**Thank you for reading!!!**

facebook.com/DaraKennyAuthor
instagram.com/darakennyauthor

Made in the USA
Columbia, SC
09 October 2022

68825254R00143